HAUNTED THEATERS

Playhouse Phantoms, Opera House
Horrors, and Backstage Banshees

Retold by Tom Ogden

Guilford, Connecticut

Copyright © 2009 by Tom Ogden

Text design: Sheryl P. Kober

Library of Congress Cataloging-in-Publication Data is available on file.

ISBN 978-0-7627-4949-2

Printed in the United States of America

10 9 8 7 6 5 4 3 2 1

*For my theater lady friends—Christine Cox,
Joan Lawton, and Betty Jean Morris.*

CONTENTS

Contents

ACKNOWLEDGMENTS

I want to thank all of the people who shared their personal spirit encounters and allow me to incorporate them into my retellings of these ghostly tales, including Deb Fox of the Grand Palace Theatre, Andrew Robley, Sally Jones, and especially Betty Jean Morris, who gave me invaluable firsthand insights about the hauntings at the Pasadena Playhouse.

I want to express my gratitude to those who provided background, contact, and tour information on the various haunted theaters, including Cyntia Leo (Disney Theatrical Productions), Allison Mui (public relations manager, the New Victory Theater), Mary Tucker and Noel (London Walks), Margaret Schmitt and Christopher Brown (McGraw-Hill), Rachel Wiegers (marketing assistant, Klondike Visitors Association), Rose Margeson (manager, Heritage Presentation & Visitor Services for Parks Canada and Dawson City), and Cheryl Fluehr.

Thank you, too, to David Shine and Michael Kurland, who helped make the writing of this book so much easier.

And of course special thanks go out to the gang at Globe Pequot—my editor Mary Norris, my project manager Jennifer Taber, my copy editor Antoinette Smith, and group publisher Gary M. Krebs—as well as my agent, Jack Scovil, for all of their continued assistance and support.

INTRODUCTION

When you're talking about theater ghosts, the words "stage fright" take on a whole new meaning.

I'd heard rumors about haunted theaters for years from both actors (I've used the currently popular form "actor" to refer to either gender throughout this book) and on back-stage tours. But it wasn't until I started to investigate some of the folklore for myself that I discovered the hard part wasn't finding theaters that are haunted. If anything, it was finding theaters that *aren't* haunted. For some reason, it seems that more spirits have taken up residence in play-houses than just about any other type of venue.

Certainly many of the apparitions people think they see can be explained away rather easily. Actors might simply be experiencing a case of the jitters during rehearsals or before a performance. A crew member might become spooked work-ing in a darkened theater or closing up alone at night. Some of the unusual sounds the staff hears in a darkened play-house can be dismissed as the customary noises you would expect in any old building, especially one with outdated pipes and heating systems.

But then there are the other cases.

Paranormal experts are quick to point out that ghosts don't typically haunt *people*. They haunt *places*.

When they do, it's usually because the apparitions were associated with the locations when they were alive. Often they return because they felt comfortable, happy, at home.

On the dark side, however, there are just as many ghosts who return (or perhaps never leave) a particular place because they have unsettled business there or their lives were tragically cut short at that spot by murder or death.

Well, it's no wonder, then, that actors come back from the Other Side. They are passionate, high-energy individuals who spend their lives pulling personal experiences from deep within themselves to create characters and illuminate a playwright's words. There's a reason why performers say, when a show is going poorly, that they're "dying" onstage.

The backstage crew, technicians, office and management staff, and even people in the audience are no less intensely involved. And just as many of them have returned to haunt theaters after their final curtains.

It might just be this quintessential energy they all share—their excitement, essence, soul, or whatever you want to call it—that either imprints itself on the theater when that person is alive or comes back to take another bow after he or she is no longer flesh and blood.

(In fact, maybe it's this "electrical spark" that causes some of the most frequent spectral phenomena in haunted theaters: lights that flicker or go on and off, seemingly of their own free will.)

One thing is certain: phantoms can't help but to command attention.

And isn't that part of what being in show business is all about? In the relatively tight confines of a playhouse, ghosts are almost guaranteed a captive audience when they come back from the Great Beyond to make one more curtain call.

The theater world has a great deal of magic and mystery about it. Because every performance is unique, it is by definition "here today, gone tomorrow." Live theater can't help but have a feel of the ephemeral—much like ghosts themselves.

The spectres you'll meet on these pages may be gone, mortally, but they're not forgotten. The supernatural performances these resident ghosts put on have been seen by dozens—even scores—of people, sometimes over several generations.

There are hundreds, if not thousands, of theaters around the world that claim to have resident ghosts. From this wealth of material, I've selected the stories in this book with great care to represent a wide variety of playhouses and different types of phantoms that haunt them. I've tried to find out as much as possible about who the spirits were when they were (as Shakespeare said) on this "mortal coil," and why they might have returned to these particular playhouses. As a result, you'll probably find these tales much more detailed than you would the typical "campfire" ghost story. But it's my sincere hope that this'll make my liberal retelling of the tales even more intriguing, grounded as they are with factual names, dates, and places.

I also wanted to give you a sense of the theaters themselves. Playhouses are not merely buildings. Each one has its own living history. And sometimes they seem to put on shows of their own.

I've broken the book down into four parts with several stories in each. (If you want, think of them as the acts and scenes in a play script.) I've started out on the Great White Way: Broadway. Part Two explores the many regional theaters scattered across America, from coast to coast. The next section jumps north to Canada; and finally, we cross the Atlantic to call on the theaters in London's West End.

Following the tales of terror, I've added two appendices that give you additional background and insight into the ghost legends.

"'Boo'ks!" is a descriptive bibliography of the books and videos I consulted while preparing *Haunted Theaters*. It also provides the addresses for some of the leading Web sites where you can find lists of spirit-infested theaters (as well as other types of venues), categorized by country; state, province, or territory; and city.

Want to visit the theaters for yourself? "Spooky Sites" is where you'll find all of the contact information, including street addresses, telephone numbers, and Web sites for all of the playhouses featured in this book.

So turn the page. It's time to go backstage to visit some of the most haunted theaters in the world.

Part One

THE GREAT WHITE WAY

Curtain up! Where better to begin our survey of haunted playhouses than on that magical street of dreams: Broadway. Our first four stops are at just a few of the theatrical houses on the Great White Way that have welcomed ghosts back into their casts.

First we'll greet impresario David Belasco, who built (and now returns to) his own theater in the heart of Manhattan. A former Ziegfeld girl still steals the show over at the New Amsterdam, the home of the Follies for many years. At least a half dozen phantoms are still "playing the Palace." And finally there's the story of Frances Alda, the fiery diva who insisted on having encores at the old Metropolitan Opera House—by staying on for more than a decade after her death.

Chapter 1

The Bishop
of Broadway

If you catch the flicker of a tall, fatherly phantom perched in a box seat at the Belasco Theatre in New York, don't be frightened. It's merely the ghost of the theater's original owner, haunting his old playhouse to catch the show.

Sitting in his private box overlooking the stage, David Belasco was in his usual state of nervous excitement on opening night. He was confident about the show itself. As usual, he had personally supervised the production. But this time he had also written the play. And it dealt with a controversial, if popular, subject: the possibility of ghosts crossing back from the Other Side.

When the play *The Return of Peter Grimm* premiered on October 17, 1911, the Spiritualist movement was in its heyday. Just a half-century earlier, in March 1848, two young girls, the Fox sisters, had started a sensation when they claimed to have communicated with a spirit occupying their family home in upstate New York. Even though they later would recant their story, the new quasi-religious movement known as Spiritualism had taken on a life of its own. By the turn of the century, there were hundreds of so-called mediums who offered their services to those wishing to contact lost loved ones. It didn't matter that many of them were exposed as frauds, caught bare-handed producing fake manifestations in the darkness of the séance room. People still wanted to believe.

Belasco had a very good feeling about his new play. His life had always been in the theater, a world of make-believe and illusion, but he was also grounded in the no-nonsense "business" world of "show." His parents had moved from London to San Francisco during the Gold Rush, and David was born in the City by the Bay in 1853. His mother enrolled him in a monastery school, but the lively young boy ran away. His real passion was the stage. Drawn to the bustling theater scene in the Bay area, he wrote his first play by the time he was twelve. Before long, he was onstage as an actor, working as a stage manager, or directing shows, and all the while writing more plays. By the time he moved to New York City in 1882, more than a hundred of them had been performed.

At first, he managed the Madison Square Theater stage while turning out scripts, and then later worked for the great producer Charles Frohman, but within thirteen years his plays were so successful that he was able to become an independent producer. In 1902, he leased the Theatre Republic (today known as the New Victory Theater). Located near the corner of Forty-Second Street and Seventh Avenue, it had been built two years earlier by theater magnate Oscar Hammerstein, grandfather of Oscar Hammerstein II, the famous lyricist and partner of composer Richard Rodgers. In typical fashion for an emerging impresario, Belasco renamed the theater for himself.

By the time Belasco took over the Theatre Republic, more than twenty-five of his plays had been performed in New York, including the one-act tragedy *Madame Butterfly*. Based on an 1898 short story by John Luther Long and produced at the Herald Square Theatre in 1900, it became one of the sources for the famous Puccini opera. His 1905 drama

The Girl of the Golden West would also be musicalized by the famed Italian composer.

Then, on October 16, 1907, Belasco opened his own theater, the Stuyvesant, on West Forty-Fourth Street. The producer-playwright-director was always interested in providing a spectacle, so the architect George Keister designed a Neo-Georgian–style theater that could accommodate all of the showman's whims. There were lamps made by Tiffany, carved woodwork, and eighteen large murals by the artist Everett Shinn.

The auditorium was deliberately wide and shallow so that all of the approximately one thousand seats were close to the proscenium with clear, unobstructed views of the stage. Belasco believed the theatrical experience depended in part upon the actors and audience being near one another.

Belasco loved to carefully paint his stage pictures by using the newest techniques in lighting, including his own pioneering work in colored silks and gels. To accomplish this, the playhouse had an immense electrical board with sixty-five dimmers—a huge number for the period.

The floor of the stage had an elevator that could be lowered to the basement workshops to lift sets into view. This complemented the enormous wing space and the traditional fly galleries.

Even though Belasco's plays were often mawkish or sentimental by today's standards, he believed in realistic sets. He would decorate them down to the smallest detail. If the play called for a kitchen, the taps in the sink had to have running water. For one play, he installed a working restaurant on the stage.

In addition to all this, there was a backstage elevator to Belasco's personal ten-room duplex apartment built atop the theater. His private rooms were decorated with a Gothic, monk-like sensibility. At some point, Belasco had taken up dressing in black and wearing a cleric's collar, sometimes even going so far as to don a cassock. His priestly attire led to his being nicknamed "the Bishop of Broadway," a soubriquet he amusedly embraced. Was it a callback to his brief Catholic schooling or mere eccentricity?

Regardless, the flamboyant Belasco could hardly be considered a saint. It was well known that, even though he was a married man, and despite his wardrobe's pretensions to celibacy, Belasco's leading ladies and up-and-coming actresses would frequently accompany him back to his penthouse. And the din from his lavish late-night parties could often be heard in the rooms below.

In 1910, the Theatre Republic returned to its original name, and subsequently, on September 17, the Stuyvesant was rechristened the Belasco Theatre—the name it retains to this day.

Now, just a year later, the curtain was about to rise on *The Return of Peter Grimm,* the new three-act play into which Belasco had placed his body and soul. In the program, he noted what had led him to write the fantasy. Ever since childhood he had wondered whether the dead might be able to return. It was what he called "the eternal riddle of the living."

When he was a boy, he had read a story in which those in the Beyond "foretold dangers to loved ones." Throughout his youth, his mother had such premonitions. One time, for example, she begged him not to go on a steamboat outing with his friends, but pooh-poohing her fears, he ignored her. Once onboard, however, the forewarning echoed in his mind. He could envision her tear-streamed face as she called out, "I wish you would not go, Davy." At the last minute, he rushed down the gangway and off the boat. During the excursion, a disaster onboard led to several people, including many of the children, being killed or injured. Was her presentiment precognition or perhaps a warning from the Other Side?

Belasco's belief in Unknown Forces was reinforced when his beloved mother returned to talk to him from beyond the grave. After a long day of troubled rehearsals for his play *Zaza,* Belasco fell, exhausted, into a sound sleep. In the middle of the night, he abruptly awoke to see his mother, dressed all in white, standing at the foot of his bed. She called his boyhood name, "Davy! Davy!", over and over. She said she was dying but that he was not to grieve. She simply had to see him one more time. And with that, the vision faded as her form slipped out of the room.

Belasco feared the worst. He jumped out of bed and roused his whole family. "My mother is dead. I know she is dead," he wailed. What else could the spectral encounter have meant? His family tried to comfort him: He was only dreaming, they said. Or perhaps it was a hallucination. But Belasco wasn't able to get back to sleep that night.

The next afternoon he went to lunch with one of his staff. The man had also been preoccupied with the difficult run-throughs at the theater, so he had forgotten to give Belasco a telegraph message that had arrived that morning. His mother had died the night before in San Francisco at the same time Belasco had seen her spirit in his room.

What finally led to writing *Peter Grimm* was his association with actor David Warfield. Discovered by Belasco in 1901, Warfield became one of the top comedy actors on the New York stage in the early twentieth century. His forte was playing kindly but cranky old gentlemen set upon by everyday mishaps and the vicissitudes of life. Belasco conceived the character of Grimm as a caring but stern taskmaster who recognizes the errors of his mortal ways when he has the chance to return as a phantom, and in Warfield, Belasco felt he had the perfect person to sympathetically portray him.

The story Belasco crafted was simple. A seemingly robust, prosperous, unmarried Dutchman, Peter Grimm enjoys his life to the fullest on his estate just north of New York City. His doctor knows the truth, however—that his friend will soon die—and, without disclosing the seriousness of his condition, gets Grimm to make a pact that whichever of them dies first will try to return to let the other person know that an Afterlife exists. After he passes over, Grimm does come back, but he discovers the difficulty of making contact and interacting with the living.

The play was filled with melodramatic flourishes and clichés, such as a greedy minister, a nosy parson's wife, a virginal young ward and her poor suitor, a deceitful cad of a nephew, a frail child "sensitive" to spirits, all wrapped up in a tale of thwarted love made right. But it also had long, lyrical passages in which the possibility of life after death was explored.

As the house lights lowered that October evening, Belasco smiled as he surveyed the murmuring audience in his magnificent auditorium. The curtain slowly started to rise. This was Belasco's favorite part of the evening: As a play begins to weave its spell, it's magic time.

The show was a huge critical and popular success. The initial production continued for six months, which was a healthy run for the time. Belasco later revealed that the play had been written during the last year and a half of his daughter Augusta's life. She liked to keep the manuscript by her bedside, and the promise of the Next World seemed to comfort her. She often remarked, "Yes, Father, it is all true. I believe every word of it." Belasco later commented that although none of them knew it at the time, "the dear child was preparing to leave the world."

Over the next nineteen years, Belasco would produce more than fifty plays at his namesake theater, including a brief revival of *Peter Grimm* in the fall of 1921, with Warfield once again in the title role.

(Also along the way, in December 1915, Belasco wrote *Van der Decken,* based on the legend of the ghost ship, the *Flying Dutchman.* The play, also featuring Warfield, toured on the road, but it was never produced in New York.)

Belasco was passionate about the theater that bore his name. He spent much of the last twenty years of his life within its walls, writing, producing, and directing. It gave him fame, wealth, and enormous happiness—not to mention a very active "personal" life. He died in New York in May 1931 at the age of seventy-one. But is it any surprise that he has never left the building?

After Belasco's death, his theater was leased, first to actress and producer Katherine Cornell, then for a time to the wife of playwright Elmer Rice. The Group Theatre took residency in the playhouse in December 1934. Formed three years earlier by theater titans Harold Clurman, Cheryl Crawford, and Lee Strasberg, the Group Theatre sought to provide a natural style of acting derived from the teachings of the Russian master Constantin Stanislavski. Among their landmark productions at the theater were Clifford Odets's *Awake and Sing, Golden Boy,* and *Rocket to the Moon.* In 1948, the playhouse became part of the Shubert Organization. Then for a few years, from mid-1949 until November 1953, NBC broadcast radio plays from the theater, but after that, legitimate plays started anew.

Throughout all this, Belasco's ghost was lurking in the shadows.

Almost immediately after his death, stage crew and actors started spotting his phantom all over the theater. But this was no wispy wraith. He could always be recognized by his white, tousled hair and the priest-like outfit, either a black shirt with collar and jacket or sometimes a monk's robe. It was unmistakably Belasco.

Sometimes his ghost could be seen sitting alone in the balcony. Or he would make his way backstage to shake hands with the actors or even give them a word of encouragement or advice. More than one actress complained that a man dressed as a Catholic parson pinched her derriere.

Late at night, after the audience had gone, crew members, cast, and office personnel would hear laughing, singing, and footsteps—even the sound of a party in full swing—emanating from the closed-off area overhead that used to be Belasco's penthouse suite. At least one stagehand reported hearing the gears and chains of Belasco's old private elevator moving, even though the lift had been disabled for some time. For many years, the stage doorman claimed that every day at 4 p.m. his dog would growl at an invisible presence. It was at that time of the day Belasco had been prone to take a leisurely stroll about the building.

The distinct odor of Belasco's burning cigar could occasionally be caught in the air backstage. Doors on set pieces might open or slam shut without assistance. And, from time to time, the front curtain would go up, pause for a few moments, then lower on its own. Was it Belasco giving a helping hand, trying to get the show to begin?

Belasco's spirit would also leave the confines of back-stage and the auditorium to wander around the theater's hallways and stairwells. An usher claimed that one night when she jokingly said, "Good night, Mr. Belasco," while closing up the lobby, all of the doors facing out onto Forty-Fourth Street suddenly swung open simultaneously by themselves.

Over time, the ghost's appearance came to be considered a lucky omen. He often showed up on opening nights in his favorite, otherwise empty, private box.

But his appearances stopped abruptly in 1970 when *Oh! Calcutta!* transferred to the theater from downtown. With its full frontal nudity, the show was quite daring at the time, but why this should have scared away the spectre of a man who was well-known for indulgences of the flesh is unknown.

Rumors persisted that the theater was haunted, although for thirty years reports of the ghost actually materializing were rare.

But apparently with the new millennium, Belasco has chosen to show himself once again. His spectre was seen during the run of *Enchanted April* when it played at the theater in 2003. The following year, several cast members of *Dracula, the Musical* heard sounds of an argument between a spectral man and woman seemingly coming from behind a large portrait of David Belasco hanging near the stage door. When the painting was lifted away from the wall, there was nothing there.

Surely one of the disembodied voices was Belasco's, but who did the other belong to? Well, Belasco always loved the ladies. Has he found a companion in the Afterlife? One actress recently claimed that while taking a shower in her locked dressing room she heard someone—or something— enter by the locked door. When she peeked out from behind the curtain, she saw a hazy, blue glow hovering in mid-air. Others have seen the Blue Lady, as some are now calling the spirit light, in the house itself. So far, there have been few sightings of this second ghostly presence in the Belasco Theatre, but once they've manifested, phantoms tend to stick around.

The Bishop of Broadway may have to get used to sharing the limelight.

Chapter 2
The Ziegfeld Girl

She was on top of the world. She was one of Ziegfeld's favorites. And she got to marry a movie star. But after a late night of revels, ex-Ziegfeld chorine Olive Thomas accidentally took her final bow. Now she's returned to the theater of her happy past.

Looking into the mirror in the bathroom of her hotel suite in Paris, Olive couldn't quite focus her eyes. It had been a wild night of partygoing. But why shouldn't she have fun? She was on her second honeymoon. Her husband, Jack, was already passed out on the bed in a drunken stupor. If only *she* could get to sleep. Maybe there was something there on the washstand she could take to calm herself down, help her doze off. There: That must be the sleeping pills. In the blue bottle.

"Ollie," as she was known to her friends, had been born Oliva R. Duffy in Charleroi, Pennsylvania, near Pittsburgh, in 1894. She married a local man, Bernard Thomas, at sixteen, but, after two years, they divorced and she moved to New York City.

While working in a department store in Harlem, she entered a contest to find the "Most Beautiful Girl in New York City," being held by the successful commercial artist Howard Chandler Christy, who was already well-known for his sketches of young, nymph-like ladies (the so-called Christy Girls).

Olive thought she had a real chance. Her skin was flawless, delicate, almost translucent. Long eyelashes rimmed her violet-blue eyes, and a curled mane cascaded over her shoulders. She won the title.

This led to her being drawn by Harrison Fisher, the "Father of a Thousand Girls," whose work, like Christy's, featured young, attractive women. Olive's wholesome yet provocative look led to her likeness appearing on the cover of the *Saturday Evening Post*.

Fisher always claimed that what happened next was a result of a letter of introduction that he wrote. Olive claimed she secured the appointment on her own. Regardless of how the meeting was arranged, the ingenue caught the eye of Florenz Ziegfeld.

Ziegfeld. The very name conjures up an image of spectacle, elaborate sets, glittering costumes, and, most important, gorgeous girls.

Although he had dabbled in entertainment at the 1893 Chicago World's Columbian Exposition, the showman got his real start by promoting the Polish-French performer Anna Held, including his scandalous press releases about her taking baths in tubs full of milk. The handsome, mustachioed impresario and the vivacious, curvaceous Held were lovers for sixteen years, until 1913, but they never married.

It was Held who first suggested to "Flo" that he produce an American version of the Parisian Folies Bergère. His first Ziegfeld Follies was staged in 1907, and they became an annual event through 1931. Over the years, the extravaganzas appeared in a number of different theaters, but its zenith coincided with its move to the magnificent New Amsterdam Theatre on June 16, 1913.

Olive remembered the first time she walked into the New Amsterdam. No wonder the *New York Times* had dubbed it the "House Beautiful" when producers Klaw and Erlanger opened its doors in 1903.

The eleven-story building, designed by architects Herts and Tallant, contained two theaters (the main auditorium and the rooftop stage), offices, broad staircases, elevators, several plush lounges, and a spacious lobby. The swirling, floral and fauna Art Nouveau decorations and walls were set in green, mother of pearl, and mauve. Murals representing the history of theater and Hendrik Hudson's founding of New Amsterdam (the early settlement that became New York City) graced its walls. The main theater sat 1,750 in three levels with twelve boxes.

Before Ziegfeld arrived, the New Amsterdam was home to classics—its opening production was *A Midsummer Night's Dream*—and musicals, including the premieres of George M. Cohan's *Forty-five Minutes from Broadway,* George Bernard Shaw's *Caesar and Cleopatra,* and Frank Lehar's *The Merry Widow*. But it was the Ziegfeld Follies that defined the ornate theater for the first quarter of the twentieth century.

Ziegfeld had a simple formula for his shows: Combine the most melodious songs assembled from Broadway's top tunesmiths, great singers, the funniest comedians from the vaudeville stage, and lavish sets with luxurious yet revealing costumes filled with strikingly good-looking women. The shows were sumptuous; the girls were ravishing. It was a match made in heaven.

From its inception, the New Amsterdam also housed a rooftop theater, originally called the Aerial Gardens. Although such stages were popular at the time, most consisted of little more than a simple raised platform placed in a nightclub setting surrounded by potted greenery. The Aerial Gardens, however, was a complete, enclosed miniature theater that could be operated year-round (although it was usually open only in the summer).

Ziegfeld renamed the space Danse de Follies when he began producing his more risqué *Midnight Frolic* there in 1915.

Some of the girls in the revue, which was most often frequented by men only, were clad only in balloons, which patrons could pop by the adroit touch of a cigar. To further titillate audiences, the showroom included a glass dance floor on a balcony, so Lotharios sitting below could peek up the skirts of the ladies overhead. The room's name was later changed to the Dresden Theatre and, in 1923, to the Frolic Theatre.

Standing on the main stage downstairs to audition for the great Ziegfeld in 1916, Olive Thomas was overwhelmed. She had heard all of the theater gossip about him. For the last five years of his relationship with Held, Ziegfeld had *another* much younger mistress, the actress Lillian Lorraine, whom he had started to feature in various shows starting in 1909. In 1914, he left both Held and Lorraine behind when he married Billie Burke, who appeared in the Follies the following year.

But the marriage didn't stop Ziegfeld's roving, womanizing ways. After all, a pretty girl is like a melody, or so said the Irving Berlin song the composer wrote for the *Follies of 1919*, so why shouldn't he play a tune whenever the opportunity present itself?

The master knew beauty, and Olive was instantly hired. Before long, she was in the *Follies,* dancing her heart out in a green beaded dress, matching feathered headband, and sash. She was such a coquette that, when the rooftop garden opened, she was moved upstairs to the friskier *Frolic.*

Olive found herself being admired and pursued by a string of wealthy gentlemen, many of whom plied her with expensive gifts. Peruvian artist Alberto Vargas convinced her to model for him, naked from the waist up. One of the other men to frequent the Frolic was movie actor and man-about-town Jack Pickford. Brother to silent film star Mary Pickford, Jack had followed his older sister to Hollywood, and by the time he met Olive, Jack had appeared in almost a hundred shorts and features.

Over the course of eight months, Pickford romanced Olive, figuratively sweeping her off her feet night after night on the dance floor. They eloped in October 1916, and although they always remained deeply in love, the marriage was far from smooth. Pickford was an alcoholic and had a wandering eye, and both of them enjoyed their libations and crazy nights. When they were together, they would fight, make up, fight, exchange costly gifts, and then fight some more. Their stormy marriage became fodder for the tabloids and movie star magazines.

Increasingly, the two were often separated by work. Independent of her husband and the *Follies*, Olive had been signed for the movies. Within just four years, she would appear in more than twenty, and in 1920, she played the title character in the film *The Flapper*, the first time that term appeared.

Meanwhile, for a time in 1918 after the U.S. entry into World War I, Pickford joined the navy, but after hushed-up accusations of bribery and his procurement of ladies for officers, he was quietly given a "medical" discharge to avoid scandal.

In August 1920 the pair decided to take a romantic getaway to Paris, and they holed up in the Hotel Ritz. On

September 9 they hit the nightclub district of Montparnasse and then stumbled home to their suite around 3 a.m. Both had been drinking, perhaps too much for their own good. Jack soon fell asleep, but Olive just couldn't get her mind to relax. So here she was, wandering into the bathroom, hoping that perhaps she could find something there that could help her get some sleep.

She stood over the washbasin and tried to read the labels on the bottles, but many of them were in French. *What is this?* she thought, picking up one of the bottles. *It's so pretty. Tinted blue. Odd, though. Almost in the shape of a tiny coffin.* She sniffed the liquid contents. A small whiff of alcohol. Even if it weren't a sleeping draught, she decided, it might help calm her nerves. She tossed back her head, tilted the bottle, and drank.

She immediately felt the burning sensation in her throat and a sharp stab to her stomach. Suddenly her mind cleared and snapped to attention. Knowing only limited French, she frantically struggled to comprehend the writing on the bottle.

"Oh, my God! Jack!"

Pickford, roused by the scream, woke to see his wife fall to the floor. He snatched up the bottle that had dropped to her side. He knew exactly what it was: the mercury bichloride that he kept to treat his chronic syphilis. What had his wife done?

He lunged for the phone and had the hotel call a doctor. Desperately, Jack forced her to drink and swallow raw eggs as she slipped in and out of consciousness to try to get her to vomit. But it was no use. Finally the physician arrived, and he pumped her stomach three times in quick succession. By 9 a.m. Olive Thomas lay in a bed in nearby Neuilly

Hospital. In the ensuing hours, she would come around, be lucid for a few moments, apologize to Jack for her dreadful accident or call for her mother, and then slip back into sleep. Throughout it all, Jack stayed by her side.

Despite all the doctor's ministrations, the amount of toxic fluid she had ingested took its toll, and her kidneys shut down. After she died, Pickford returned his wife's body to the United States for burial. After a packed service at St. Thomas Episcopal Church in New York City, she was laid to rest in Woodlawn Cemetery in the Bronx on September 29, 1920.

Although Pickford always swore he had been asleep in the next room when Olive drank the poison, a small scandal later suggested that he had left the hotel and was out on the streets looking for drugs. Rumor also had it that she was high on cocaine at the time and that, far from it being an accident, she had actually committed suicide. The truth will never be known.

Jack would go on to marry twice after Olive's death, both times to former Ziegfeld girls. He died in Paris in January 1933 in a room that overlooked the hospital where his beloved Olive had died.

Almost immediately after her death, Olive's faded ghost began to appear backstage and in the lower lounges at the theater. But one of the most widely reported occurrences didn't take place until 1952 when a workman twice claimed to have seen the pale spectre of a Follies girl in a white dress wearing a gold sash with the name Olive emblazoned on it. Both times she abruptly vanished right before his eyes. He recognized the apparition as Thomas; he had been on the *Follies* crew as a young man when she performed in the theater, and he had always adored the dazzling showgirl.

The years were not kind to the New Amsterdam. In 1927 Ziegfeld opened his own playhouse (the aptly named Ziegfeld Theatre) on Sixth Avenue and Fifty-Fourth Street, and he moved his Follies there. (It was also where he produced one of the seminal works of American theater: *Showboat*.)

At first the New Amsterdam, which had always housed other shows between Follies seasons, continued to flourish. Its new productions included *Whoopee, The Band Wagon, Face the Music,* and *Roberta*. It was even home to rival Follies-like shows, including *Earl Carroll's Vanities* in 1930 and *George White's Scandals* in 1935.

But by then the Great Depression had forced many Broadway theaters to close or switch to movies or burlesque. After having shuttered temporarily in 1936, the New Amsterdam, the last holdout on fabled Forty-Second Street, finally succumbed in 1937, becoming a movie palace—ironically reopening with the Max Roach film version of *A Midsummer Night's Dream*.

Over the next half century, the interior of the once-splendid jewel box wasn't maintained, and it quickly deteriorated. Due to lobbying by preservationists, the building, both inside and out, was declared a New York City landmark in 1979, and the Nederlander Organization purchased it three years later with the hopes of restoring it. But the damage from the many years of decay turned out to be far worse than initial inspections had suggested, and the theater was sold to the state.

Amid the blare of the action films that had become the theater's staple fare throughout the 1960s and 1970s, Olive went into hiding and eventually was all but forgotten.

⊹

Dana woke with a start and looked at the clock on his bed stand. It was after 2 a.m. Who would be calling him at this hour? But he worked for the Disney corporation, and they could be a hard taskmaster, especially when Dana was in charge of refurbishing their newest acquisition, the New Amsterdam Theatre. Disney hoped to make it the flagship for their bold new stage venture, Disney Theatricals, and in 1993, for an estimated $35 million, they began restoring the faded grand lady to its former glory.

"Mr. Amendola, sir, you won't believe what I just saw," said the voice at the other end of the phone. "I want out of this place. Now!"

The panicked night watchman rattled on about what he had encountered. In the gloom, his eyes made out the glowing image of a striking young woman, shimmering on the darkened stage. He raised his flashlight and caught her full in its beam. The beads from her Follies dress, headpiece, and sash sparkled in the glare, and in her hands, the security guard could make out a big blue bottle.

"Miss," he called, "stop. Who are you? You shouldn't be in here."

A demure smile formed on the girl's lips. She turned, drifted across the stage, and continued out of the building—right through the solid wall of the Forty-First Street side of the theater.

Amendola *could* and *did* believe what the man told him. During research for the theater project, he had stumbled across the story of the sad fate and the purported spectral comeback of Olive Thomas. He hadn't told the security staff— why would he want to worry them with a ghost story?—but the theater workers, mostly men, had been running into the spectre throughout the restoration, onstage and sometimes in one of the dressing rooms. She was usually dressed in her beaded green gown, and she always carried that blue flask. On some occasions she even spoke to them. Still a flirt, she would whisper, "Hi, fella," and bat her eyes before suddenly disappearing. Or her disembodied voice would call out, "Hey, how're you doin'?" Other times, objects moved on their own, rearranged by phantom hands.

The New Amsterdam opened to the public in May 1997 with a staged concert of *King David,* followed by *The Lion King* and *Mary Poppins.* Even after he became a vice president of operations, Amendola continued to hear tales of sightings.

The casts and crews have reported that Olive is a semi-regular guest at the theater, never appearing until after the audience has left for the night. On at least one occasion she is said to have made the sets shake and another time caused all of the lights to blow out in the offices on one of the upper floors. She's most often seen when changes of any kind take place in the theater or when any of the dwindling number of living original Follies girls visits. And now and then she's spotted on the rooftop, floating in the area where the glass dance floor used to be located.

Since the theater was reopened as a legitimate playhouse, two portraits of Olive Thomas, looking radiant and full of life, have hung backstage. Actors are a superstitious lot, so when they pass one of them, they often make it a point to greet Olive—and her spirit.

Good night, Olive, and welcome home.

Chapter 3
Playing the Palace

In vaudeville days, you knew you had made it when you finally "played the Palace." Hundreds of acts, from unknowns to the biggest names in show business, appeared at the theater when it was home to a variety showcase. Now many have chosen to return to the place where they achieved the pinnacle of their success.

Don't look down.

It's the number-one rule. He knew it as well as he knew his own name.

Louis Borsalino, part of the acrobatic team the Four Casting Pearls, was making his solo walk on a tightwire strung from a stage-right box to the front of the mezzanine, high above the heads of the rapt audience twenty or thirty feet below.

He'd done the walk a hundred times before in theaters and fairs, indoors and out, all across the country. But this was the "big time." He was "playing the Palace."

Since at least the early nineteenth century, itinerant entertainers and variety acts had been appearing regularly in saloons, town halls, and seedy theaters across America. One of the first uses of the term "vaudeville" came in the 1870s when H. J. Sargent organized a revue show he called Sargent's Great Vaudeville Company in Louisville, Kentucky. Tony Pastor, a former circus ringmaster–turned–theater owner, was instrumental in popularizing the entertainment format when, in October 1881, he opened a "clean" vaudeville, with acts suitable for one and all, in New York City. The new sensation caught on.

From the early 1880s until the 1930s, vaudeville was perhaps the leading form of theatrical entertainment throughout the United States. On a single show, the audience could see a half dozen or more variety acts—trained animals, magicians, jugglers, acrobats, dancers, singers, musicians, comedians, pantomime artists, actors in short vignettes—all on the same bill, topped by a headliner.

In July 1885 two former circus men, B. F. Keith and Edward Franklin Albee II (the adoptive grandfather of playwright Edward Albee), opened the Boston Bijou Theatre, in which performers on the bill repeated their acts, one after the other, from 10 in the morning until 11 at night. As with the old circus sideshows or ten-in-ones, you could pay your admission, come in any time, and stay as long as you liked. Keith and Albee later opened the Union Square Theatre in New York City before moving on to Philadelphia, Boston, and other cities throughout the Northeast and Midwest. Before long they controlled a huge theater route, popularly known as the Keith circuit—*and* the acts to perform on it.

In 1906 the men formed the United Booking Office, which charged artists a 5 percent commission for booking them. In addition, they sewed up contracts with several rival theater chains, so that in the early twentieth century it became almost impossible to perform in the better vaudeville theaters in the eastern United States unless Keith Albee represented you.

Enter Martin Beck. Beck had moved to the United States from Austria in 1883 at the age of sixteen. By the early 1890s he had settled in San Francisco, where he became involved with the Orpheum Theatre. After Morris Meyerfeld bought the playhouse in 1899, Beck helped him expand until he owned a chain of theaters, which became known as the Orpheum circuit. By 1905 Beck was managing the company.

Keith, Albee, and Beck were the titans of vaudeville, and every act courted their favor. Performers on their circuits might struggle for years in near-anonymity in the "small time" in rural towns and minor cities, performing multiple shows a day for low pay in rundown theaters or other buildings pressed into service as theaters. If the acts did well, they would be promoted to the "medium time," which offered better pay for just two shows a day in theaters specially built for vaudeville use. Then, if they were talented enough and gained a loyal following, they would graduate into the "big time," performing in theaters in major cities. The higher the act's name was on the bill, the better the prestige and, usually, the better the pay, sometimes into the thousands of dollars a week.

And at the top of the rung, the mecca to which all acts aspired, was the Palace Theatre.

When Martin Beck decided to make a stand in the Big Apple, he engaged architects Kirchoff and Rose to design a new flagship theater for him that would sit in the middle of Duffy Square, right on Broadway near the corner of Forty-Seventh Street. The Palace was roomy: The house could seat more than 1,700 people on three levels and was handsomely decorated in crimson and gold.

But Beck was the new boy in town, and Keith and Albee had no inclination to make it easy for him. They had an exclusive lock on some of the best talent in the country, having placed them under contract to work in their houses. Albee demanded that Beck give up three-quarters of his shares in the Palace, or he wouldn't allow any of his acts to perform there.

The agreement was further complicated by the fact that theater owner Oscar Hammerstein operated a rival variety house, the Victoria Theatre, at Broadway and Forty-Second Street. He had already negotiated a deal with Keith and Albee to be allowed to act as an agent for any of their acts in that part of the theater district. Beck was finally able to come to terms with Hammerstein: He paid him $225,000—an astronomical sum—to be allowed to book the acts directly.

Finally, with all the deals in place, Beck was able to open the Palace on March 24, 1913, promising the best family entertainment on Broadway. Two shows were to be performed daily, with a $1.50 top price for matinees, $2.00 in the evening. Headlining the bill at the premiere was the great clown Ed Wynn.

Audiences were amazed by the theater's splendor. They weren't as impressed by what was onstage. Even the show business trade paper *Variety* was unenthusiastic, complaining about the quality of the acts as well as the high ticket prices.

Beck took drastic measures. Just a few weeks after opening, he convinced Ethel Barrymore, then the First Lady of the American Stage, to appear on the bill in a one-act play. Then, in May, Sarah Bernhardt made her first New York vaudeville appearance at the Palace. The theater's fortunes seemed to turn overnight.

The Palace's reputation grew, and it quickly became *the* place to perform. To "play the Palace" became synonymous with having achieved the height of success as a variety act. Acts clambered to appear there.

Over the next twenty years, most of the top names in show business headlined the bill at the Palace, including Jack Benny, Milton Berle, Fanny Brice, Burns and Allen,

Eddie Cantor, W. C. Fields, Bob Hope, Harry Houdini (whom Beck had discovered performing in a beer hall in St. Paul, Minnesota, in 1899), George Jessel, the Marx Brothers, Ethel Merman, Kate Smith, Sophie Tucker, and Will Rogers.

There were also a few notable exceptions. Among them was Al Jolson (whose ghost is said to haunt the Royal Alexandra Theatre in Toronto). During the Palace's early years up until his retirement from live performance in 1926, Jolson was the most famous and highly paid entertainer in America, but he was under contract to Lee Shubert, the owner of the competing Winter Garden Theatre. As a result, Shubert never allowed Jolson to appear at the palace.

Ironically, 1927, the year Jolson's film *The Jazz Singer* opened, is often cited as the date vaudeville died. The movie business had already begun to divert audiences away from live entertainment. For a time, acts were forced to share the bill with movies, performing on the stage between screenings. But when the Great Depression hit, most theater owners were forced to face the inevitable: It was much more profitable to run a movie several times a day than to pay for performers, stagehands, and a live orchestra.

The Palace tried to hold out as long as possible. In 1929 the owners increased the theater schedule to three performances a day. Three years later they moved to four shows a day and drastically lowered ticket prices. In November 1934 they dropped vaudeville from the bill completely and (except for a brief return to variety shows in 1936) operated as a movie house until the end of the 1940s.

In the 1950s the Palace tried to revive live entertainment at the theater by presenting concert appearances by stars, often supported by opening variety acts. It's believed that it was during one of these shows that wire-walker Borsalino took to the air in the theater.

This performance will be no different than all of the others, he thought. Inching forward, he knew the trick was to not look down at his feet. If he did, his eyes would play tricks, and his focus would shift between the thin cable and the audience far below. Instead, he had to concentrate on a fixed spot at the end of the cord. One foot in front of the other. One step at a time. Equilibrium. Balance.

He knew that if anything went wrong, there was nothing to break his fall. Wire-walking by its very nature was a duel with death. Working without a safety harness or net was what made the act exciting for the audience: There was always the possibility that the acrobat might meet his doom. Borsalino was well aware of the risk, but working with a net was out of the question. Wasn't that what made the Flying Wallendas world famous when they debuted at Madison Square Garden in 1928 without the usual safety rigging?

The Wallendas themselves would fall from a wire in 1962, killing two members of their act, and sixteen years after that Karl Wallenda, leader and patriarch of the group, would plunge to his death while attempting to walk an open-air cable stretched between two hotel rooftops in Puerto Rico.

No one ever found out what caused Borsalino's fall. Did the taut wire go slack without warning? Did something momentarily distract him, or was there a slick spot on the cord? Whatever the reason, one second the daredevil was in supreme control, hovering high above the heads of the crowd; the next second, he had lost his balance and was plummeting downward.

People scattered as Borsalino struck the seats on the floor level. Pandemonium broke out as women screamed or fainted. Mothers covered their children's eyes or rushed them out of the theater. Men leapt to their feet and crowded around the helpless entertainer.

The orchestra momentarily stopped. Then the conductor, prepared for such an emergency, sprang into action and had his band strike up a lively march. Behind the main curtain, word spread instantly among the other performers. The stage crew rushed to the acrobat's aid. Amazingly, he had not died instantly, but he was fatally injured. They gently lifted Borsalino and hurried him backstage to await the ambulance that would rush him to the nearby hospital where he died several hours later.

An announcement was made that the great daredevil was only slightly injured. With a nod from the stage manager, the orchestra leader struck up a waltz. The house lights dimmed, signaling people to return to their seats.

The show must go on.

Even Louis Borsalino would have agreed. That's showbiz. But for him, his last show at the Palace was never going to end.

The same would become true for one of the most talented entertainers in American history, one whose "comeback" performances at the Palace are the stuff of legend: Judy Garland.

Between 1951 and 1957, the Palace welcomed a succession of superstars such as Harry Belafonte, Betty Hutton, Danny Kaye, Jerry Lewis, Liberace, and Frank Sinatra. But the first of this series of headliners, Judy Garland, premiered on October 16, 1951.

Although an international film, recording, and concert performer, Garland was always troubled by insecurities and self-doubt. This had led to a nervous breakdown and a suicide attempt, which, coupled with an addiction to drugs dating back to her studio days, had recently resulted in her being fired from three high-profile movies, *The Barkleys of Broadway*, *Annie Get Your Gun*, and *Royal Wedding*.

Following a concert tour of the United Kingdom to reinvigorate her career, Garland opened at the Palace to ecstatic reviews. Her vaudeville-style, two-show-a-day run lasted for nineteen weeks, breaking all box office records at the theater and resulting in her receiving a special Tony Award. After filming *A Star Is Born*, a foray into television, and five weeks of shows in Las Vegas, Garland made a triumphant return to the Palace in 1956.

In 1965 James Nederlander and the Nederlander Organization (which at that time operated theaters in Detroit and Chicago) purchased the Palace to make it a house for legitimate theater. They brought in designer Ralph Alswang to restore the playhouse. It was repainted in crimson with gold gilt, the original crystal chandeliers were hung, the side boxes were renovated, and the lobby was elaborately decorated and filled with artwork. The theater had its grand reopening on January 29, 1966, with the premiere of *Sweet Charity*.

Since then the theater has enjoyed a steady run of musical and straight shows, with a few star concerts sprinkled in along the way to remind audiences of the theater's roots in vaudeville. The first of these headliner acts took the stage in July 1965 when Garland returned for a final sixteen shows in *At Home at the Palace*. Subsequent concert artists have included Eddie Fisher, Buddy Hackett, Shirley MacLaine, Bette Midler, Diana Ross, and Garland's daughter Liza Minnelli (in 1999's *Minnelli on Minnelli,* a tribute to her father, Vincente Minnelli, and 2008's *Liza's at the Palace*).

Ever since its reincarnation as a playhouse in '65, the Palace Theatre has had the reputation of being inhabited by several spirits. With the hundreds of entertainers who enjoyed their greatest triumphs there and the thousands of audience members who thrilled to their performances, it's of little surprise.

The unidentified spectres include a forlorn little girl who leans over the rail to peer down from the balcony, a small boy who rolls toy trucks on the floor at the back of the mezzanine level, and a man in a brown suit who walks past the manager's office at night. Another is a cellist dressed in a white gown who's observed in the orchestra pit—most recently by one of the stars of *Beauty and the Beast*.

Without a doubt, the most famous ghost at the Palace is Judy Garland herself. Although her apparition has never been seen, her troubled spirit has been felt by dozens of people as they passed or stood by a door that was specially installed for Garland at the back of the auditorium so she could make her entrance through the audience.

And then there's Louis Borsalino. For years, actors peeking out from behind the curtain while waiting for the show to begin have reported seeing his ghost floating above the heads of the audience as if he were walking across a spectral tightrope. If they watch long enough, they see him tumble and hear the disembodied voices of an invisible audience scream in horror. Needless to say, it's considered bad luck to see him or hear the shrieks. Still another legend says that anyone who catches sight of the wire-walking ghost will die within a year.

If *you* attend a show at the Palace, you can go home when the curtain falls. But for many people whose goal in life was to one day "play the Palace," their spirits can never leave. So be careful: If you spot the wrong phantom in the theater, you may one day be joining them in the playhouse forever.

Chapter 4
A Night at the Opera

They say, "It ain't over 'til the fat lady sings." Maybe it's not over until she comes back from the Other Side either. The ghost of Madame Frances Alda, the singer and wife of managing director Giulio Gatti-Casazza, didn't just return for the music: She loved to dish the dirt on her fellow divas as well.

Located on the west side of Broadway at Thirty-Ninth Street, the old Metropolitan Opera House was built as a monument to culture. No one knew at the time that it would also become home to a famous ghost.

The hauntings didn't start until the early 1950s, and they stopped abruptly when the opera company made its move about ten years later to Lincoln Center. Ironically, this helped ghost hunters confirm the identity of the phantom female who was making a ruckus in the parterre. But then, it had never been that difficult to figure out. The apparition was so distinct that several regular operagoers were able to recognize her at first glance: world-renowned soprano Frances Alda.

Born Fanny Jane Davis in Christchurch, New Zealand, in 1879, Frances Alda became one of the most dazzling and colorful sopranos of the early twentieth century. She spent most of her childhood in Melbourne, Australia, before going to study in Paris at the age of twenty-two.

She made her debut at the Opéra-Comique in 1904, singing in Massenet's *Manon*. Within two years she was appearing at the Royal Opera House in London and, for the 1906–1908 seasons, she took up residence at La Scala in Milan.

It was there that her life became entwined with her future husband, the renowned opera manager Giulio Gatti-Casazza.

Gatti-Casazza, born in Udine, Italy, in 1869, was educated as a naval engineer and marine architect, but in 1893 he succeeded his father as the manager of the municipal theater in Ferrara. After just five years, he was invited to become the manager of La Scala. He was there when Alda made her debut, and they remained close even after the impresario moved to New York in 1908 to take up his new position as manager of the Metropolitan Opera. Two years later they married.

The love of opera was well established in the United States by that time. As early as 1850 showman P. T. Barnum correctly gambled his fortune and reputation by bringing the Swedish Nightingale, soprano Jenny Lind, to America for a series of concerts. In 1854 the Academy of Music opened its doors on Fourteenth Street in lower Manhattan as the first established opera company in New York.

By 1880 a group of newly wealthy businessmen, feeling that they were being snubbed by the "old money" society that ran the Academy—among other slights, they never had access to the private boxes—decided they needed their own opera house in which they, their friends, and their families (including the Morgans, Astors, Vanderbilts, and Roosevelts) could feel comfortable. They formed the Metropolitan Opera Association and immediately began searching for a site to build a theater.

They found it at 1411 Broadway. Taking up the whole block between West Thirty-Ninth and Fortieth Streets in the Garment District, the Metropolitan Opera House was designed by J. Cleveland Cady. The exterior was hardly enticing. In fact, its stern industrial appearance gave rise to a notorious nickname, the "Yellow Brick Brewery." Nevertheless, it opened its doors on October 22, 1883, with a performance of Charles Gounod's *Faust* under managing director Henry E. Abbey.

Nine years later, on August 27, 1892, a devastating fire ravaged the theater. The entire next season had to be canceled while the edifice was rebuilt. The results were amazing.

With a new interior by architects Carrère and Hastings, the auditorium was painted in a lustrous gold, and an immense chandelier hung over the heads of the audience. The wide, gently curved proscenium was emblazoned with the names of six great composers—Beethoven, Gluck, Gounod, Mozart, Verdi, and Wagner. As audiences waited for performances to begin, they faced an enormous gold damask curtain, which became a trademark of the theater.

Not the typical look of a "haunted house" by any means.

The next sixteen years brought several glorious "firsts" to the Met. From 1892 to 1903 a new managing director, Maurice Grau, attracted the top names in opera to New York. He was followed by Heinrich Conried, who remained for five years.

Enrico Caruso made his Met debut in 1903, and his association with the theater outlasted Conried's. In fact, in some ways the Metropolitan Opera House became Caruso's second home. Before he died, he had performed there more times than he had appeared at all of the world's other opera houses combined.

By the time Gatti-Casazza took over the reins, the Met was already well on its way to becoming one of the top opera houses in the world. But under his stewardship it flourished.

At his invitation, in 1908 conductor Arturo Toscanini (with whom he had worked at La Scala) made his debut with the Metropolitan Opera. In fact, under his management there were two seasons in which both Toscanini and Gustav Mahler were guest conductors!

Gatti-Casazza felt it was important that the Met produce at least one opera by an American composer with a libretto in English every season. Although the results met with various degrees of success, and few if any of them have become staples of the opera repertoire, it was a bold gamble to make the Met a uniquely progressive institution.

Gatti-Casazza commissioned new operas from European composers as well. One, Giacomo Puccini's seventh opera, *The Girl of the Golden West,* had its world premiere at the Met on December 10, 1910. If its name sounds familiar, it's because the opera's libretto was based on the 1905 play written by David Belasco, whose ghost still haunts the Belasco Theatre, just blocks away.

In fact, many American and world premieres would take place at the Met under Gatti-Casazza. Among them was Walter Damrosch's 1913 *Cyrano,* based on the 1902 Edmund Rostand play *Cyrano de Bergerac.* The opera, which starred our future ghostly diva Frances Alda in the role of Roxanne, did not arrive without incident. The French playwright strongly protested the adaptation of his work without his permission. But in that era, international copyright laws didn't protect him, so his objection was all but ignored.

Although not as regular a presence at the Met as one might suspect given her marriage to the managing director, Alda would nevertheless appear in several productions during

Gatti-Casazza's time there. For example, she performed the title role in the 1914 world premiere of Victor Herbert's second opera, *Madeleine*. Six years later she sang the title role in Henry Haldey's *Cleopatra's Night*, another world premiere.

She also was feted for her appearances in *Faust, La Boheme, Manon Lescaut, Martha, Mesfistolfele,* and *Otello*. Also during her years at the Met she started recording for the Victor Talking Machine Company.

Alda made a triumphant return to New Zealand in 1927. The temperamental star divorced Gatti-Casazza the following year, and in 1929 she ended her association with the Met—at least while she was alive.

Gatti-Casazza remained at the helm of the opera company until 1935, when he retired and moved back to his native Italy. To date, he still has had the longest tenure of any of its managers. A year after his death, several articles he wrote were collected and published as an "autobiography," *Memories of the Opera*.

Meanwhile, Alda, still celebrated for her technique and timbre, continued to perform in concert, on recordings, on radio, and in vaudeville. She remarried in 1941 and even after retirement spent much of her year traveling the world. The colorful lyric soprano died of a stroke while in Venice, Italy, in 1952 at the age of eighty-three.

But did she stay there? No.

Gatti-Casazza had been succeeded at the Met first by Edward Johnson, from 1935 to 1950, and then by the larger-than-life Sir Rudolph Bing. Among the celebrated divas who made their Met debuts during the Bing years were Marian Anderson, Maria Callas, Birgit Nilsson, Leontyne Price, Dame Joan Sutherland, and Renata Tebaldi. Since 1950 the Met has had a succession of general managers.

The interior of the old opera house also changed over this period. In the 1940s, after ownership of the theater was transferred to the not-for-profit Metropolitan Opera Association, the private boxes in the second tier were replaced with additional rows of seating. Then, shortly after her death, Frances Alda began to appear in the parquet circle.

It's a well-founded cliché that operatic sopranos often berate the talent of their tenors. Alda was no exception, and her comments could be bitter and caustic. Indeed, her 1937 autobiography was titled *Men, Women, & Tenors*. But she perhaps held her highest scorn—even after death—for her rivals, her fellow divas.

Her ghostly manifestations always took the same form—and always during the first act of a performance. A patron would become aware of a striking woman of advanced years, handsomely dressed, and ostentatiously decked out in jewels sitting either next to her or at the end of the same row. The figure would mutter to herself, making disapproving comments about the performance of the soprano onstage. She could be overheard clicking her tongue or impatiently tapping her program. Sometimes the lights would catch her dismissively waving her hands in the air, in obvious displeasure or even disgust.

How rude!

The house manager and head ushers became used to the many complaints about the mysterious woman. For a time in the mid-1950s, they become almost commonplace. Usually the staff would simply agree to take care of the impolite lady's boorish behavior. But they knew it wasn't necessary. The bad-mannered spectre never returned for the second act.

The hauntings came to an abrupt end on April 16, 1966, when the old Metropolitan Opera House closed its doors forever. Almost all of the stars on the Met's roster took part in the final performance that night. The auditorium was filled with invited guests from the company's illustrious past, but if Alda's spirit was in attendance, she kept her peace.

The Metropolitan Opera moved to the modern Lincoln Center for the Performing Arts on Broadway at Sixty-Fourth Street. The new theater was long overdue. Although the original building was elegant and had brilliant acoustics, the space was inadequate to properly stage many major operas. Often, sets had to stand outside the structure while scenery was being changed. The new theater, on the other hand, seats around 3,800, and, in a nod to tradition, still has a gold damask main curtain—the largest of its type in the world.

An attempt to obtain landmark status for the old Met failed, and in 1967 it was demolished to make way for an office building. The visitations by Frances Alda, which can never again be experienced in the house, are now only the stuff of memory and legend.

For whatever reason, she decided not to move with the company to Lincoln Center. Perhaps her spirit was simply too attached to the old hall, or she just didn't feel at home in the new surroundings.

But, if she changes her mind, a ghost moving from one theater to another is not unprecedented. So if you find yourself being annoyed by a disruptive dowager during a production of *Turandot* at the Met, don't be too surprised. It might be Frances Alda come back to critique the new girl in town.

Part Two

GHOSTS OF THE AMERICAN STAGE

Not all actors make it to Broadway. And neither do all theater ghosts. But don't worry: There are plenty of stages throughout America where spirit entities walk the boards. Some of the spectres were actors; some were members of the audience; others were dedicated workers, volunteers, or staff.

A few of the phantoms were famous. Take John Dillinger, who still haunts the movie theater where he was gunned down, or John Wilkes Booth, who has returned to the theater where he assassinated President Abraham Lincoln. But most were everyday, ordinary people—like the teenage usher at the old Guthrie playhouse, the theater manager who couldn't bear to leave backstage, and the actress who went into her dressing room, locked the door, and was never seen again.

They came from all walks of life. But they have one thing in common: All have returned to bask in the spotlight.

Chapter 5
No Exit

The Harvard Exit Theatre in Seattle, Washington, isn't your average, everyday movie theater. In addition to what's shown on its two silver screens, at least four ghosts—three female and one male— dwell within. One predates the building; the others may still be there from its days as the city's premier women's club.

Janet Wainwright didn't like the looks of what she saw. As the new theater manager of the Harvard Exit Theatre, she unlocked the doors as usual that night at 5 and entered the main lobby to find a warm blaze already glowing from the immense fireplace. Who could have started it? She was always the first to arrive for the night, and even if someone else had come in early, the entire staff had strict orders not to leave the fire unattended.

She looked around the room. Still decorated much like it was back in its days when the building served as a private club, the lobby was furnished with a grand piano, a chandelier, cozy chairs, and small tables flanking the working hearth. The intent of the owners who transformed it into an art house cinema back in 1968 was to give patrons an inviting, comfortable place to gather while waiting for the auditorium to open before that evening's film.

Odd. Wainwright realized the chairs by the fireplace had been turned slightly toward each other, as if to encourage people to engage in conversation. They hadn't been that way when she closed up the night before.

Suddenly her eyes were attracted to a slight movement to her left, and she focused on a high-backed wooden chair. The lamp on the table next to it was on, and from its dim light Wainwright could see a woman sitting there, reading a book. Part of the stranger's long hair was pulled up into a bun while the rest neatly framed her ashen face, and she was wearing a calf-length floral dress of a style popular several decades earlier. Her silent presence was unsettling enough, but she also seemed translucent. The phantom female turned to Wainwright, and their eyes met. Was it just for a few seconds or several minutes? As the theater manager stared, incredulous, the figure slowly faded into nothingness.

Wainwright would remain at Harvard Exit for ten years, but that was the last time she saw that particular vision. However, it was far from the last haunting that would occur during her stay there.

The story of her unearthly encounter was retold many times, and before long legend had it that the fire was *frequently* burning when the evening personnel arrived. Sometimes it was said that instead of vanishing, the spectre would rise, turn off the lamp, and walk out of the room. Or she would turn the lights on as an employee entered the darkened lobby. Supposedly she also appeared on photographs of the lobby, even though no one was ever visible in the room when the shots were taken.

The spirit was soon identified. Or at least it was decided who she was: Bertha Knight Landes, one of the early presidents of the Women's Century Club, for which the building was constructed and that still meets there to this day.

To be honest, it's entirely possible that the spectre that's most often seen is not Bertha Landes at all. No positive ID has ever been made. But it's usually assumed that she's the oldest and most austere-looking of the female spirits that show up.

That's right: She's not alone. But more about the others in a moment.

Located on the corner of Roy Street and Harvard Avenue in the trendy, bohemian Capitol Hill section of Seattle, Harvard Exit Theatre is recognized for its showing of avant-garde and independent films. It got its unusual name because, although the box office and entrance to the theater are on Roy Street, the main auditorium exits onto Harvard Avenue.

A private house was originally located on the site, but it was ripped down so the current three-story brick building could be constructed in 1925 as a home for the Women's Century Club. The organization was founded by Carrie Chapman Catt in July 1891 and became a member of the General Federation of Women's Clubs the following year. Catt had become president of the national suffrage movement when Susan B. Anthony retired, and after years of traveling and lecturing on behalf of the right-to-vote faction, Catt eventually settled in Seattle.

Washington seemed a natural place for Catt to put down roots. Women had been allowed to vote in the state since 1883 in its territorial days. When Catt founded her new club, she created its name in the belief that women would finally achieve full equal rights in the next century.

Nowhere in its early days could the aspirations of the Women's Century Club be better exemplified than in Bertha Knight Landes.

Bertha Knight was born in Ware, Massachusetts, in 1868. She graduated with degrees in history and political science from Indiana University in 1891, and after teaching at Classical High School for three years, she married a geologist,

Henry Landes, whom she had met while they were students. They moved to Seattle when Henry became a professor in the College of Science at the University of Washington, and they raised a family of three children.

Bertha felt that being active in the community was a necessary role for women, and over the next few years she took leadership roles in several women's groups in Seattle, including the Women's University Club, the Washington State League of Women Voters, the Women's Auxiliary of University Congregational Church, and, of course, the Women's Century Club. She became its president in 1918 and remained its head for two years.

In 1921 her organizational skills as president of the Seattle Federation of Women's Clubs impressed the mayor, and she was invited (as the only woman) to join a commission on unemployment. The next year, with her husband's strong support, Landes ran for the city council and won.

But this was only the start of her political career. She was reelected two years later and was named city council president. Then, in 1926, she ran for mayor, promising to clean up corruption with "municipal housekeeping." She soundly defeated the incumbent Edwin J. "Doc" Brown, and in doing so she became the first female mayor of a major city in the United States.

When she came up for reelection two years later, she was endorsed by city newspapers, the Central Labor Council, the Prohibition Party, and various women's clubs. But a whisper campaign had started almost from the time of her inauguration that a city as large and important as Seattle should not have a woman as its mayor. Despite her general popularity, the "sex card" was successfully played, and Landes went down in defeat to Frank Edwards, a political nobody.

Although Landes's time in the Seattle political spotlight was over, she remained active in women's issues up until her death in 1943. It was a long and distinguished career, both locally and later nationally. So, of all the places with which she was associated over the years, why would she choose to haunt the building that was once owned by the Women's Century Club? After all, it had not even been built when she was the club's president. She was serving on the city council by the time the clubhouse opened.

Who's to say? Surely she visited the building often, and she had great affection for the organization that used it as its headquarters. Perhaps she figured, "Why not stick around to make sure everything remains copasetic?"

In 1968, two Boeing engineers and self-avowed cinema buffs, Art Bernstein and Jim O'Steen, purchased the Women's Century Club's home and transformed it into a movie theater. The spacious lobby retains its 1920s charm from when it was the clubhouse's reception area; the second main auditorium on the ground floor now seats four hundred and includes a small balcony.

From the start, the newly dubbed Harvard Exit Theatre specialized in contemporary foreign language movies and independent films, as well as American and foreign classics—the sort of fare not normally on view at traditional commercial theaters. For many years Bernstein personally welcomed the audience and introduced the film each evening. The theater's reputation led to its being named one of the original host cinemas of the Seattle International Film Festival and the Gay and Lesbian Film Festival.

Landmark Theatres/Seven Gables purchased it in 1979. In the 1980s a former ballroom on the third floor was converted into a second movie theater called the Top of the

Exit. Dedicated patrons must climb two steep flights of stairs (with landings in between) to get there, because there's no elevator. Recent renovations to the building have added an indoor box office, enlarged concession space, and wheelchair-accessible restrooms on the lobby level.

The second floor, not generally seen by the public, is used for offices, with several rooms opening onto a central corridor.

And, of course, there are the ghosts.

Several apparitions—female apparitions and at least one male—have been seen at the Harvard Exit Theatre dating back to the middle of the twentieth century.

Although the spectre in the lobby thought to be Bertha Landes also occasionally manifests just outside the third-floor theater, what's most often experienced up there is an indistinct but overbearing negative force that appears to be laying claim to the territory. Luckily, so far no one's been hurt. Some parapsychologists and ghost hunters who've studied the Harvard Exit Theatre—and there have been many—suggest that the entity might not be an individual spirit. Rather, they claim it might be the collective energy of several spirits, perhaps former strong-willed suffragettes, trying to protect their clubhouse.

A female ghost (who may or may not be a different phantom) has made her way onto the second floor, where the sad spectre sometimes frightens the staff working in the offices as she floats down the hallway. She's even been heard crying, and at least one employee approached the unfamiliar person to see if he could help. When he got near, the apparition instantly disappeared.

Then there's the female form that sometimes shows up in the balcony of the main auditorium. Most often, people merely sense her presence, but she's been known to be visible from time to time, wearing a late Victorian–era dress. Her identity is unknown, but because of her short height, she's not believed to be Landes.

Some think she's the ghost of a woman who, it's said, was suffocated somewhere in the building in the 1940s. But there are plenty of other candidates. Many women resided in second- and third-floor apartments at the house during its early years, and a few of the flats were utilized all the way into the 1970s. Over the past eighty-plus years, hundreds of women have passed through the building's doors and held it close to their hearts. Any one of them could be the phantom visitor in the balcony.

As for the ghostly male figure that shows up now and then, some think it might be a man who was killed in a fight in the old house that was torn down to make way for the present structure. Regardless, Peter, as he's been nicknamed, is fascinated by the movies. The portly, slightly transparent form sometimes brushes the back of moviegoers' necks as they watch the film. Or he'll appear standing down in front, just off the corner of the screen, joyfully watching the movie himself.

Other times he (or some other spirit) plays tricks, though never malicious ones. Projectionists will come in to discover film canisters strewn about the floor, and on occasion the movie is already playing when they arrive. In such cases, the projection booth is always locked from the inside.

If you're in the mood to catch a fascinating flick the next time you're in Seattle, the Harvard Exit Theatre is a good bet. But it might not be a simple, lighthearted night out at the movies. That person sitting next to you in the dark may be not all she or he seems. It could be one of the resident ghosts paying another visit.

Chapter 6

Vex Not
His Ghost

They say the role of King Lear is the Mount Everest of the Shake-
speare canon. So it's little wonder that the ghost of that giant of an
actor Charles Laughton, who planned to portray the monarch at
the Oregon Shakespeare Festival, returns to haunt its stage.

Over the years, the four-acre campus of the Oregon Shakespeare Festival has played host to some of the biggest names
in theater. And they don't get much bigger in fame or frame
than Charles Laughton.

Located just off Interstate 5 a few miles north of the
California border, Ashland, Oregon, is a bucolic, close-knit
community. The city is home to about twenty thousand year-
round residents, although it attracts another hundred thousand each year to the stages of the festival playhouses.

Today, the Oregon Shakespeare Festival, or OSF, as it's
often called, produces eleven plays (four or five of which are
by the Bard of Avon) on its three stages over a nine-month
season from February to October. Usually three of those productions are performed during the summer months on its
original space, the outdoor Elizabethan Stage.

And that's the one Laughton, whose plans to perform
there were cut short by his death, now haunts.

In the late 1800s the Chautauqua movement, that unique
brand of live entertainment and educational lecture, was
in full swing. Often its performers appeared under canvas,

but in July 1893 Ashland opened a permanent structure to host the touring companies. The theater's capacity was expanded eight years later to seat 1,500 patrons. Then, in 1917, the structure was replaced with a magnificent domed structure.

Unfortunately, by the time the new theater was completed, Chautauqua was breathing its last, and the stage fell into disuse. The dome was removed for public safety, but the walls were allowed to stay in place.

In early 1935, Angus L. Bowmer, a theater professor at Ashland's Southern Oregon Normal School, made a startling proposition to the city. To him, the partially remaining wall of the now roofless building resembled the round theaters of Elizabethan times, so he suggested to civic leaders that the space be used to perform Shakespeare plays during the summer.

Given permission to put together a season—provided he also include boxing matches to guarantee the program showed a profit—that summer Bowmer arranged his First Annual Oregon Shakespearean Festival, which consisted of just two plays, *Twelfth Night* and *The Merchant of Venice*. They were a huge success with the community; in fact, the money made off the shows paid for the loss incurred by the boxing matches.

The idea for a larger festival took off.

Originally Bowmer built a thrust stage (projecting out into the audience) within the twelve-foot-high, circular walls. The Elizabethan Stage, as he called it, was divided into three performance areas: a forestage, a middle, and an inner stage with a balcony. It was damaged by fire in 1940, and the festival was suspended during World War II. The stage was rebuilt in the shape of a trapezoid for the 1947 reopening, with added upper performance areas flanking its balcony.

Renovated once again for the 1959 season, the theater had a third story (and accompanying backstage space) added to the stage's facade. Additional structural changes were provided to make the theater resemble, as closely as possible, the known configuration of Shakespeare's lost Fortune Theatre as it appeared in 1599 London.

That was how it looked in 1961 when Charles Laughton came for a visit. He had been asked to perform at the OSF for many years, but up until then, he had resisted Bowmer's entreaties. The natural setting and the receptive audiences entranced him, however, and he immediately approached Bowmer about the possibility of performing *King Lear* at a future festival.

Laughton had been born in Scarborough, England, in 1899. Initially entering the family hotel business, he acted only for pleasure in a local amateur society. At the age of twenty-six, though, he decided to move to London to study at the Royal Academy of Dramatic Arts, the school founded in 1904 by Sir Beerbohm Tree at Her Majesty's Theatre (which today is haunted by Tree's ghost).

Laughton made his professional debut in the West End in 1926. He was rotund, not exactly the typical "leading man" type, but as a character actor he was brilliant . . . *and* memorable. He was quickly cast in a string of plays, including one called *Alibi* based on Agatha Christie's *The Murder of Roger Ackroyd,* in which he became the first person to portray the novelist's famous detective, Hercule Poirot.

He made his first Broadway appearance in 1931, which immediately resulted in work in Hollywood movies. (He'd already acted in several silent British shorts while still appearing on the London stage.) In short order he turned out amazingly varied roles in a half dozen films, including a deranged submarine commander in *Devil and the Deep* and Nero in Cecil B. DeMille's *The Sign of the Cross*. But it was his magnificent performance in the title role in 1933's *The Private Life of Henry VIII* that secured his place in film history. His outsized portrayal of the royal glutton won him an Oscar for Best Actor in a Leading Role.

Laughton's passion was Shakespeare from the time of his youth, and he always yearned to be accepted as a classical actor. In 1933, just after his movie *Henry VIII*, he was asked to perform a repertory season at the Old Vic Theatre in London, and he jumped at the chance. The results were disappointing. Whatever the reason, his first efforts at portraying Macbeth, Henry VIII, and Prospero on the stage were poorly received by the critics.

Laughton returned to films with a vengeance. Throughout the 1930s he seemed to specialize in historical costume dramas, and he's still remembered for his astonishing interpretations of such characters as Quasimodo (*The Hunchback of Notre Dame*, 1939) and Captain Bligh (*The Mutiny on the Bounty*, 1935, for which he was nominated for his second Academy Award).

Regrettably, most of his 1940s films are forgettable, including one that is nevertheless worth mentioning here because of its subject matter. In 1944 he starred in *The Canterville Ghost*, very loosed based on the Oscar Wilde short story. *Very loosely* because, other than the fact there's a spectre haunting the Canterville family manse, the original story and the movie's screenplay have nothing to do with each other.

Wilde's tale concerns an American family that buys an English manor purported to be haunted. Indeed, they encounter the ghost almost at once, but instead of being frightened off by the pesky spirit, they decide to make *his* life miserable. By the end of the story, they manage to make peace with the phantom and help him make his way onto the Next Plane.

In the film version Laughton played a cowardly noble from the 1600s who ran away from a duel and hid in the family castle. Disgraced, his father walled him up alive. The man's ghost becomes fated to haunt the mansion until one of his descendants breaks the curse by performing a heroic act. His chance comes when troops, including one of his distant relatives, are stationed there during World War II.

Throughout this period, Laughton made regular returns to the theater. In 1936 he'd made a memorable Captain Hook opposite a Peter Pan played by his wife, Elsa Lanchester. For his celebrated 1947 English-language version of *Galileo,* Laughton (who starred as well as directed) worked closely with author Bertolt Brecht. Three years later he directed and appeared as the devil in an all-star concert version of George Bernard Shaw's *Don Juan in Hell.*

Two of his biggest successes in the theater came from plays he only directed: his 1953 stage reading of Stephen Vincent Benét's *John Brown's Body* and his biggest hit, the 1954 stage version of Herman Wouk's *The Caine Mutiny Court-Martial,* starring Henry Fonda.

The 1950s saw Laughton playing everything on the silver screen from a comic pirate in an Abbott and Costello movie to Herod in *Salome.* He even revisited Henry VIII in 1953's *Young Bess.* In 1955 he directed his one and only film, *The Night of the Hunter,* now considered a classic but unsuccessful in its initial run. Two years later, in 1957, another Agatha Christie role brought him his third Best Actor Oscar nomination in the screen version of *Witness for the Prosecution.*

The British actor, a U.S. citizen since 1950, felt that he had too long been away from the boards in his native country, so in 1958 Laughton returned to the West End as director and star of a minor play, *The Party*. It turned out to be his last performance on the London stage.

There's a superstition in the theater world that it's bad luck to want something too much. A perfect example might be Charles Laughton's lifelong desire to portray King Lear. He'd always dreamed of one day playing what many consider to be, with perhaps the exception of Hamlet, the hardest role in the Shakespeare canon. In private, Laughton dissected, studied, memorized, and practiced the role. In 1959 he was finally invited to perform *Lear* at the Royal Shakespeare Theatre in Stratford-upon-Avon, the playwright's birthplace.

The production had every chance for success. The company included Vanessa Redgrave, Albert Finney, and Ian Holm. Because of his years poring over the part, Laughton was "off book," working without a script and his lines fully memorized, from the first day of rehearsal (even though this, too, is considered by many in the theater world to be bad luck).

According to all accounts, Laughton was magnificent during the first few run-throughs. But, unfortunately, there were six more weeks of rehearsal to go, which must have seemed endless to someone who had carried the role with him for so many years. Then, the actor's nightmare: On opening night, Laughton completely blanked, forgetting his very first line. After a very noticeable prompt, he immediately got back on track, but by then the damage had been done. Afterward, critics and the audience weren't particularly kind, and the reputation of his Lear had been cemented, if not as a disaster, as a bad miscalculation. Laughton, crushed, returned to the States and went on tour, primarily in concert readings.

Then, in 1961, he came to Ashland. After seeing the superb surroundings, he relished the chance to revisit Lear, and preparations began at once. There were even discussions that he would also play the role of Falstaff in their already-announced 1963 production of *The Merry Wives of Windsor*.

But none of the plans were to be. On December 15, 1962, Laughton succumbed to bladder cancer, and he was buried in Los Angeles. But perhaps his will to perform at the festival was so strong that he refused to accept death as his final act. In his heart, he must have felt his best scenes were yet to come.

The Merry Wives went on as planned. Throughout the performance loud, resonant—and oddly familiar—disembodied laughter was frequently heard backstage. And to one actor it was more than an aural illusion. A stout, full-bearded Falstaff strode into view confidently, resplendent in sixteenth-century doublet, hose, and feathered cap. But it wasn't the player who was scheduled to perform the role that evening. It was Charles Laughton!

Word soon spread that the great actor had returned from the grave. The next year, when the production of *King Lear* in which Laughton had hoped to perform finally had its first performance, an ethereal, indescribable noise, almost but not quite that of a human voice, rushed through the audience and up onto the stage. Was Laughton back again howling his anguish?

The last scene of the play, in which Lear would die, flashed through the actors' minds. The monarch's loyal subject Edgar beckons him to rise, but the king's servant Kent stays the thought, saying,

> Vex not his ghost: O, let him pass! he hates him much
> That would upon the rack of this tough world
> Stretch him out longer.

Laughton's ghost was *clearly* in the house, no doubt vexed that he had been unable to triumph as Lear himself.

Ever since, almost every season, the invisible phantom of the corpulent star of stage and screen has been heard singing or moaning somewhere in the theater, especially when *King Lear* is being performed. If he deigns to materialize, it's most often backstage on the third level of the Elizabethan Stage.

Many changes have occurred at the festival in the past forty years. In 1970 a second, indoor playhouse, the Angus Bowmer Theatre, was added. Bowmer himself retired the next year, and a succession of managing directors has followed. A third stage, the Black Swan, was built for small, experimental works in 1977, to be replaced by the New Theatre in 2002.

The festival was recognized in 1983 with a Tony Award for outstanding achievement in regional theater, and five years later its name was officially changed to simply the Oregon Shakespeare Festival. In 1992 the Elizabethan Stage, now seating 1,200, was enclosed by the Allen Pavilion to improve acoustics, lighting, and other amenities.

Throughout it all, Charles Laughton has remained. And perhaps he'll stay until the day he finally gets to tread the boards at the OSF.

In the meantime, please, vex not his ghost.

Chapter 7

"Not Now, Gilmor"

Gilmor Brown, the founder of the Pasadena Playhouse, spear-headed its productions until his death. The merry man may be deceased, but that doesn't deter him from pulling pranks all around the theater—often to the chagrin of crew and cast.

Betty Jean Morris just wasn't in the mood. The ghost wouldn't cooperate.

It had been a long day. The audience at the matinee had been unusually spirited and hard to get back into their seats after intermission, and the evening performance had been filled with longtime subscribers—many of whom, for some reason today, seemed more interested in sharing their reminiscences of the early days of the theater than seeing the play that was currently onstage. Were they somehow sensing that there was definitely a presence, an old friend, in their midst that night?

At first Betty Jean hadn't been sure it was Gilmor. As house manager, she was, as usual, the last living soul in the building. Even the tech and backstage crew had long since closed down their areas. Betty Jean had helped the ushers close up the auditorium, making sure it was cleared of patrons and dropped programs. Then, after she said good-night to the remaining staff, she closed the doors between the lobby and the orchestra seating level and, as was her routine, checked both restrooms to make sure the lights and water taps were off. Finally, she turned to make one last visual sweep of the lobby.

That's when she noticed that her binoculars were gone. She had brough her personal set from home because, on slow nights, she sometimes watched the show from the balcony and loved to check out small details on the set. She knew that everyone else had been gone by the time she had put the binoculars down on the desk in the lobby, and no one had come in after that.

Slowly she walked over to the desk and brushed her hand along the polished tabletop. The entire foyer had been decorated as a hotel lobby for the production of *Room Service* that was currently playing, so there was a large imitation front desk complete with a sign-in registration book, an old-fashioned "ring for service" bell, and a mannequin dressed like a bellboy standing at attention. (In fact, the ushers, too, wore rented bellhop uniforms throughout the 1987 run.)

She *knew* she had put the binoculars on that desk. Or was she mistaken? From her new vantage point, she looked around the room. No, they were nowhere to be seen. She leaned over and checked beside and behind the table. No, they weren't there either.

Gilmor must have taken them.

Who knows why? Maybe he was upset because his oil portrait, which usually hung in the lobby, had temporarily been replaced as part of the makeover for *Room Service* by a painting of the supposed head of the White Way Hotel, where the action of the play takes place.

More likely, it was just Gilmor being Gilmor.

Pasadena lies just ten miles outside downtown Los Angeles, but in 1917, the year Gilmor Brown moved there, it might as well have been in another state entirely. The road that most directly connects the two didn't become a modern freeway—California's first—until 1940. The highway started as a wagon trail that followed the Arroyo Seco, a stream that passed through the San Gabriel Mountains on its way toward the coast. A commuter rail line and a partial cycle path later snaked between the cities, but in 1917, when Brown moved to Pasadena, the motorway was still decades away.

The Pasadena area was inhabited by the Hahamog-na tribe when Spanish missionaries arrived to found the Mission San Gabriel Arcángel (or San Gabriel Mission) in 1771. California rancher and politician Benjamin Davis Wilson became the first non-Hispanic owner of Rancho San Pascual, which included the property that is today Pasadena, around 1860. Beginning in 1873 he began selling parcels of the land, primarily to asthmatic patients of one his friends, an Indiana doctor who recommended that they move west for the climate. By the next year, the so-called Indiana Colony needed a name for their new community, so on April 22, 1875, the town's leaders decided on Pasadena, which in the language of the Minnesota Chippewa Indians meant "of the valley."

By the turn of the century, easterners were moving into the area in droves. This included wealthy entrepreneurs in search of new opportunities, and their European-styled mansions were soon lining Orange Grove Avenue. Pasadena became a stop on the Atchison, Topeka and Santa Fe Railroad, and major hotels opened for the influx of tourists. An active arts scene flourished in the rapidly growing community. And if all that wasn't enough, the new city achieved national fame when it inaugurated its annual Tournament of Roses Parade in 1889.

Enter Gilmor Brown. Betty Jean knew all about the man who could rightly lay claim to being Pasadena's patron saint of theater.

Born George Gilmor in 1886, the future actor and theater manager spent his first six years on a sheep and wheat farm twelve miles outside Salem, North Dakota. His parents then moved to Denver, and the change was electrifying to the young, artistic boy.

Sneaking into a vaudeville show at Elitch Gardens, Brown was mesmerized by what he saw, and the theater bug bit hard. He organized some of the neighborhood children into his first group of players, the Tuxedo Stock Company, and they were soon putting on shows in his home and for a local church. His passion for the stage led him, at the age of seventeen, to enroll in the Johnson School of Music, Oratory and Dramatic Art in Minneapolis and, later, the Chicago Auditorium. He toured college campuses throughout the States with a group of British actors that included Sidney Greenstreet, gained further experience in Canada, and then made an unsuccessful stab at New York.

Regrouping back home in Denver, he formed his own repertory touring group, the Comedy Players. After it disbanded, he went back to variously acting, managing, or directing for a series of other troupes, one of which, the Crown Stock Company, took him to Pasadena for the first time in 1913.

Four years later he returned with a reconstituted group of actors, the Gilmor Brown Players. He booked a season at Tally's, a rundown burlesque house that had been rechristened the Savoy Theatre, located on unfashionable North Fair Oaks Avenue.

From his years on tour dealing with civic leaders and their society wives, Brown knew how important it was to get the community on his side—especially since there were already at least six amateur groups of players in town vying for his all-important audiences and (as it would turn out) contributors.

From the start, local participation in his productions was part of his plan, and when the doors to his first show opened on September 17, 1917, an influential socialite and president of the Maskers club, Marjorie Sinclair, was in the cast. As the weeks proceeded, the supporting roles (and, now and then, some of the leads) were filled by townspeople. Brown also ran amateur shows, pageants for the Red Cross, contests, and receptions to boost additional interest from the residents.

In November his retitled Community Players moved from the Savoy to the Shakespeare Club. (In his cast was a young dancer/actress who would become world famous, Martha Graham.) Before long, however, the troupe moved back to the Savoy and renamed it the Community Playhouse. The stage was narrow, the roof leaked, and the dressing rooms and single bathroom were in a dark cellar, but he was making theater!

The next year his volunteers became an official organization, the Community Playhouse Association of Pasadena. To offset operating costs, Brown convinced regional artists to contribute sets, props, and costumes. Full of energy, Brown oversaw adventuresome stagings (sometimes dictated by the limitations of his space) that included an eclectic mix of classics and crowd-pleasers. For his efforts, by the early 1920s, Brown and the Community Players were getting national attention in the pages of such publications as

Theatre Magazine, Billboard, Variety, and the *Christian Science Monitor.*

In 1922 the fire department condemned the Community Playhouse as a fire hazard. But what initially seemed to be a setback turned out to be a blessing in disguise. Brown had long wanted a modern home for his players, and with the strong community support he had built up over the years the Playhouse Association was able to organize a successful fund-raising campaign to build a new theater.

The following year land was purchased on El Molina Avenue, just off Colorado Boulevard, the main street through the center of Pasadena. A ceremonial cornerstone was laid on May 31, 1924, in conjunction with the national convention of the Drama League of America, which fortuitously was meeting in the City of Roses. Actual work on the theater began in September, and the Pasadena Playhouse opened its doors in May 1925.

(In the interim, Brown had not been idle. Somehow, performances were allowed to continue at the old Savoy almost until opening night at the new theater. Also, Brown was experimenting with a new form of staging in the Playbox, a theater located in his home, in which the audience sat in a horseshoe shape around the actors and the stage. Although this style had its predecessors in Europe, Brown is generally credited with being the first to open a theater with what is now technically called "flexible staging" in the United States.)

But back to the Pasadena Playhouse, which is, after all, the place Gilmor chose to return to as a ghost. The theater's Spanish Revival exterior was designed by architect Elmer Grey to evoke the mission history of Southern California. A central courtyard contained a tiled fountain and was bordered on both sides with boutiques. Farther down a covered passage on the north side of the main auditorium were spacious rooms for the storage and construction of wardrobe, sets, and props, as well as a dye room. (Later much of that space would be converted into office spaces, a recital hall, and theaters.)

Large wooden doors opened into a lush ivory-colored foyer decorated with gilded sconces. A second floor contained areas for what would become a prestigious theater library and a meeting room for the board of directors.

Inside, the auditorium raked gently toward the stage. The 820 seats in both the orchestra and balcony levels were grouped into three sections, separated by central and side aisles. Lavish plastered masks lined the walls, and "Juliets" (or workable boxes for balcony scenes) flanked the proscenium. Perhaps the most beautiful feature architecturally was overhead. What appeared to be elaborate wooden tiles was actually a sheet of burlap painted into intricate geometrical squares, hanging beneath an acoustically recessed ceiling.

The theater boasted state-of-the-art technology both in the booth and backstage, and a large loading dock adjoined the performance area. A soaring fly gallery allowed for the hanging of drapes and flats. Under the stage was an enormous green room where the actors (some of whom were still local residents) could relax and meet guests after the show. For the audience's convenience, the green room could be accessed from an outside entrance or through a small passage in the orchestra pit at the front of the house. There were ten three-person dressing rooms whose doors opened into the green room, and the substage area also contained chorus makeup rooms, toilets, showers, a costume room, and even a kitchen to prepare food for the actors or receptions.

Almost overnight, the Pasadena Playhouse became one of the most important theaters in the country. With the advent of sound movies, it was perfectly poised to provide Hollywood with a steady stream of trained actors who could speak well. There seemed to be agents and industry insiders at every performance. Film royalty such as Mary Pickford, Douglas Fairbanks, Charlie Chaplin, and Will Rogers were early visitors, and over the years innumerable movie stars would grace the playhouse's stages.

With the new facilities in place, Brown opened the School of Theatre in 1928. Students came from across the nation, most to be instructed in acting for the stage, but others, no doubt, arrived with hopes of becoming a star on the silver screen in nearby Tinseltown. Alumni of the school would include Charles Bronson, Ruth Buzzi, Jamie Farr, Gene Hackman, Dustin Hoffman, Mako, Rue McClanahan, Robert Preston, Sally Struthers, Barbara Rush, JoAnne Worley, and hundreds more.

During a trip to MGM Studios in 1933, legendary British playwright George Bernard Shaw visited Pasadena and reportedly dubbed it the "Athens of the West." No doubt this was due in large part to the contributions of Gilmor Brown and the Pasadena Playhouse.

In 1936 the theater became the first American stage to perform all thirty-seven Shakespeare plays in their entirety. Also that year a towering six-story building was added behind the theater, and the sorely needed additional space was promptly used for set production, storage, classrooms, dance studios, and rehearsal space. The following year the state legislature, by a unanimous vote, declared Pasadena Community Playhouse to be the State Theatre of California.

In its first twenty-five years alone, the theater produced more than 1,300 plays, including 23 U.S. and 477 world premieres—an astounding legacy. But by 1950 Gilmor Brown was slowing down. As he became frail, others began handling more and more of the day-to-day artistic operations. Then, a car accident led to his having to use a wheelchair, and eventually the impresario who was synonymous with Pasadena theater died in January 1960.

By that time the world had changed, and the theater was entering financial straits. In 1938 Actors Equity had unionized the playhouse, and Brown had to give up his popular practice of including talented amateurs in his casts. This no doubt led to some loss of economic support from the community, compounded by the fact that many of the well-heeled society ladies who were his early backers and the playhouse's most enthusiastic supporters had passed on.

The theater was forced to shutter its doors in 1968, and when bankruptcy was declared the following year, most of its contents were auctioned off. In a desperate attempt to avoid demolition of the building, supporters had the playhouse designated a historical monument.

But the theater then sat empty, unused, a pitiful shell subjected to the ravages of weather and vandalism, for ten years until investors negotiated a deal to restore the property. It took six more years, until 1986, before the main auditorium was able to reopen with a season of plays. That year a dream was realized when the Pasadena Playhouse was named to the National Register of Historic Places.

The hauntings started to take place soon after the theater reopened. By the time Betty Jean was hired as house manager, everyone associated with the place knew Gilmor had returned. Or, perhaps, that he had never left.

All of the phenomena were mere mischief, as if the ghost was simply trying to let the current occupants know it was there. Personal items actors or staff left lying in one place magically turned up in a completely different part of the theater. Other times the objects, including people's keys, Morris's binoculars, and the stopwatch she used to time intermissions, disappeared completely. (Staffers joked that somewhere in the playhouse there must be a secret stash where Gilmor has everything hidden.)

Doors would open on their own. Other times they would seemingly become locked, only to unlatch effortlessly just minutes later. Disembodied footsteps could be heard walking around the building. Actors and crew often felt the invisible presence of someone standing behind them, looking over their shoulders.

The ghost has never been seen, but it became identified as being Brown when the elevator in the six-story building attached to the back of the theater began stopping of its own volition on the third floor. For many years that's where Gilmor Brown had kept his office.

And, after all, the staff decided, why wouldn't Gilmor return? Gilmor Brown *was* the Pasadena Playhouse.

Before long, anything out of the ordinary that happened at the theater was being blamed on Gilmor's ghost, and people soon figured out a way to stop his pranks. If the spectre started acting up, all they had to do was gently but sternly scold him and the activity would immediately stop.

There was the time, for example, that one of the box office personnel was having difficulty getting her numbers to balance at the end of an evening. She later told fellow staffers that she simply called out, "Not now, Gilmor, I'm busy. Cut it out," and the next time she tried the figures, they tallied perfectly.

Betty Jean had personally been present when two successive series of hauntings took place. For several weeks, every time the tech crew returned to the booth after intermission, they discovered that the dials had been altered and their headsets had been moved. They started to lock the door when they left; they closed the work panel; they posted an usher to guard the room. But whenever they came back from a break, the controls had been reset. Then just as suddenly as the phenomenon had started, one day it stopped.

Then, in 1989, during the run of *Groucho, A Life in Revue,* a set of events took place that no one could deny because everyone in the theater—cast, crew, and the audience—experienced it. At one point as part of the play, a blank pistol was used on stage. For six weeks during the Sunday matinees, but only the matinees, as soon as the shot was fired, all of the house lights came up. Every week, at exactly the same time. Needless to say, the tech crew checked out the lighting boards. Even the master electrician was eventually called in. But no one ever found the cause. Is it possible that Gilmor just didn't like having a gun go off in his theater?

Now it was the binoculars. Oh, well, Betty Jean decided. They weren't coming back, at least not tonight. She clicked off the lights in the lobby and walked into the cool night air, firmly securing the doors behind her. Was she locking people out or locking Gilmor in?

No need to worry about that, she thought. Gilmor literally put his life into the Pasadena Playhouse. His spirit is in its walls. He wasn't going anywhere soon.

Chapter 8

Only a Ghost in a
Gilded Cage

The Bird Cage Theatre in Tombstone, Arizona, was your typical Wild West saloon: part dancing hall, part gambling hall, part brothel. The days of the Wild West are long gone, but the tombstone terrors from that era continue to belly up to the bar, as one fan of the Old West was about to find out.

As she walked around Tombstone, Arizona, Charlene didn't realize that at almost every turn she ran the risk of coming face to face with a real-life ghost. All she knew was that she loved the Old West.

Her friends had always teased her about her obsession with the Wild West as she grew up. After all, she wanted to play Cowboys and Indians instead of dolls and jump rope, and that was considered pretty weird for a little girl in the 1950s. She enjoyed reading about wagons trains and Buffalo Bill, not fairy princesses and little mermaids like everyone expected of her. Why hadn't she been born a hundred years earlier? Maybe she could have grown up to be a famous cowgirl like, oh, Annie Oakley or Calamity Jane.

Her youthful dreams had been set aside as she left school and entered the business world. But now she was in her fifties, and, independent and secure, she could afford to indulge her childhood fantasies. Three years ago she had spent a couple of weekends on a dude ranch. (Was she a "dudette"?) Two summers back she'd camped out under the stars, taking part in a cattle drive. Last year she'd traveled along the old prairie highways, walking along the preserved historic sections of the Chisholm, Santa Fe, and Overland Trails.

And now here she was, driving around the Southwest, trying to hit as many of the cattle, cowboy, and pioneer towns as her time and pocketbook would allow. Dodge City. Abilene. The names were like magic words ringing in her ears.

Today she had hit a goldmine—or more correctly, silver mine—in Tombstone, Arizona, because the small town where she stood, 170 miles south of Phoenix and just 63 miles from Tucson, didn't start up as a ranch or cattle town. No, the "Town Too Tough to Die" made its name as one of the richest silver mining camps of the Old West.

When prospector Ed Schieffelin made his way to the southern Arizona Territory in 1877, other miners were already searching the waterless creek beds for signs of ore. He was just one more, with little chance for success. Each day he set out from Camp Huachuca and Brunckow's cabin, a small, ramshackle house where prospectors often stayed, to explore the dry washes out on the cactus-filled prairie, hoping to spot a few specks of gold or silver sparkling up at him from the desert floor.

It was a dangerous business, not just because of the relentless heat, rattlesnakes, and scorpions. This was Apache territory, and they didn't take too kindly to the ever-increasing number of outsiders roaming their land: A soldier warned young Schieffelin that all he'd be finding out there in the desert was his tombstone.

But that was no deterrent to the hard-edged Schieffelin. He'd already spent years throughout the West trying to strike it rich. Then, after just a few months, he finally hit the mother lode when he discovered an outcropping of almost pure silver ore on the shelf of a remote mesa called Goose Flats. Remembering the soldier's words, he named his claim Tombstone, and the mining camp that grew up nearby almost overnight soon adopted the moniker.

As more and more stakes were claimed in the area, Tombstone became a boomtown. Prospectors, gamblers, prostitutes, businessmen, and investors alike came to make their fortunes. When an actual town was laid out in 1879, there were only a hundred residents and forty small cabins. Within a year the population had swelled to three thousand, and by 1881 it topped seven thousand.

At the end of the decade, around fifteen thousand people were living there and almost $38 million in silver (and some gold) had come out of the mines. But by the mid-1880s the silver in the mines had run out. Then the workers hit water, and the mines soon flooded. The boom went bust, and by 1900 fewer than seven hundred people were still living in Tombstone.

During its heyday, though, the wild frontier town was known throughout the country for its lawlessness and vice. At one point President Chester A. Arthur almost declared martial law. One incident in particular is legendary. On October 26, 1881, Deputy U.S. Marshall for the territory Virgil Earp and his brothers Wyatt and Morgan, along with Doc Holliday, fought a band of outlaws known as the Cowboys that included Ike and Billy Clanton, Frank and Tom McLaury, Billy Claiborne, and Wes Fuller in the celebrated shootout that became known as the "Gunfight at the O.K. Corral." In the thirty-second exchange of gunfire, the McLaurys and Billy Clanton were killed.

Today the historic center of Tombstone, about a six-block area, is maintained to look the way it did in the late 1880s. This was what Charlene had come to see.

In two disastrous fires in June 1881 and May 1882, most of the wooden structures from the original mining camp were destroyed. Then over the years most of the other early buildings either collapsed or were replaced. But a few are standing to this day, among them St. Paul's Episcopal Church, the *Tombstone Epitaph* newspaper offices, and the Crystal Palace Saloon, still operating and decorated with many of its original furnishings.

But the most famous of all—perhaps "notorious" would be a better word—is the Bird Cage Opera House Saloon.

Of course, it wasn't an opera house in the same sense we think of one today. In the nineteenth century, and even into the early twentieth century, the word "theater" often carried a negative connotation. Many people considered the shows that appeared in them to be frivolous and sometimes downright indecent, certainly not the sort of diversion an upright family might attend.

Indeed, the entire acting community was looked down upon. Actors were considered little better than common street gypsies. Hotels and boardinghouses, afraid that itinerants would steal anything not nailed down in the rooms, would post signs out front saying, "No actors or dogs allowed."

One way civic leaders got around people's apprehension about attending a theater was to simply call it something else: an opera house. The term alone gave the playhouse a thin veneer of respectability, suggesting that patrons would be able to attend an evening of refined, proper, and polite amusement.

Although theaters for real opera were being built in the major cities throughout America, few if any of the playhouses in small or even medium-size cities actually used them to perform opera. If they did, it was only the occasional touring artist. Instead, these so-called opera houses became all-purpose entertainment venues for everything from educational and inspirational lectures to traveling vaudeville revues and theater companies. In a pinch, the opera house might double as a community center for dances or civic meetings.

And some of the opera houses, like the one in Tombstone, had little or nothing in common with either the grand monuments to culture on the coasts or the rustic public halls of Middle America.

No, Tombstone's opera house was a down-and-dirty combination of saloon, dancing hall, gambling joint, and house of ill repute. And it was known across the country! In 1882, the *New York Times*—two thousand miles away—called it the "wildest, wickedest night spot between Basin Street and the Barbary Coast."

It was opened by William Hutchison as a legitimate playhouse called the Elite Theater Opera House on Christmas Day 1881. It very quickly changed its focus, turning into a bar and gambling hall and staying open nonstop, twenty-four hours a day, for the next eight years.

Its name changed quickly, too, as Charlene, who was a student of western lore, loved to tell anyone who would listen.

High above the heads of the patrons of the opera house saloon, which were usually all men, fourteen small booths were suspended along the two walls, seven on each side. Inside these red-velvet-curtained cubicles, ladies of easy persuasion could privately entertain their clients.

British lyricist Arthur J. Lamb, standing by the bar one night, mused that the women in their hanging (euphemistically named) "cribs" reminded him of birds trapped in cages. In a flash of inspiration, he came up with the words to the song that would become a nineteenth-century standard:

> She's only a bird in a gilded cage,
> A beautiful sight to see.
> You may think she's happy and free from care,
> She's not, though she seems to be.
> 'Tis sad when you think of her wasted life
> For youth cannot mate with age;
> And her beauty was sold for an old man's gold,
> She's a bird in a gilded cage.

The song, first sung from the Elite Theater stage by Lillian Russell, resulted in a name change for the theater itself. From then on it became known as the Bird Cage Opera House, and it earned every bit of its national reputation as the tawdriest tavern west of the Mississippi. But even the earthiest audiences want "real" entertainment from time to time, and with the hundreds of thousands of dollars coming out of the silver mines, being spent on liquor, poker, and women, the opera house could afford to pay for genuine headliners.

At one side of the main room was a raised, curtained platform, and over the few years the opera house was in business such stars as comedian-dancer Eddie Foy performed there. But usually the stage was reserved for the females of the species, which was more to the liking of the men in the rough-and-tumble town. Besides Russell, other sirens who treaded the boards included British beauty Lillie Langtry, courtesan and Spanish dancer Lola Montez, and Montez's protégée, red-headed singer, dancer, and banjo player Lotta Crabtree.

Charlene was in luck. As she walked up to the entrance of the Bird Cage Theatre Museum, a tour was just about to begin and she eagerly joined it. Inside, the opera house was exactly the way she already envisioned it in her head. There were the "cages," the long bar, and the poker tables that had hosted such names as Bat Masterson, Diamond Jim Brady, and George Randolph Hearst. As the group walked through the hall, the guide pointed out a few of the bullet holes from the numerous gunfights that had broken out inside the saloon.

There was the famous hand-painted stage. A man dressed in black, wearing a visor, and carrying a clipboard busied himself near the back curtain. *Maybe he was a stagehand or the pianist,* thought Charlene. Or perhaps he was one of those "atmosphere" people amusement parks and historical sites hire to dress up in costume to interact with guests.

Next the tour visited the dressing rooms, then descended the stairs from the backstage area to the lower level where a high-stakes poker game had been played continuously for eight years, five months, and three days. Along the wall were a few small, private rooms where gamblers could visit the higher-paid girls of horizontal pleasure.

Back upstairs, Charlene took one last look around. *The place was amazing,* she thought to herself. The theater had originally escaped destruction in the devastating fires of 1881 and 1882 because, as opposed to the wooden structures in town, it was built out of concrete. When Tombstone emptied out in the late 1880s, Hutchison reluctantly decided to close the Bird Cage Theatre on Christmas Eve 1889. But the saloon won a reprieve of sorts because he boarded it up with everything inside intact. The opera house stood that way, a time capsule, for forty-five years until it was opened as a tourist attraction in 1934. It was like stepping back into history.

"Any questions?" asked the tour guide.

Charlene, realizing that it was getting late and the Bird Cage was closing for the day, was puzzled. "Yes. Are you reopening tonight? Will there be a show of some sort?"

"No," the guide replied sadly. "We don't have performances in here anymore. If you're staying in town tonight, though, there's live music over at Big Nose Kate's Saloon, and . . ."

"I just wondered," Charlene interrupted, "because I saw the man onstage setting up, and I thought that maybe he was getting ready for later tonight."

The smile left the guide's face. He looked closely at Charlene, trying to decide whether she was joking. Then he glanced over toward the stage. It was empty. "No, I'm sorry," he said after the briefest hesitation, the fixed smile returning to his lips. "That was someone else."

He cordially thanked the visitors as he saw them out the door. "Excuse me. Miss?" he called after Charlene. "May I speak to you for just a moment?"

It was then that Charlene discovered that Tombstone was no dusty, dried-up waxwork. The past was still living and breathing all around her.

"The man you saw," the guide started cautiously, "well, he was one of our ghosts."

All of Tombstone, Charlene soon learned, seemed to be haunted. People visiting the O.K. Corral have reported seeing the pale spirits from the shootout, sometimes with guns drawn as if they were forced to fight the gun battle over and over throughout eternity. A different phantom, Marshall Fred White, who preceded Virgil Earp as deputy marshall and was accidentally shot in 1880 by Curly Bill Brocius (another one of the Cowboys) is said to walk the streets at night.

And then there's Boot Hill Graveyard—so called because many of its residents had been in gunfights and died with their boots on. Between 1878 and 1884, more than 250 people were interred in the old cemetery just a few miles north of town. Among them were the McLaury brothers and Billy Clanton. Visitors to the graveyard sometimes come across strange lights and sounds, and now and then an apparition actually materializes. Now and then, spectres appear in photographs shot there, even though nothing unusual was seen when the pictures were taken. Legend also has it that from time to time Clanton can be seen rising from his grave or walking the highway from the cemetery back into town.

But the most haunted site of all is the Bird Cage Theatre. Charlene had thought the sign she saw saying DON'T DISTURB OUR 26 RESIDENT GHOSTS had been a joke. But apparently some or all of them do regularly return, rearranging furniture and moving small items. Visitors have been known to smell whiskey and cigar smoke, though neither alcohol nor tobacco is allowed on the premises anymore.

Occasionally an unidentified (and unseen) woman can be heard softly singing, and employees have heard the unexplained voice of an unknown man speaking over the sound system after closing. A few people have claimed to see the ghost of a young boy who died of yellow fever in the mining camp. And, as in many haunted places, there are the usual abnormal cold spots.

Passersby at night are sometimes shocked to hear the spectral sounds of music and merriment emanating from inside the empty, locked saloon. If they peek in, they might catch a glimpse of the bar in full swing, with phantom ladies dancing and ghostly gamblers wagering at the tables. It's only after a moment's pause that they realize the ethereal vision is doubly impossible: Although people on the street could see directly from the front doors to the stage in the 1880s and '90s, today a wall separates the entrance from the main room.

Charlene shivered. She had come to Tombstone only to soak in the surroundings of one of the best-preserved towns of the Wild West. Nobody told her she might bump into one of its original residents. On some level she was comforted, though. It was nice to know that the past—the Old West she loved so much—would never completely die.

But she didn't want to be trapped in it either. It was time to go. She walked out into the red glow of the setting sun, out of the Bird Cage, free.

Chapter 9
Little Boy Lost

The spirit of a small boy who was killed in a boiler explosion in New Mexico's KiMo Theater still romps throughout the playhouse. The lad is more or less well-mannered—just long as the staff leaves him a stack of his favorite doughnuts backstage!

Bobby Darnall was like any other six-year-old in 1950s Albuquerque. Happy. Carefree. Full of life.

And what fun it was to see a movie from the balcony! He loved walking up the soft, carpeted stairs, slowly making his way into the gallery that overlooked the people far below. There in the upper reaches of the KiMo, nestled in his favorite row of seats, he felt like he was in his own private world. He was free to imagine himself up there on the screen, right next to the Hollywood stars, maybe as a cowboy, or a cop, or maybe even a robber. Wow, wouldn't *that* be fun?

But that Thursday afternoon, August 2, 1951, as he whiled away a summer day at the movie with friends, disaster struck. Normally Bobby wasn't easily frightened, but when the sound of a loud siren suddenly blared off the screen he just wasn't expecting it. Involuntarily he let out a small scream and jumped out of his seat. Without thinking, Bobby bolted out of the balcony, ran down the stairs, and dashed into the lobby. He was halfway across when it happened.

A hot water heater underneath the concession stand exploded, mercilessly shooting metal debris and scalding liquid in all directions. At least seven people were severely injured. Little Bobby was killed.

But the impish youngster must have felt content there at the KiMo, because he's apparently never left.

Today Albuquerque is famous for many things in popular culture. It's the setting of Disney's *High School Musical* and the city from which, in the movie *Little Miss Sunshine*, a comically dysfunctional family set out for a beauty pageant. Ethel Mertz, the fictional character played by Vivian Vance on TV's *I Love Lucy*, supposedly came from Albuquerque. And the city is, amazingly, featured in songs by such disparate performers as Neil Young, Frank Zappa, Johnny Cash and Bob Dylan, "Weird Al" Yankovic, and the Partridge Family. Not to mention, it's also where up to seven hundred hot-air balloons are set aloft every October as part of the annual International Balloon Festival.

And it's home to the KiMo Theatre.

The KiMo was the dream of one man, an Italian immigrant named Oreste Bachechi. The Atchison, Topeka and Santa Fe Railroad had come through Albuquerque in 1880, and five years later it brought Bachechi and his wife, Maria, to the growing town of eight thousand. Founded in 1706 as a Spanish colonial settlement, the original village was laid out around a central plaza, bounded by government buildings and a church. When the railroad decided to build its station two miles east of what is now called Old Town, however, a new community quickly sprang up closer to the tracks.

It was there by the rails in 1885 that Bachechi set up a small but successful business in a tent. Before long the young entrepreneur owned a grocery store and, with a partner, started the Consolidated Liquor Company. In 1905 Bachechi opened the swank (for turn-of-the-twentieth-century New Mexico) Savoy Hotel. Meanwhile, his wife ran a dry-goods store in the Elms Hotel while raising six children!

By 1919 the Italian businessman had joined with another partner, Joe Barnett, to form the Bachechi Amusement Association, and together they owned and operated the Playtime Theatre.

But Bachechi's dream was to have a theater of his own. And why not? Many of Albuquerque's playhouses had been started up by new settlers coming from Italy. Perhaps foremost among them were two venues, the El Rey Theater and Puccini's Golden West Saloon, both housed under one roof, the historic Puccini Building. And yes, it was *that* Puccini, or at least the same family. The owner was Luigi Puccini, a cousin of the famous opera composer, Giacomo Puccini.

(For those of you into synchronicity, Puccini wrote his opera *Madame Butterfly* after seeing the nonmusical play of the same name, written by David Belasco, at London's Duke of York's Theatre. That playhouse is now haunted by Violet Melnotte, a former owner. Meanwhile, Belasco's ghost haunts his namesake theater on Broadway. And Puccini's later opera *The Girl of the Golden West,* also based on a Belasco play, first appeared in the original Metropolitan Opera House in New York City, which was haunted by the spectre of an opera diva, Frances Alda. Small world, isn't it?)

In 1925 Bachechi decided the time was right to build his theater. He contacted Carl Boller of the Boller Brothers architectural firm, in Kanasas City, Missouri to design a grand movie palace that would rival the faux-Chinese and pseudo-Greek motion picture playhouses then in vogue throughout America. The Bollers had already produced two ostentatious theaters, one in a combination Spanish/Babylonian style in St. Joseph, Missouri, and the other in a mixture of Western and Rococo in San Antonio, Texas.

But Bachechi's would be different. He wanted to celebrate the culture of the Southwest that had brought him such wealth and happiness.

Carl Boller was up to the challenge. For research, he traveled throughout New Mexico, visiting Navajo tribes and pueblos of the Acoma and Isleta. He studied the natural colors of the region as well as the shapes, flora, and fauna found in the arid desert. He came up with a work of genius in a brazen style known as Pueblo Deco, which married Southwest Native American motifs with the then-popular Art Deco.

The theater's exuberance amazed everyone from the start. Its massive interior was adorned throughout with painted thunderclouds and birds. Turtle images that were used to decorate the proscenium symbolized strength, and icons on opposing exit doors represented the rising and setting suns. There were also several swastikas, which symbolize life and fulfillment to the Navajo and Hopi. (The figure appears in many cultures, but, needless to say, they were temporarily covered during and immediately following World War II due to the shape's association with Nazi Germany.)

The beams on the ceiling, some up to seventy feet long, were constructed of steel, concrete, and plaster, but they were painted to look like logs. Chandeliers were made to resemble dugout canoes and war drums; ornamental imitation buffalo skulls had lights set into their eye sockets. Overhead grates for the air conditioning were decorated to look like woven rugs.

Nine large murals by Carl Von Hassler covered the walls, and the rest of the theater was accented in tones of white (representing the rising sun), yellow (for midday), red (the setting sun), and black (for the gathering storms).

Bachechi spared no expense to create this masterpiece of fantasy. On top of the $150,000 it cost to construct the theater itself, $18,000 was spent to install a gigantic Wurlitzer pipe organ. (This was, after all, the time of silent movies, which needed musical accompaniment.) In addition, the building housed the Tawa Curio gift shop, the Kiva Lo diner, and the Kiva Hi restaurant.

True to Bachechi's independent spirit, he held a contest to name the theater. The winner, Pablo Abeita, invented the word KiMo by combining two native Tewa terms that, taken together, mean "king of its kind." The playhouse opened with great fanfare and a grand ceremony on September 19, 1927. In addition to showing movies, it immediately became a headliner stop on the vaudeville and variety circuit.

Sadly, within a year of opening his theater's doors, Bachechi was dead.

The theater carried on, at first under the management of his sons. Touring shows and stars such as Gloria Swanson, Mickey Rooney, Ginger Rogers, Tom Mix, Sally Rand, and even Vivian Vance appeared on its stage. And of course there were the movies.

But then in 1951 tragedy struck when that boiler blast took the life of young Bobby, our ghost-to-be. Disaster hit again in 1963 when fire destroyed the original stage and damaged the entire building. Repairs were made, but the era of the majestic film palace had faded. As was occurring throughout the rest of America throughout the 1960s and '70s, people were moving to the suburbs. Downtowns were emptying out, and audiences weren't coming back into the city just to see a movie.

The KiMo Theatre soon fell into wreck and ruin, and was closed in 1968. The theater was slated to be razed, but then, in a burst of civic pride, the City of Albuquerque decided to buy the theater and restore its majesty. Today, as downtown has become revitalized and Old Town itself is a tourist destination, the seven hundred–seat KiMo Theatre, now an arts center for live entertainment, shines as a testament to the vision of one of its early leading lights.

Over the years actors and staff have come to realize that even when there's no audience in the theater, they're not alone. Bobby Darnall is there.

As a rule, he's well behaved. When he appears, he's seen dressed in a striped shirt and blue jeans, usually playing or dawdling on the staircase that leads from the balcony down to the lobby. But he's been spied all over the theater.

More often he stays invisible. And like many children, he can be quite mischievous. His unseen spirit has been known to trip people or make noise backstage during performances.

To stop him from being so rambunctious, a tradition started of putting out doughnuts for him around the playhouse. Soon people began threading the tasty pastries onto a string and hanging them on a pipe that runs along the wall backstage. According to legend, doughnuts left out overnight were usually gone by morning. Any that remained had tiny human bite marks in them.

And anyone who ignored the tradition was in for trouble. According to a longtime technical manager at the theater, in the 1980s a no-nonsense director of a Christmastime production insisted that the doughnuts be thrown out. They were taken down, and almost immediately, things started to go wrong in the theater. Actors stumbled onstage or "went up" (forgot their lines); windows began to open or slam shut on their own; the soundboard went haywire; lightbulbs inexplicably blew out.

The doughnuts were returned.

A few years ago the crew built a shrine backstage to replace the practice of hanging the sugary treats. For good luck, performers began to leave small gifts on the table for Bobby, and today it can be found filled with anything from toys to coins and candy—and now and then an occasional doughnut.

And get this: Bobby's not alone! They say the apparition of an unidentified woman also walks the corridors. She never seems to interfere with or bother anybody. Nothing is known about her, but because she's always seen wearing an old-fashioned bonnet, she may come from the theater's earliest days.

But more likely than not, if you run into a wraith at the KiMo, it's probably going to be Bobby. Don't be upset if he becomes too high-spirited, though: He's simply having fun. What else would you expect from a six-year-old boy?

Chapter 10

Take Me Back to Tulsa

Even when the curtain has fallen, some artists have to return to the stage. Enrico Caruso was known to bring down the house while he was alive. Some say he's returned to do it again now that he's dead. If anyone has a ghost of a chance of making it back, it might be the man many think was the greatest tenor in history.

Caruso in Tulsa? At first it almost sounds like an oxymoron. But it's true: When Enrico Caruso, then the most famous operatic tenor in the world, first made his way to Oklahoma around 1913, the new state wasn't just wide-open plains and cattle ranches. It was also the "Oil Capital of the World."

Tulsa was settled in 1836 by the Lochapoka and Creek Native Americans on what was then Indian Territory. The tiny village expanded as pioneers moved westward, and the town was incorporated in 1898. It was still a small community when oil was struck in 1901. When a large deposit of the liquid gold was discovered four years later in what is today nearby Glenpool, the territory began to grow in leaps and bounds.

Money was flowing as freely as the oil, and among the many benefits of the newfound wealth was the construction of what is now called the Brady Theater. Residents needed a place to hold large civic events and meetings, and they wanted a landmark theater that could attract the top names in entertainment to the prairies.

The architectural firm of Rose and Peterson was brought in from Kansas City to design a grand building that could suit both purposes. The result was the Tulsa Convention Hall, which opened to the public in 1910.

Tulsa soon became one of the top stops on the vaudeville and concert circuit for artists traveling through the Midwest. And the city could afford to bring in the best.

Caruso was just one of hundreds of performers who passed through the doors of Convention Hall in the first quarter of the twentieth century. But he wasn't just any entertainer. Born in Naples, Italy, in 1873, he was, by any measure, one of the great opera singers in history. Fortunately for modern lovers of the art, he made more than 250 recordings in his all-too-brief lifetime, so his rich tone, phrasing, and style can be marveled at and enjoyed to this day.

Caruso was a star at leading opera houses all over the world: La Scala in Milan, the Royal Opera House, Covent Garden in London, and New York's Metropolitan Opera House (haunted, starting in the 1950s long after Caruso's tenure there, by the diva Frances Alda). Caruso had even sung *Carmen* in San Francisco the night before the 1906 earthquake, and he was still in the city when it struck the next morning.

To 1913 Tulsa, he was a revelation, and the theater was the site of a great triumph for both the city and the tenor. Could the international sensation have been so moved that his spirit would one day return?

Just eight years after that glorious concert, the hall played a small part in a very different evening: a night of race riots rocking Tulsa that some consider to have been the worst in the nation's history. The events were set in motion when a nineteen-year-old African-American man was accused of assaulting a seventeen-year-old white girl in an elevator. In the early evening of May 31, 1921, about two thousand whites gathered outside the courthouse where the suspect was being held. After an armed confrontation with fewer than a hundred black men, the mob stormed the prosperous but segregated Greenwood section of Tulsa populated mainly by African-Americans that was known as the "Black Wall Street."

By dawn thirty-five city blocks had been burned to the ground, causing almost $2 million in damage—more than $20 million in today's dollars. Ten thousand people were forced from their homes; eight hundred were hospitalized. Officially, only thirty-nine people died, more than two dozen of them African-Americans, but the Red Cross set the number of black deaths at closer to three hundred. There were apocryphal reports, though, that as many as three thousand might have actually been killed in the evening's chaos.

During the ten hours of rioting, the local National Guard and police moved hundreds of African-Americans, both men and women, into makeshift detention centers in various facilities around the city—one of which was the basement of the Brady Theater. The Oklahoma National Guard arrived in Tulsa the next morning, established martial law, and finally quelled the violence.

But some of the souls of those kept in the cellar of the Brady that night may still be captive there.

In 1930 the interior of the convention hall was completely renovated by designer Bruce Goff. The result was a 2,800-seat Art Deco palace, accented with white and gold-trim paneled walls, a ceiling set in blue, green, white, and gold acoustic tiles, and five enormous green-and-white chandeliers. Further changes were made in 1952 when the hall's name was changed to the Tulsa Municipal Theater.

In 1978 the playhouse was remodeled once again, into what was then called Western Classic Revival style, and the following year the Brady Theater, as it was by then known, received the honor of being listed on the National Register of Historic Places.

The theater has another distinction as well. It is definitely haunted.

A man's dim, dark spectral figure has been seen crossing the catwalk and walking through a doorway on the fly gallery level backstage. At some point it was decided that the phantom was the ghost of Enrico Caruso.

Caruso? Why Caruso?

Some ghost enthusiasts have claimed that Caruso's spirit has come back to the Brady because he sang his last concert there. But his final public performance was really at the Met on Christmas Eve 1920. He died the following year, probably of peritonitis, in Naples, and for many years his body was put on public display in a glass coffin. He was later laid to rest in a small chapel-like tomb.

The fact is that even those who believe the spectre seen in the theater's fly gallery is the celebrated singer don't really have a good explanation for his returning to Tulsa. But the story persists nonetheless. And why not? On the other hand, if it *is* Caruso, it's amazing that after all these years and so many changes to the theater he even recognizes the place.

The boiler room beneath the massive auditorium hasn't changed all that much, however. It's still dark and slightly sinister, the way it was that sorry night in 1921. Anyone who spends even a few minutes there can imagine the emotions—hate, fear, panic—that must have filled that subterranean vault while the innocent citizens were being held captive simply because of their color. It's easy to believe that the unexplainable cold breezes experienced in the underground chamber and the mysterious orbs of light that appear on photos and video that are shot down there could be the tortured souls and broken spirits of those who were imprisoned within its dank walls.

Actors, staff, and audiences alike have felt unseen presences in the auditorium as well. They've described the sensation as having someone standing behind them and watching them with invisible eyes. People have also heard and even encountered doors slamming shut on their own.

Today many theaters and performance centers are scattered throughout Tulsa, but the jewel of the downtown arts district remains the Brady Theater. Almost a century has passed since the playhouse received its first visitors. Hundreds of performers and thousands of patrons have passed through its doors, with an untold number of reasons why some might want to return from the Next World. Who knows how many ghosts might actually be "living" there, haunting its historic halls?

Chapter 11
Exit, Dying

Percy Keene, who was stage manager at the Grand Opera House in Oshkosh, Wisconsin, from 1895 up until his death in 1967, still shows up for duty. And he may not be the only ghost that has made the theater its final abode.

As the film drew to an end and the credits began to roll, Bob Jacobs was pleased. The screening had been a success. As much a labor of love as anything else, *Exit, Dying* was his baby. The University of Wisconsin-Oshkosh professor had written, directed, edited, and produced the two-hour made-for-TV movie, and much of it had been filmed right there in the Grand Opera House in Oshkosh.

The Grand had been built in 1883 after several businessmen decided that their city, with a population of around twelve thousand (then the second largest in the state), deserved an opulent entertainment palace.

A local architect, William Williams, who had already designed many of the buildings in town, was engaged to draw up the plans. They couldn't have asked for better results. The theater had almost perfect acoustics, exquisite Queen Anne–style decor, and 668 plush velvet seats. Tall columns rose up the sides of the proscenium flanking the hand-painted main curtain, and cherubs decorated the ceiling. Tapestries accented the walls. Extra seating could be squeezed into the hall to accommodate up to 1,224 people.

The opera house premiered its first show, a production of Michael William Balfe's opera *The Bohemian Girl,* on August

9, 1883. The playhouse converted to electricity two years later, and a fire escape and a large marquee were added right around the turn of the twentieth century.

By the 1920s the playhouse had become one of the top stops in the Upper Midwest on the vaudeville and lecture circuit. Over the years artists and speakers such as Mark Twain, Harry Houdini (who grew up just twenty-one miles down the road in Appleton), John Philip Sousa, Enrico Caruso, the Marx Brothers, Charlie Chaplin, Susan B. Anthony, Sarah Bernhardt, and President Howard Taft all graced the stage.

Improvements to the heating, plumbing, lighting, and ventilation were made in the late 1920s, and somewhere along the line a name change was made to the Granada. As elsewhere in the country, the age of vaudeville drew to a close, and the playhouse was sold in 1948. It reopened as the Civic Theater, showing films and hosting a few local civic events.

But by then the opera house's luster had faded. Two years later, despite a new name proclaiming it to be the Grand Theater, almost eight feet of the stage had been chopped off to add more seats for moviegoers.

Then in 1965 local citizens were galvanized when the nearby Victorian-era Athearn Hotel, built in 1891, was torn down. They couldn't let that happen to their historical playhouse as well!

But things didn't look good for their cause. The theater had been showing second-run movies for more than a decade, and by 1970 it had become a home for adult flicks. Nevertheless, the preservationists persevered, and in 1974 it was placed on the National Register of Historic Places. At least it couldn't be removed without a fight!

Yes, the theater had been through a lot over the years, thought Jacobs. That's why it had been the perfect choice when he needed a stand-in for the rundown, small-town, Midwestern theater in his film. He had begun shooting *Exit, Dying* back in 1976, when the Grand was undergoing yet another round of renovations and its future was still up in the air.

In the movie, a businessman (played by Henry Darrow, best known for his work in episodic TV) buys up, refurbishes, and resells dilapidated theaters. He gets more than he bargained for when it turns out that this particular place has a resident ghost—and it's not particularly nice.

What a perfect night for an advance screening, thought Jacobs, *given the subject matter.* It was just two nights before the movie's premiere on Halloween 1979. Not only that, the Grand Opera House was supposed to be haunted for real!

Jacobs knew all about the spooky legends surrounding the playhouse-cum-cinema, and his company *had* had a few unusual, and in some instances unnerving, incidents.

Take that time one of the actors had been hoisted over the stage and suspended for one of the scenes in the movie. After almost an hour, and take after take was finished, he was slowly lowered to the floor. The instant his feet touched the ground, the rope that had been holding him aloft snapped and fell in a pile around his feet. If it had broken only minutes before, he would have fallen and been seriously injured or killed. Had something supernatural been holding him up all that time until he was safely back down?

Then there were the two grips—technicians who put lighting and rigging in place—who saw a shadowy male figure walk up out of the orchestra pit and go through a door into one of the stage-level boxes. When they went to investigate, the compartment was empty, even though there would have been no other way out for the stranger.

And what about that girl, also on the crew, who swore that while she and a female colleague were exploring the passageways under the theater she saw an inexplicable humanoid form emerge from the ground? And before she could escape the tunnels, she felt an invisible hand grab her ankle.

But every theater has its mysteries, thought the rational Jacobs. There are always dark corners and strange noises as the floors creak and foundations settle. And given the movie's subject matter—a malevolent spirit trying to keep control of its domain—it's no wonder that the crews' imaginations had run wild.

Jacobs's eyes wandered from the screen as he took in the theater's faded decor, the discolored curtain, the stained wood. Up above him the closed balcony loomed ominously.

Wait! No one was supposed to be in the balcony, but there, *almost* plain as day, stood an elderly, balding, gray-haired man, dressed in a crisp white shirt. The eyes in his cheery face were bright, piercing in fact, behind a small set of round spectacles. He smiled down at Jacobs benevolently. The director studied him, puzzled. Was the unknown visitor signaling his approval of the movie?

Then, as suddenly as Jacobs had noticed the man, the spectral uninvited guest simply vanished. But the director wasn't alone in seeing the apparition. The man in the booth had also spied the ghost.

"Did you see that guy?" the projectionist called out to anyone and everyone.

He and a few others searched the balcony, but nothing out of the ordinary was ever found, that is, except for a single folded-down seat where the ghost had been standing.

People with the film company were at a loss for an explanation. But actors and staff who regularly worked at the theater knew what—and who—had most likely been causing the strange phenomena.

It was Percy Keene.

Keene, who died in 1967 and precisely matched the description of the spirit given by Jacobs, had been the stage manager at the Grand Opera House for as long as could be remembered. No one was ever sure about his age, but rumor had it that he had been at the theater doing one job or another since 1895.

The theater's staff had been aware of Percy's ghostly presence for years. They had often felt him protectively watching over them. Lights would go on and off by themselves, unidentifiable sounds reverberated through the empty space, and there were sudden drops in temperature. All Keene's doing, they would say.

In 1980 the City of Oshkosh acquired the theater and two years later began a full restoration. Today the only original parts of the playhouse are the proscenium and the balcony. Everything else has been lovingly and carefully re-created. On October 3, 1986, 102 years after its opening night, the Grand Opera House flung wide its doors with a new production of its first show, *The Bohemian Girl*.

In the years since, hauntings have diminished. But they haven't disappeared. Occasionally a white or orange-tinted mist will hover over the stage or drift into the wings. Others have seen Keene looking down from the balcony since that movie screening. And remember the single seat that was lowered? It wasn't an isolated incident, either. It's been discovered that way several times since, and even if you fold it back up, it will somehow manage to drop back down on its own when no one's looking. Was it Percy's favorite chair? Members of the Drama Lab, an area theater group working out of the Grand, regularly experienced slamming doors and disembodied footsteps all over the playhouse. One guy even ran into Keene's ghost, who was wearing clothing from the turn of the twentieth century and carrying a program from a show that had played the theater in 1895.

Mind you, Keene isn't the only phantom in the opera house. The apparition of a man—who may or may not be Keene—wearing glasses, a sweater, and blue jeans has materialized in the halls and the lobby. But, now and then, other spectres wearing late-nineteenth-century clothing pop up, including an old stagehand named Jack Stanton. A ghost dog thought to be Stanton's has been spotted on the stage and elsewhere in the building as well.

But overseeing it all is the kindly stage manager, Percy Keene. And why not? He's been there over a hundred years. What's another century or two more?

Chapter 12

The Stained-Glass Spirit

When the Grandstreet Theatre in Helena, Montana, reinstalled the Tiffany window that had graced the building when it was a Unitarian church, it got more than it bargained for. The woman to whom the glass was dedicated suddenly returned to the "congregation."

Clara was content. She was particularly devoted to the youngsters in her husband's congregation, and in the two years the couple had been in Helena, Montana, the Sunday school had grown from twenty children to more than a hundred. Modest to a fault, she refused to take credit for any of it, but indeed the swell in the enrollment among kids and young adults was due in large part to her enthusiasm and support. A former kindergarten teacher, she knew just how to let her charges know they were valued, respected, and loved.

Her husband, the Reverend Stanton Hodgin, had been called to the church in 1903. At that time the city was only thirty-nine years old, and the state capitol building had been completed just the year before. The place had grown up around Last Chance Creek when gold was discovered in 1864, and Last Chance Gulch, the main street that winds its way through town, is named after and pretty much follows the stream's original path.

Over the next twenty years, more than $3.5 billion worth of gold (in today's dollars) was discovered in the area, and in 1888 at least fifty millionaires were living in the city. Yes, in

Helena, Montana! It's hard to believe, but according to some sources, at the time there was a greater percentage of millionaires in Helena than in any other city in the entire world.

Of course, a city's citizens have spiritual needs, and in 1901 a Romanesque stone building was constructed on Park Avenue at a cost of $20,000 to tend to many of Helena's devout Unitarians.

One of the faith's major tenets is that the church should be an active part of the town in which it's located, and, as such, the sanctuary was planned so it could also be used for get-togethers, lectures, and theatrical presentations from the very beginning. A proscenium stage was built where the altar alone usually stands, and the main floor was deliberately sloped to allow better viewing by the congregation and/or audiences.

Its very first pastor, the Reverend Leslie Willis Sprague, pronounced that its rooms would "be in demand for various sorts of gatherings for clubs, classes, social events and all the rest. . . . It is not our purpose to so consecrate this building that it cannot be used for all sorts of conventions, meetings, entertainments, and in fact, for anything that tends to build up the better life."

When the Hodgins arrived, Clara immediately took full advantage of the space. She directed the church's youngsters in plays and other short performance pieces—anything that would give the children a chance to shine. Hidden away she had a box full of notes for activities that she one day hoped to arrange.

If only there had been time.

In January 1905 Clara became sick, and after a short illness, she passed away. She was gone at the tender age of thirty-four.

The parishioners were devastated. In her memory, they raised money to purchase and install an original Tiffany stained-glass window.

And what a window it was: Vines of yellow and burnt-orange leaves framed blue lakes and gently rolling hills. The darkening reddish glow of a late afternoon sky shone over majestic purple mountains off in the distance. At the very base of the glass were the words:

IN LOVING MEMORY
CLARA BICKNELL HODGIN
1905

Time passed.

In 1933 the church was donated to the City of Helena to replace its library, which had been severely damaged during a series of earthquakes. (Helena's in an active seismic area, and significant earth tremors have been recorded there in 1869, 1877, 1897, 1925, and, the most destructive, 1935.) As part of the renovation for the building's new use, the floors of the church were leveled, a mezzanine was installed, and the beautiful Tiffany glass was carefully removed, crated up, and put into storage in the civic center.

Jump forward forty-two years. In 1975 Carl Darchuck, a Montana native who had founded theater companies in Tacoma and Fort Townsend, Washington, and Fort Peck, Montana, decided to start up a resident troupe in Helena. He set up shop in the ballroom of the old Placer Hotel at the corner of Grand Street and Last Chance Gulch, and, using a bit of logic to help patrons find them, he named the new acting ensemble Grand Street Theatre.

The following August the former Unitarian church/city library became available for lease, and the actors (under the aegis of an enterprise named Broadwater Productions) picked up stakes and moved lock, stock, and greasepaint over to North Park Avenue. To help let audiences know they had relocated, they changed their name slightly to Grandstreet Theatre.

The company went into action refurbishing the hall. First they removed the false flooring so the auditorium would once again be raked and put back the balcony, complete with tiered seating.

Most important to our story, however, the Tiffany window, which had almost been forgotten, was found and lovingly restored.

And along with the stained-glass panes came the ghost of Clara Bicknell Hodgin.

Almost as soon as the window was in place, both actors and crew began to sense a presence in the theater. At first it was simply felt, with no physical manifestations. Before long, everyone decided Clara was back in their midst.

Like many spirit entities, the phantom likes to create havoc with the lights, dimming them unexpectedly or turning them on and off. Now and then small electrical appliances in the building, such as radios, are affected.

Often, folks know Clara is in the house by her footsteps. Her most frequent path is from the front door, up the stairs, and into the main auditorium. Her paces were even heard during the brief period that the stairs were being fixed in the 1970s.

Clara's walks are not confined to the front stairs. Those working on the theater's lower level have heard her careful steps on the stage overhead. In fact, the gentle sound of her feet crossing the floor has echoed throughout the building.

She also seems to like to clean up. Many times after props have been set on the stage, crews have found the objects backstage where they're normally kept.

When Clara does appear, it's often in the form of a spectral fog hanging in the balcony. And apparently Clara enjoys herself up there, because quiet, bright laughter has been known to float down from the rafters.

A few people have also seen a bluish-white mist floating down that staircase by the entryway. At least one woman has reported that a feminine face has materialized above the mist, but no full-form apparition of Clara has ever been seen.

In 2005 another large window was installed over the main entrance. It was specially designed to complement the Tiffany panes already enshrined in the hearts and souls of Grandstreet Theatre and the rest of Helena.

Fortunately, there are no plans to remove or replace the stained glass, and everyone seems to welcome Clara's benevolent presence. If you visit the theater as you pass through the Treasure State, don't be surprised if you catch a glimpse of Clara yourself. No, that's not a trick of the eyes. Those sparkling rays of light dancing around the antique Tiffany window may very well be the ghost of Clara Bicknell Hodgin.

Chapter 13
The House of Usher

A student commits suicide after his parents force him to quit his job as an usher at the famous Guthrie Theater in Minneapolis. But that doesn't stop him from roaming the aisles—and sometimes hovering too close for comfort.

It's never clear why people do such things. Even when they leave behind a note, you always have to wonder whether they've told you the real reason . . . or given the full explanation.

No one had noticed that he was depressed or even unhappy. He always seemed to have a ready smile for anyone he ran into at the theater: cast, crew, and audiences alike. Who could have predicted such a thing?

And then there are always those questions that linger afterward: Shouldn't I have seen it coming? Wasn't there something I could have done to prevent it, to talk him out of it? Was it somehow my fault?

Eighteen-year-old college student Richard Douglas Miller enjoyed being part of the tight-knit acting community at the theater. And he took great pleasure in dealing with the public, even in such a mundane task as helping patrons to their seats.

Sure, it was only a part-time job. But that's not why Miller was doing it. He didn't need the money. His father was a physician with a successful practice just outside St. Paul, Minnesota, and his parents were more than willing to support him in his studies. No, Miller simply loved being at the theater. And he knew he was privileged to be, if only in a small way, involved with one of the greatest and most storied regional theaters in America.

No wonder after his suicide he returned to continue his ushering duties as a ghost.

The Guthrie Theater opened its doors on May 7, 1963, the brainchild of (Sir William) Tyrone Guthrie. The internationally acclaimed director had been born in Tunbridge Wells, Kent, in England in 1900. Active in student theater at Oxford, after graduation Guthrie went on to produce and write radio plays for the BBC. He also began directing for the stage, first for the Scottish National Players, then for the Shakespeare Repertory Company that was in residence at the Old Vic in London. Before long he was bouncing between continents, in demand as a director and producer of radio, theater, and opera in England, Canada, and the United States.

Then in 1952, Guthrie was asked to be the first artistic director for a new repertory theater dedicated to performing Shakespeare's plays in Stratford, Ontario, Canada. When the Stratford Festival Theatre (now known as the Stratford Shakespeare Festival) opened on July 13, 1953, the company, which included Alec Guinness and Irene Worth, performed its first production, *Richard III*, in a large tent on the banks of the River Avon. Today the festival runs for eight months each year, from April through November, with shows in five theaters. Its mission grew to include renowned works by other writers as well as contemporary plays and even musicals.

Guthrie would be involved with the Stratford Festival for the next several years, but by the end of 1950s he had set his sights on a new challenge: founding a repertory regional playhouse in America that would take on all the great classics of dramatic literature. In a 1959 article in the *New York Times*, he asked whether any city in the United States would want to join him in the grand undertaking. Seven responded, and eventually Guthrie settled on the Twin Cities in Minnesota as the most passionate and sincere contender. A foundation was soon set up, a site in Minneapolis was acquired, and ground was broken. It was in 1961, during the planning and construction of the theater, that Guthrie received his knighthood, which could only have galvanized the already fervent community in its support for the project.

On May 7, 1963, the Guthrie Theater premiered its first production, *Hamlet*, starring George Grizzard. Others in the company that first season included Jessica Tandy and Zoe Caldwell. Since then, some of the top names in the acting profession have been drawn to the theater. The appeal of the Guthrie to actors and directors has always been the opportunity to work on their craft far away from the commercial demands of Broadway.

Guthrie remained as artistic director until 1966, and he would continue to direct there for three more years after that. He died back in Ireland on May 15, 1971.

By that time poor Richard Miller was no longer among the living.

On February 5, 1967, he asked to borrow some money from his mother. Dressed in his usher's uniform, he drove the family car to a large department store on Lake Street, where he purchased a rifle and ammunition.

Concerned about their son's education and worried that he wasn't concentrating on his studies, his parents had insisted that he quit his job at the Guthrie. They didn't know that the teen's confidence and sense of self-esteem were tangled up in what little time he got to spend at the theater—in fact, it was the only thing that brought him joy and satisfaction.

Parked in the huge lot outside the store on that lonely, wintry day, the despondent boy raised the loaded gun to his head. He took careful aim . . . and fired.

It was almost two days before a store employee happened to peek into the abandoned car and notice the body. A suicide note explained that "ushering was the best thing I've ever done." Miller asked to be buried in his uniform and that his fellow theater attendants be allowed to act as pallbearers.

Almost immediately the young man was back at his post.

The hauntings started simply enough. One of the patrons, distracted by the incessant pacing of one of the ushers throughout the first act of a play, complained at the front office during intermission. The house manager was confused. He knew that none of his ushers had been standing in the aisles during the show, so he asked the woman if she had been able to see the person's face. Fortunately, she had, she said, and as she described the boy, down to a small mole on his cheek, the blood drained from the staffer's face. The person the lady had seen was Richard Miller!

Before long, several audience members, especially those sitting in or around Row 18 (which had been part of Miller's assigned section when he worked at the playhouse), began to see the spirit. He never spoke or, indeed, made any sound at all. But he would walk up and down the side aisle and sometimes return a stare.

Over the years his spectre was seen by dozens of actors and crew members throughout the theater, most often floating in the aisles but also in a special seating area known as the Queen's Box and on the catwalks above the stage.

According to legend, late one night in 1968 after the theater had closed, three of the male ushers tried to contact Miller using a Ouija board. After receiving some jumbled, indecipherable responses as the planchette at their fingertips moved among the letters, one of the boys is said to have seen Miller's luminous spirit floating above them.

And on at least one occasion, the ghost decided to venture outside the theater to become a phantom hitchhiker. An actress reported that earlier that day her eyes had been drawn to a solitary figure watching her throughout rehearsals. As she drove home past the front of the theater that night, that same (to her) unknown teenager—Miller—was suddenly sitting in the seat beside her. Just as quickly as the apparition had appeared, he completely faded away.

In 1993 extensive renovations were done to the theater's interior. The following year the crew supposedly brought in a paranormalist, very discreetly, to "exorcise" Miller's ghost. It's not that his visitations had become all that bothersome. But the theater personnel really hoped to help release the captive spirit from whatever bonds were holding him back, keeping him from Moving On.

After that the hauntings noticeably decreased. But they never completely disappeared.

The company moved to a new three-theater complex on the shores of the Mississippi River in May 2006. Coming full circle, the last production at the original Guthrie was *Hamlet*. The old theater was demolished, and a park and sculpture garden are planned for the site.

Is Richard Miller's ghost gone but not forgotten?

Perhaps it's too soon to tell. Maybe he's finally been able to go on to his Great Reward. At least so far he hasn't turned up at the new theater. But anything's possible. Although a ghost moving from one site to another is very uncommon, it's not unheard of, even in the theater world.

So if the next time you're seeing a show at the Guthrie you find yourself being shown to your seat by an unusually quiet, deathly pale, yet strangely incandescent young usher, you might want to take a second look at him. That person handing you your program might just be the phantom of Richard Miller himself, back where he always felt most alive.

Chapter 14
The Ghost of DD113

A rejected actress nicknamed Elvira has returned to the opera house in Woodstock, Illinois, after her death—supposedly by suicide. She even has her favorite seat in the theater.

The name Elvira resonates through popular culture. In 1981 the Oak Ridge Boys recorded their cover version of a 1966 song by that name and went to number one on the *Billboard* country music charts. It's also the name of TV's buxom hostess of late-night horror films, the self-styled "Mistress of the Dark."

In ghost lore, Elvira is another type of mistress of the dark. She's the seductive, malicious apparition found in Noël Coward's 1941 comedy *Blithe Spirit*. But Elvira is also the sobriquet that's been given to the beautiful wraith who wafts her way through the opera house in Woodstock, Illinois.

Woodstock is a bucolic city of around twenty-four thousand located just fifty-one miles northwest of Chicago. It's so picturesque that it was a perfect choice when producers were looking for a town to stand in for Punxsutawney, Pennsylvania, when they were filming the 1993 movie *Groundhog Day*. The city even has its own hometown weather prognosticator, Woodstock Willie, who peeks out of his hole to look for his shadow every February.

Another celebration, Dick Tracy Days, takes place there every summer to honor local resident Chester Gould, who created the iconic comic strip character. Woodstock is also known as the boyhood home of actor Orson Welles, who became involved in dramatics when he was a student at the Todd School for Boys (and whose ghost is said to haunt one of his hangouts, the Sweet Lady Jane Bakery in Los Angeles).

The Woodstock Opera House, the largest building in the community, borders one side of the town's center square. Built in 1889, it was designed by architect Smith Hoag to house the city council rooms, the court chambers, the offices of the fire department, the library, and most important to our tale, a second-floor auditorium with a proscenium stage.

The four-story, $25,000 building was constructed of limestone, sandstone, and white brick, along with decorative fieldstone and terra cotta. It was topped by a tall bell tower, which could be accessed by a winding staircase from inside. The exterior is a cacophony of different styles: Victorian, Gothic, Moorish, and Early American; the interior of the auditorium was intended to mimic the stages found onboard showboats that were still plying American rivers.

The first performance in the opera house was the Patti Rosa Company production of *Margery Daw* on September 4, 1890. The playhouse immediately attracted touring theater companies, minstrel shows, speakers, and, later, traveling vaudeville artists. In 1934 Roger Hill, headmaster of the Todd School, produced a summer season of Shakespeare in the hall, starring internationally famous actors Louise Prussing and Micheál MacLíammóir and featuring nineteen-year-old Welles.

In 1947 a repertory group called the Woodstock Players made the theater its home. During the group's tenure such actors as Shelley Berman (who would later become better known as a comedian), Tom Bosley, Lois Nettleton, Paul

Newman, Betsy Palmer, and Geraldine Page passed through the Woodstock Opera House doors.

Today, along with a series of individual concerts ranging from dance and music to educational lectures, the Town-Square Players and the Woodstock Musical Theatre Company present their seasons at the city-owned historic venue.

Also, at some point Elvira moved in.

Legend has it that she's the ghost of a distraught actress who threw herself out of the bell tower, either after not being cast in a ballet role she yearned for or after a love affair went awry. Other versions of the tale say she hanged herself in the belfry or jumped off a catwalk in the fly gallery above the stage. The only thing all the stories agree on is this: She's dead. And for some reason, as unhappy as she was during her days at the opera house in life, she's returned to haunt it after crossing the Veil.

Of course, places in which deaths occur, especially murders or suicides, are ripe for hauntings. And perhaps, deep down inside, the young woman really loved the theater and was simply driven to her unfortunate end by out-of-control passions.

No one knows when the event took place or even who she was. Indeed, there's no record of a suicide actually having taken place in the building. And even though she's believed to be from the theater's earliest years when meticulous records might not have been kept, surely news of such a sensational death would have appeared in local newspapers had it occurred.

Nevertheless, sometime after World War II people started calling the theater ghost Elvira.

Shelley Berman is among the many who have admitted to experiencing ghostly phenomena in the comfortable 424-

seat auditorium. He heard Elvira's spectral footsteps rever-
berate from empty parts of the theater, and he witnessed
her favorite trick: She invisibly turned down five seats in
one of the rows in the balcony as he watched, dumbfounded.
And before you jump to conclusions, the chairs are spring-
loaded and won't fall down on their own. Someone—or
some*thing*—has to press them down. But that day no one
was there.

The same story has come from several people. In fact,
Elvira seems to have a favorite seat, DD113, the fourth row
on the stage-right aisle in the balcony. Actors, tech crews,
and theater staff have looked on in amazement many times
as the seat has lowered itself on its own accord during
rehearsals, as if Elvira had invisibly settled in to watch the
run-throughs.

Elvira is also a critic. Actors and crew sometimes hear
her disapproving, wistful sighs if a show is going badly.
(Mind you, she *does* register appreciative support from time
to time as well.)

She'll let people know she's around by pushing small
props off shelves or tables on the stage. Or the items will
simply not be there when actors go for them, even though
crew members swear they've properly set the items in place.
Elvira's even been known to untie the back supports for the
scenery flats, hoping they'll fall over. Whether she's doing it
out of malice or mischief is unknown.

Her ghost isn't seen very often, but when Elvira does
materialize she's invariably described as slim, wearing a
flowing, translucent, almost shimmering dress and having
long blonde hair that cascades down below her waist.

If you're an actress and are about to take part in a production at the playhouse in Woodstock, look out! Over the

years, more than one young woman has confessed that she had to fight a sudden, inexplicable urge to flee the stage and rush up the staircase into the bell tower.

Is this a case of life imitating art? In *Blithe Spirit* the ghostly Elvira has a murderous bent, but her macabre hijinks are supposed to be funny. If such a thing happened in real life, however, it would certainly be anything but.

Is the impulse to run into the perilous bell tower simply a case of naive, impressionable girls being influenced by the ghostly stories surrounding the Woodstock Opera House? Or is Elvira looking for company and reaching out from beyond the grave?

Chapter 15
The Apparition
of the Alley

It reads like a gangster movie: Criminal kingpin John Dillinger is gunned down in an alleyway after leaving a Chicago cinema, the Biograph Theater. But he doesn't escape: His spirit is trapped there for eternity.

Derrick needed his nicotine fix.

He and his girlfriend were walking down Lincoln Avenue toward the Biograph Theater, where they planned to see a film, when he thought to ask. "How long is this movie, anyway?"

"I think it's around three hours. Why?"

"Then I need a smoke."

Jennifer wasn't pleased. She'd asked him to give up cigarettes—or at least *try* to give them up—months ago. But so far, no such luck. It was one of the main reasons that so far she'd resisted his invitations to move in with him. His apartment smelled like an ashtray.

But she understood. She was one of the few in her circle of friends who didn't smoke, and she knew how many of them had tried to stop but failed. But before her relationship with Derrick could become anything more serious, the cigarettes had to go.

"Give me a minute," he begged. "If you want, go get the tickets. I'll be there in a sec."

Jennifer gave him a withering glare, then headed off for the movie theater, just three storefronts away. *If looks could kill,* thought Derrick.

He turned the corner into the alley by the Fiesta Mexicana restaurant to get out of her sight. He pulled a cigarette from the pack, popped it into his mouth, and lit up. Leaning back against the wall, he took a deep drag and closed his eyes.

It was one of those dead, airless July nights, so as he exhaled, the smoke didn't drift but stayed in tight around his head. Derrick glanced down the alley. *Odd that no one was taking it,* he thought. Normally people coming over from Halsted used it as a shortcut. Instead, everyone seemed to be passing behind the restaurant, then walking all the way down to the corner of Lincoln; well, that wasn't his concern.

One more puff.

Wait. There *was* someone walking down the alley after all. It had gotten dark early, so through the lingering cloud of smoke Derrick could barely make out the form. Then he realized that the man was walking away from him. How had he gotten past Derrick without him noticing?

Something else was strange about the guy, too. He seemed almost out of focus, his outline a hazy, almost bluish blur. The mysterious figure looked over his shoulder, put his right hand into his pocket and pulled out—was that a gun?!

Panicked, Derrick dropped to the ground. What the hell was going on? Was he gonna die in this alleyway over a cigarette?

He raised his eyes to see if the creep was pointing the pistol at him, but the man was gone. Whoever, or whatever, it was had disappeared. No one had come toward him, and he could see the length of the building and beyond, all the way to Halsted. The alley was empty. The guy had simply vanished.

Slowly Derrick stood up and brushed off his clothes. He looked down at the still-glowing cigarette that had fallen from his hand. He crushed it out under his sole, walked back out onto Lincoln, and turned toward the Biograph. There was Jennifer, staring impatiently in his direction and pointing at her watch.

How was he going to explain what had just happened? Should he even try? No, he decided. She'd think he was smoking something stronger than tobacco.

It was a pity he was too spooked to tell her. If Derrick *had* mentioned the bizarre experience, she would have had an explanation: He had seen the ghost.

Jennifer had lived in the neighborhood from the time she was a little girl, so she knew all about the Biograph Theater and the spirit that supposedly haunts it. She couldn't *not* know. That alley where Derrick stopped was the spot where gangster John Dillinger was gunned down on a sultry July evening after watching a flick at the Biograph.

By 1934 Dillinger was number one on the FBI's Most Wanted List. Born in Indianapolis in 1903, he quit school in his teens and started work in a machinery shop, which might have been okay with his strict father, a grocer by trade. But when the boy started staying out to all hours carousing with friends, his dad had had enough and moved the family to Mooresville, Indiana, figuring the small farm community (without even a semblance of a night life) would straighten the boy out.

He was wrong. After a run-in with the law—a car theft—young Dillinger joined the navy. But the rebel soon deserted and was given a dishonorable discharge. He moved back to Mooresville and tried to settle down. But it seems Dillinger was not the "settling down" type.

In 1924 he and a friend robbed a local store but were quickly caught. With his dad's advice, Dillinger pled guilty, hoping to receive a light sentence. Instead, he got ten to twenty years and wound up serving eight. (His partner in crime, meanwhile, went to trial and received only a two-year sentence.)

Soon after his parole on May 22, 1933, Dillinger held up his first bank. This led to a string of bank robberies in which the dapper bandit, often clad in a straw hat, would effortlessly jump over the counter to empty out the drawers, earning himself the nickname "Jackrabbit." Four months to the day after his release, he was arrested again and sent back to prison.

But during those months of freedom, Dillinger had put plans in motion to help friends he had made in the Indiana State Prison escape. The breakout was successful, and three of the men in turn stormed the Lima jail where Dillinger was being held and broke him out.

Dillinger and his gang set out on an almost unprecedented crime spree. Along the way several law enforcement officers were killed, one of whom Dillinger personally shot during a bank heist in East Chicago. The men not only robbed banks but also broke into police stations to get guns, ammunition, and bulletproof vests. (Cars, they stole along the way as needed.)

Two members of Dillinger's gang went into hiding at the Hotel Congress in Tucson, Arizona. When a fire forced everyone out onto the street, a fireman recognized one of the men from a newspaper photo and tipped off the police. Before long, four members of the gang, including Dillinger, who had recently arrived in town to meet up with the boys, were caught and arrested. Three of them were shipped back to Ohio for killing a sheriff during their prison break in Lima. Dillinger was extradited to Indiana to stand trial for murder.

Despite the fact that he was put behind bars in what was supposed to be an escape-proof prison, on March 4, 1934, Dillinger managed to bluff his way out of the Crown Point, Indiana, jail by using a fake gun. Dillinger boasted that he had carved it out of wood; some said later that it was probably merely blackened soap.

It was perhaps during this escape that Dillinger made his biggest mstake. By stealing a car and driving it over a state line into Illinois, he violated federal law, and soon the FBI was called in. (Amazingly, bank robbery itself was not against federal law until a few months later.)

Once free, Dillinger fled to Minnesota's Twin Cities and immediately whipped together a new gang, one of whom later became famous on his own as Baby Face Nelson. Only two days after his escape, Dillinger returned to work—this time a bank heist in South Dakota. A week later they pulled off another job in Iowa, and while making their escape, Dillinger was wounded.

Nevertheless, their bank robberies continued. Because of the large distances between the banks and their being in no seeming order, the gang appeared to be everywhere at once. Although there's no evidence to support the myth, somewhere along the way Dillinger gained the reputation of being a kind of Robin Hood. It was probably just wishful thinking on the part of people in the midst of the Depression, but reportedly Dillinger was sharing his ill-gotten gains with the needy.

The mythos also grew up because Dillinger had style. He didn't always simply barge in and yell "Stick 'em up." Sometimes he would pretend to be a security expert selling alarm systems so he could case the joint as bank officials freely showed him their vaults and defenses. Other times he might claim to be making a movie so locals would stand by peaceably as the "bank robbery sequence" was supposedly being shot.

On April 20, 1934, Dillinger and his gang went into hiding at the remote Little Bohemia Lodge in northern Wisconsin. Tipped off by the owners that Dillinger was there, FBI agents headed by Melvin Purvis (who was in charge of the Chicago bureau) surrounded the property, but in the ensuing melee, the entire gang managed to escape (although one died later from a gunshot wound he received as the car in which he was riding barreled off).

The heat was on. Dillinger found a plastic surgeon to alter his face. A few days later the doctor used acid to try to remove Dillinger's fingerprints. By June the gangster was back in the bank business.

On July 1, 1934, Dillinger met with his girlfriend, Polly Hamilton, who was renting a room from Anna Sage, a Romanian who was accused of being a madam and was fighting deportation. Sage discovered Dillinger's true identity and informed the FBI. She told Purvis and Samuel Cowley, who was specifically assigned to the Dillinger operation, that, in exchange for the cash reward and help with her immigration problem, she would lead them to Public Enemy No. 1. They said the cash would be hers, but all they could do was put in a good word with the Labor Department, which at the time was the agency handling immigration. Sage agreed to the arrangement.

On July 22 she called to say that she, Hamilton, and Dillinger were going to see a movie that night at either the Marbro or the Biograph. She would wear a red dress to identify herself to agents (causing newspapers to later designate the mystery woman as simply the Lady in Red).

The FBI split into two teams, with Purvis heading the one covering the Biograph. The redbrick theater, designed by Samuel N. Crowen in 1914, was a traditional cinema of its era. Located in the Lincoln Park district of the Second City, it had a ticket booth kiosk separate from the main lobby standing under a marquee. One of the theater's main attractions was its air conditioning, especially on hot summer nights.

At around 8 p.m. the trio entered the theater, which, ironically, was showing the MGM gangster movie *Manhattan Melodrama*. As soon as Dillinger entered, Purvis called Cowley, who hurried with his men to join the others staking out the Biograph. The place was soon surrounded. They were not going to have another mishap like the embarrassing snafu at the Little Bohemia Lodge.

At 10:30 Dillinger and his companions left the theater. Purvis, standing just left of the entrance, lit a cigar to signal his men to move in. Dillinger, looking Purvis in the face as he passed, sized up the situation immediately. Instinctively his radar became aware of the other men as they started to slowly move toward him. He tore his gun from his right pants pocket and made a quick turn to the left, ducking down that infamous alley. Agents fired five shots at him; three found their mark. The fatal bullet hit him in the back of the neck and exited under his right eye.

Dillinger was taken to Alexian Brothers Hospital, where he was pronounced dead. From there it was off to the morgue. At both places, crowds gathered to catch a glimpse of the notorious outlaw and take photos. Thousands showed up for his burial at Crown Hill Cemetery. Within four months all of the surviving members of Dillinger's gang had been killed or captured. Two years later, despite her cooperation in the Dillinger case, Sage was deported.

Rumors began to circulate almost immediately that the FBI had gotten the wrong man in that alleyway. During the autopsy it was noticed that the corpse had different colored eyes than Dillinger as well as a rheumatic heart condition that, if it had been noticed during a navy physical, would have kept him out of the service. Then, at first, Dillinger's father didn't recognize him because of the bad plastic surgery. Some claimed that the FBI had actually shot a small-time hood named Jimmy Lawrence and was covering up its tracks.

To keep curiosity seekers from digging up the coffin to find out for themselves whether Dillinger was in the grave, his father had three feet of concrete poured over it. But that apparently didn't keep Dillinger—whom partial fingerprints and his sister had positively identified—from returning to the Biograph.

Within months of Dillinger's death, people began to report seeing a misty male form floating down the alley where he died. Sometimes it would pull a gun before it fell to the ground and faded away. In addition to seeing the apparition, onlookers would feel a sudden chill or an icy breeze. Before long, locals stopped walking down the pathway. If they had to get from Lincoln to Halsted, they'd take the long way around.

As for the Biograph itself, over the next few years it went through several owners. At some point, its seats were replaced, and some of the old chairs—including the one Dillinger sat in that fateful night—were sold to the now-haunted Winter Garden Theatre in Toronto.

In the 1970s the large movie theater was broken up to hold three separate screens, and it finally closed in 2001. Although briefly opening the following year, its doors remained shut until July 2004, when the Victory Gardens Theater company purchased the Biograph to turn it into a legitimate playhouse. Reopened to the public two years later, the main theater now seats 299 and has a proscenium-thrust stage. A restored grand staircase leads up to a second-floor rehearsal space and a 135-seat studio theater. Other renovations include a green room, two dressing rooms, trap space under the stage, and a wider lobby.

If you want to see the interior of the theater where John Dillinger enjoyed his last movie, you'll have to attend a play. But the open alley can be visited anytime, day or night, night or day. Just don't be shocked if you too are confronted by the ghost of the Most Wanted Man in America.

Chapter 16

Mary, Mary, Quite Contrary

No one is sure how Mary, the little girl whose playful ghost haunts the Orpheum Theatre in Memphis, died. But you always know where to find her, right there in her favorite seat in a box in the mezzanine.

There are 2,333 seats in the Orpheum Theatre in Memphis, Tennessee. It's an immense playhouse, with up to six levels, depending how you count them. The bulk of the mezzanine overhangs Row Z in the rear orchestra, but its front lip curves so that some of its seats are directly above the tenth row of the orchestra. The front boxes along the side walls on the mezzanine level contain six seats each. Above all this are the four-row Grand Tier, an eight-row balcony, and a lower and upper gallery.

You'd think with so many places to choose from, the theater's ghost could sit anywhere she pleased. But little Mary has one she likes best.

Memphis, founded in 1820, is located in southwest Tennessee on the Mississippi River. When the state seceded from the Union in 1861, Memphis became a Confederate stronghold, but only for about a year. The city was a strategically important port, so Union forces quickly targeted it. Memphis fell in June 1862, and it remained in Northern hands for the remainder of the Civil War. As a result, it flourished, and in the postwar years the citizens wanted a premier theater in which to present entertainment.

The first Orpheum Theatre in Memphis was built in 1890 as the Grand Opera House, located at the corner of South Main and Beale Streets. Its name was changed when it became part of the Orpheum vaudeville circuit in 1907. For sixteen unbroken years it presented concerts and variety bills, but all that came to an end when fire broke out in 1923 during a show featuring the singer/actress Blossom Seeley. The playhouse was completely consumed in the blaze.

Five years later a phoenix rose from the ashes. The new Orpheum Theatre, built on the same site, was twice as large and cost a staggering $1.6 million. It boasted massive crystal chandeliers, brocade curtains, and a gigantic Wurlitzer organ.

Unfortunately, by the time the theater was completed, vaudeville was dying. In 1940 the Malco movie chain bought the variety house and turned it into a first-run movie palace.

In 1976 the company put the cinema up for sale. Word on the street was that the Orpheum, once billed as the "South's Finest Theatre," would fall to the wrecking ball, so the following year concerned citizens formed the Memphis Development Foundation to save it.

Five years later, on Christmas Day 1982, they temporarily closed the theater to begin a two-year, $5 million refurbishment. The idea was to return the Orpheum to its original grandeur, and succeed they did. Plush red and gold carpet now passes beneath patrons' feet. Two enormous crystal chandeliers weighing two thousand pounds each are suspended over their heads. Today the Orpheum hosts touring Broadway companies and major concert artists as well as the city opera and ballet companies.

Seeing it all since the 1920s has been little Mary.

Even for a ghost story, this legend has so many variations that it's hard to tell which parts are to be believed. The only things that are "certain" are that a young girl, about twelve years old, was killed in the street outside the Orpheum during the Roaring Twenties and, not long after, her ghost started to haunt the theater.

That being said, research has turned up no local newspaper reports about such a tragedy happening in the '20s. Thus, even if the story is true, there's no way of knowing what the youngster's name really was, but at some point people started calling her Mary.

No one knows for sure whether she was in the theater before the accident that afternoon or was just passing by. Some versions of the yarn have her darting into the street and being hit by a car, and others by a trolley. One has her being run over by a horse and carriage. It's also unclear whether the incident occurred on Main or Beale and whether the girl was carried back into the lobby or, as some paranormalists suggest, her freed spirit simply floated back into the playhouse from the street.

One account even has Mary dying not from a street accident but by falling from the balcony of the Orpheum during a show.

Most people seem to agree that Mary liked to attend shows at the theater, and she always tried to get the same seat—which would explain why her apparition is usually seen in the same location: Seat C-5, Box 5, on the right-hand side of the auditorium facing the stage. But she's also been spotted in the lobby and the corridors.

And what does she look like? Always the same. A simple white dress, brown hair with pigtails, black stockings, radiant skin. And she normally doesn't smile or frown; she usually has a blank gaze on her face, making it impossible to read what she might be thinking.

She's seldom troublesome when she's watching a performance, and she usually sits there quietly. But she's been known to turn all of the chairs in her favorite box away from the stage if she doesn't like a performance.

Many, many actors have reported seeing Mary, especially since the 1970s. Her appearances apparently became almost routine during performances of *Fiddler on the Roof* in 1977 and Yul Brenner's tour of *The King and I* in 1982.

House organist Vincent Astor is among the staff who have been very open about Mary's presence. He's said that she seems to like children's music, especially the song "Neverland" from *Peter Pan*. While Mary was always on her best behavior around him, Astor was careful never to say anything hurtful or unkind about her. (After all, you can never be too careful with a ghost.)

Often patrons can't sit in the theater boxes because they're used to house spotlights and other technical equipment. If anything goes wrong with any of the gear during a performance, guess who's blamed?

Mind you, Mary doesn't always materialize. But people know when she's around because they're hit by a sudden drop in temperature, which is a frequent manifestation of spectres. Doors will slam shut or open on their own, lights will flicker, or the pipe organ will start to play seemingly all by itself. And other times people hear disembodied laughter and footsteps as she glides down the halls.

If you visit Memphis, you won't lack for things to do. It's the home of Elvis Presley's Graceland and the famed Pink Palace Museum of history and science. There's Mud Island

River Park, where you can walk barefoot through a minia-ture scale model of the Mississippi made out of concrete.

And then there's the Orpheum Theatre. If you attend one of the many shows presented there and get to sit in Box 5, you may want to leave seat C-5 free. And if you're lucky, someone special might join you: the ghost of little Mary.

Chapter 17

Nightmares in
Nashville

Three spirits roam the halls of a celebrated theater in downtown Nashville: a superstar, a relative unknown, and a mystery man. Yet all of them belong there and have a legitimate claim to being the "house ghost."

He and his friends thought they'd get a pretty good laugh out of it. When Thomas G. Ryman decided to head down to the tent pitched at the corner of Broadway and Eighth Avenue there in Nashville to heckle the new evangelical preacher in town, he was a hard-drinking, fun-loving forty-three-year-old. Tall and rugged, he was a riverboat captain and the successful owner of the Cumberland River Steamboat Company, and his buddies were used to following his lead.

The revivalist, Samuel Porter Jones, was already well known on the circuit. Just thirty-eight, he had a huge following in the South, especially in Georgia, Tennessee, Kentucky, and Alabama. He was the grandson and nephew of Methodist ministers, and he had studied law, gaining admittance to the Georgia bar in 1868. But drink ruined his early promise, and within four years he was reduced to stoking furnaces for a living. But in 1872, after a deathbed plea from his father, Jones repented, gave his life to Christ, and entered the ministry. Having been a laborer himself, Jones was able to reach out to the common man as he railed in his sermons against sin and hypocrisy.

Ryman thought the reverend would be an easy prey, simple to ridicule and a hoot to harass. Instead, when he stepped under that canvas on May 10, 1885, the riverboat baron was struck by the words he was hearing and was instantly converted. Looking around him there in the tent, the wealthy entrepreneur decided that Jones needed a sanctuary suitable for the important message he was delivering. He told the evangelist that he planned to build him a temple, to be called the Union Gospel Tabernacle, as a home base.

Ryman sketched out a few plans for the building, and they were realized by architect Hugh C. Thompson. In May 1890 Jones held his first revival meeting within the walls of the unfinished hall. (A canvas tarp was used to cover holes in the roof.) Two years later, work on the auditorium, with seating for 1,255, was completed.

From the very beginning the building was also used for educational and inspirational speeches as well as classical programs. One of the first lectures took place in April 1893 when Lieutenant Richard Perry gave a talk about his Arctic explorations. A month later the New York Symphonic made a guest appearance. In 1901 a permanent stage was built at one end of the hall to accommodate the New York Opera Company's touring productions of *Carmen, The Barber of Seville,* and *Faust.*

From the time of his conversion, Ryman not only "talked the talk" but also "walked the walk." Overnight he stopped the impetuous wild ways of his youth. He became known for his integrity and charity work, and when he died on December 23, 1904, he was truly mourned.

At the funeral service, the Reverend Jones urged that the name of the tabernacle be changed to Ryman Auditorium.

The suggestion received a standing ovation and was approved by acclamation. (The name wasn't legally changed, however, until 1944.)

Jones's good work continued up to his death on October 15, 1906. But by that time, beginning shortly after Ryman's death, the auditorium had begun to expand its schedules to include shows that were pure entertainment. Although the hall was never transformed into a vaudeville house per se, its programming started to include theater (such as the 1907 production of *Peter Pan*, starring Broadway actress Maude Adams) and variety (such as comedian Harry Lauder's appearance in 1912).

Although the public seemed happy enough, one person certainly wasn't pleased: Thomas Ryman.

Apparently the founder was so attached to his temple that even after death he remained, watching over it. If a show appeared there that was not to his liking, especially if he considered it risqué, his spirit created such a racket of disembodied noise that it would disturb people seated throughout the theater.

Fortunately, *his* spectre seems to have settled down over the years, and not much is heard from him these days. A second ghost, however, also dating back to the turn of the twentieth century, is still showing up from time to time.

In 1897 a massive balcony was added to the auditorium, more than doubling the capacity of the hall to 3,755 (although the hall has since been reconfigured for a maximum of 2,362). The new seating area, which is still in use, was called the Confederate Gallery in honor of the Confederate Veterans Convention and Tennessee Centennial Exposition for which the balcony was inaugurated.

It's there that the second apparition is almost always seen, and—get this!—it's a male figure dressed all in gray, the shade worn by Confederate soldiers. Merely a coincidence? The Gray Man is not dressed in uniform, though, and his identity has never been known. When he materializes, it's usually during rehearsals or after shows are over for the night. He merely sits there quietly in the gallery, disturbing no one. But if you try to approach him, he simply evaporates!

Two ghosts down; one to go. The third phantom of the opera house is associated with the longest-running tenant of Ryman Auditorium: the Grand Ole Opry.

From 1943 to 1974 the Ryman played host to the most famous country radio show of all time. The Grand Ole Opry started out in 1925 as *WSM Barn Dance*, broadcast from a studio in the radio station's headquarters in the center of Nashville. The show got the name by which it's now known on December 10, 1927, from its announcer and program director George D. Day, who was affectionately known as the "Solemn Old Judge." He noted on the air that *Barn Dance* followed the NBC Radio's Network's *Music Appreciation Hour* of classical music and opera, so he flippantly remarked that audiences who had just listened to an hour of Grand Opera would now get to hear the "Grand Ole Opry." The name caught on, and that's what it's been called ever since.

The show became so popular that the station decided to broadcast it from a theater so a larger live audience could attend. It moved from one venue to the other, three in all, before finally settling into Ryman Auditorium on June 5, 1943, where it stayed for the next thirty-one years.

Over those three decades, everyone who was anyone in country-and-western music appeared on its stage. Among its galaxy of stars was Hank Williams (now often referred to as Hank Williams Sr., because his son and grandson, Hank Williams Jr. and Hank Williams III, are also country performers). The composer and singer of such timeless songs as "Cold, Cold Heart," "Jambalaya (On the Bayou)," "I'm So Lonesome I Could Cry," "I Saw the Light," "Take These Chains From My Heart," and "Your Cheatin' Heart" was born in Alabama in 1923. By his mid-teens, Williams was a professional with his own radio show on WSFA in Montgomery. Before long he was invited to become a member of the Grand Ole Opry.

Throughout his life Williams was plagued by alcoholism and, later, addiction to several painkillers, including morphine. His use and later dependence was no doubt brought on, at least in part, by the fact that he was born with a mild form of spina bifida, and he was seeking relief from constant back pain throughout his short life.

As his condition and behavior worsened, it was hard for the singer to keep band members. Often his drinking was costing more than the shows were taking in. He would even turn up drunk for his own radio show. Finally in 1952 it led to Williams's being fired from the Grand Ole Opry.

He died in 1953 at the age of twenty-nine in the back of a car while being driven from Knoxville, Texas, to a gig in Canton, Ohio. A couple of cans of beer were found by his side, but he had also injected himself with morphine before leaving his hotel. Williams is buried back in Montgomery, and his funeral is thought to have drawn more people than any other ever held in Alabama.

On March 16, 1974, the Grand Ole Opry relocated to its current home at the 4,400-seat Grand Ole Opry House outside the Opryland USA theme park, nine miles east of downtown Nashville. The show may have moved on, but it left at least one ghost behind. Hank Williams led a troubled life, but he seems to have found peace back on the stage of Ryman Auditorium.

In a 2003 Country Music Television list of the "40 Greatest Men of Country Music," Williams came in second, behind only Johnny Cash. His face is so etched into country music history that it would be almost impossible for anyone in the industry not to recognize his apparition if it appeared backstage at the Ryman. And it does, and people have!

Besides roaming the hallways, Williams shows up on the stage itself, where he often first materializes as a hazy white mist. He then slowly forms into the identifiable figure still beloved by country fans throughout the world. And he doesn't remain cooped up indoors. It was no secret that Williams liked to tip the bottle a bit, which might explain why his ghost has also been spied in the alleyway between the Ryman Auditorium and Tootsie's Orchid Lounge next door.

The Ryman has never completely closed its doors, but the loss of the Grand Ole Opry significantly changed its fortunes. It sat mostly unused for years, although scenes from several movies and an occasional TV special were shot there, and now and then it housed a concert or other show. Then in 1992 Ryman Auditorium celebrated its centennial, and the following year Gaylord Entertainment, which owns and operates Opryland, began an $8.5 million restoration of the hall. The Mother Church of Country Music, as the Ryman is endearingly and reverently nicknamed, officially reopened as a major performance venue and museum in June 1994. Tours are even available, so whether you see a show or just duck in during the day to take a peek, you have a chance to catch one of the theater ghosts for yourself.

A final note: In some circles it's said there was a Grand Ole Opry curse, because as many as thirty-five of the acts who appeared at the Ryman had their lives cut short under terrible circumstances: in plane crashes, car accidents, house fires, or murder.

So if your ambition in life is to become a great country singer and one day appear at the Ryman Auditorium, beware! It already has three ghosts, but there's always room for one more.

Chapter 18
The Spectral Sweeper

Akron Civic Theatre is still the working address for the ghost of its longtime custodian, Fred. And shades of the catacombs in Phantom of the Opera: *The spectre of a young woman who drowned herself in a canal under the theater has also come back.*

The two kids broke into the building easily. There wasn't anyone to stop them. Hell, it was a run-down movie house. Why would anyone guard that?

The theater, glorious in its heyday, had fallen into disrepair. But it still had most of the original furnishings from when it first opened. True, most of the exquisite woodwork had lost its polish and veneer over the years, but a lot of the bric-a-brac could fetch a fair amount if it got to the right collector or some disreputable dealer. And there were plenty of odds and ends the boys could carry off, if that's what they had been there for.

But rumor had it that the city was going to take over the old movie palace and turn it into a grand theater for live entertainment. The whole place would have to be fixed up, top to bottom, so what difference would it make if in the meantime two guys decided to tag the whole thing with graffiti? They figured that if they wanted to go for it, it was now or never.

Ohio's Akron Civic Theatre was originally known as Loew's Theatre, built by Marcus Loew and opened on April 20, 1929.

The cinema replaced the Hippodrome playhouse, which had stood there on Main Street, unfinished, since 1918. But the plain three-story facade and functional front marquee of the new theater, designed by architect John Eberson, gave no clue as to the opulence inside.

The interior was meant to evoke a Mediterranean-style Moorish castle and garden. An entrance hallway, with a terrazzo floor and exposed beams overhead, led to the Grand Lobby. There, a massive chandelier hung from the intricately carved ceiling, and plush red carpet patterned with blue and beige diamonds was laid underfoot. Handcrafted iron railings lined the two-tiered staircase, and a wide, decorated arch spanned the top of the stairs.

Inside the auditorium an elaborately detailed proscenium framed the top of the stage, and the stylish wood paneling continued several feet along the walls on both sides into the house. Actual antiques and Italian alabaster columns were installed as part of the decor, and a full-size concert Wurlitzer organ was mounted on an elevator so it could be raised from beneath the stage.

Before the performances, clouds lazily drifted across the sky, as stars twinkled from the heavens. Okay, the stars were small lightbulbs set into the ceiling plaster, and the clouds were projected, but still. Today the Akron, which cost $300,000 to build, is one of a handful of still-operating "atmospheric theatres" built in the 1920s and '30s by Eberson, who was considered the best in the business. It's the last remaining theater of the eleven Loew originally opened in Ohio.

The young men moved silently through the auditorium toward the front lobby. Why were they tiptoeing? It wasn't like anyone was going to hear or stop them. Entering the foyer, they found the perfect spot to vandalize: two soaring bare walls, painted Etruscan gold, on either side of the grand staircase. No one could miss seeing their marks.

"I'll take this side; you take the other."

"You know whatever we do's not gonna be here for long, right? These walls'll be the first thing they repaint when they start to fix the place up."

"Yeah, but 'til then they'll know that we—well, someone—was here."

They reached into their bags and pulled out two huge cans of black spray paint. The sound of the metallic balls rattling echoed as they shook the cans. The kids popped off the tops and aimed.

"Hey, I changed my mind. You get the walls. I'm gonna get the bird."

When the theater first opened, two live macaws were placed in the lobby to greet patrons as they arrived. Although the birds were beautiful to look at, they were aggressive, and one of them, Loretta, bit the finger of an audience member who got too close. A lawsuit was settled out of court and, curiously enough, Loretta died under mysterious circumstances just about the same time.

No, she doesn't haunt the theater. But she *is* still there. Loretta was taken to a taxidermist, stuffed, and placed in an alcove just to the left of the top of the grand staircase. In spite of everything, she goes on welcoming guests. (In fact, she's so well known that the bird is part of the Akron Civic Theatre logo.)

If the tagger had gotten to his intended victim, he wouldn't have been the first. Years before, the macaw's colorful tail feathers had fallen out, and someone had taken it upon himself to spruce her up with a bit of paint. But this night the boy never got that far.

As the kid looked at the steps, a white glow slowly appeared at the top of the staircase. The orb then started to grow, taking the shape of a shining, male figure: an old but still robust man. The glimmering shape started rapidly coming toward the teenager—and the ghost wasn't happy.

"Hey, dude. Look! What the hell is that? Let's get outta here!"

The pair turned and ran. They sprinted through the auditorium, ran backstage, and found that the door they had jimmied open was somehow ajar. Without pausing, they ran outside, slammed the door behind them, and took off.

Back inside the theater, a smile crossed the lips of the shining sentinel as it faded and disappeared.

In June 2001 the cinema, by then owned by the city, underwent a complete restoration, and today, after about $20 million, sixteen months of refurbishment, and a name change, it's once again a marvel to behold.

And, of course, it has its ghost. Or should we say "ghosts"?

At least two and possibly three spirits haunt the Akron Civic Theatre. Besides the protective spectre, the apparition of a weeping woman is also sometimes seen. She appears standing beside a water channel that runs underneath the theater's foundations.

We're not talking *Phantom of the Opera* here. Parts of the Civic, including the Grand Lobby, extend over a section of the old Ohio Canal. Akron was founded in 1825 near a major set of locks of the Ohio and Erie Canal system that was used to transport goods and passengers across America from 1827 up until the 1860s.

Although the canal hadn't been used since 1913, the

City of Akron still owned the property when the theater was constructed, and it wouldn't allow the waterway to be closed. Loew leased the air rights, and Eberson built the Grand Lobby over the canal. Unseen by the public, thick concrete "stilts" actually support the floor of the foyer.

Due to the ghost's manifestations near the hidden channel, it's assumed that she dates back from the time the canal was an important water path winding its way throughout Akron. But no one knows for sure. Both her appearance and clothing are nondescript, so it's impossible to tell in what period she lived. According to legend, she committed suicide by drowning herself in its depths.

In addition to her phantom, an unidentified male spook is sometimes spotted sitting in the balcony of the Civic, quietly looking on during rehearsals. Again, no one knows who he is, but it's assumed that he must have been involved with the theater in some capacity when he was alive.

But the theater's main ghost and the one that's most often seen is the one we first met. The apparition that guards the playhouse against unwelcome visitors is known as Fred the Janitor, or just simply Fred. The longtime custodian worked at the Civic back when it was still Loew's Theatre. He died in the theater, but that didn't stop the loyal employee from staying on the job. He most often appears when special events are being held there; other times he's been known to scare off more than one intruder.

So this tale should be a lesson to all burglars and vandals. Be forewarned: Just because a theater is unoccupied, it doesn't mean it's uninhabited.

Chapter 19
Without a Trace

Home to at least three ghosts, the Victoria Theatre in Dayton is now the primary residence for Vicky, an actress who mysteriously disappeared from her dressing room one night, as well as Lucille, a woman who was assaulted in a stage-right private box.

"Vicky, hurry up. What's keeping you?"

The door to Vicky's dressing room had been closed for quite a while, which was unusual for the young actress. True, she was modest—too much so for the Roaring Twenties, according to some of her friends—so she always swung the door closed when she was changing her clothing, but that usually only took a couple of minutes, at most.

Her friend knocked at the door. And again. No answer. She turned the knob. It was locked.

What is going on? she wondered. Vicky never slipped out without saying goodnight. She rushed down to the stage doorman, who was sitting behind his desk checking out the *Daily Racing Form.*

"Hey, did you see Vicky leave? I can't find her anywhere backstage, and she's not in her dressing room."

"No, sorry, sweetie. I woulda seen her if she had gone out this way. I guess she coulda gone out the front, but I've never known her to do that."

"Okay. Thanks."

Now she was worried. Where could Vicky be?

She went out into the theater, where the stage manager was setting out the ghost light. The actress knew all about the theatrical tradition—some would say superstition. It's been around for as long as anyone can remember.

A "ghost light"—a single, bare light bulb perched on top of a pole about six feet tall—is always placed center stage after the audience has gone for the evening. It's turned on and allowed to burn throughout the night.

Now, the lamp *does* have a practical purpose: preventing accidents. A solitary bulb might not give all that much illumination, but if someone's trying to negotiate a stage or auditorium, it's better than complete darkness.

But the *other* reason the ghost light is left on—isn't it obvious from its name?—is to scare away any stray spirits in the theater that might be in the mood to create havoc. (And, perhaps, given the relatively few problems caused by the countless number of theater spectres that have been reported over the years, it would seem that ghost lights work.)

But Vicky's friend had more immediate concerns: Someone was missing! The stage manager was a pretty smart guy. He'd know what to do.

"Well," he explained, "if Vicky hasn't left the theater, which she most likely did—that lazy guy at the door probably missed her; always has his mind on the horses and never takes his nose outta the—oh, right, Vicky. And you checked her dressing room?"

Although he didn't like to do it, the stage manager finally agreed to use his spare key to open Vicky's room and let her friend take a quick peek inside. The actress *could* just be asleep, but she might be sick, or worse. It would only take a second to check.

The two made their way to the dressing room. They knocked, then called out the absent actress's name just to warn her, in case she *was* there, that they were coming in. Sam turned the key in the latch, and . . .

The room was completely empty. Well, not empty, of course. Vicky's personal effects were there, as well as her costumes; makeup and brushes were spread out over the table in front of the long mirror. And there was the lingering scent of the rose perfume that had always been her favorite. But Vicky herself was gone.

And she was never seen again.

Lucille hated to go to the theater alone. But this was a show that she really wanted to see, and despite her rather heavy-handed hints to several beaus, none had asked to take her to the performance.

It wasn't exactly improper, but it was still considered rather déclassé for a young lady, especially if she were still single, to be seen in public on her own. Lucille didn't quite understand why: It was the twentieth century, after all! But, still, in polite society, rules are rules.

That's why, instead of sitting in her preferred seat in the center front of the balcony, she had hired the private box so she could remain, for the most part, out of sight. The box where she sat on the upper level of the left side of the house was actually split into two small sections. The front half, nearer the stage, had only two seats, partitioned off from four seats in the rear of the box.

Lucille had taken the front compartment for herself, demurely sitting in the inner seat. That way, her presence was less conspicuous as she sat in the dimmed auditorium.

But it also placed her closer to the door. Which is exactly

what made her attacker think he wouldn't be seen. The assailant reached out through the darkness, quietly slipping both arms around the unsuspecting Lucille. In a single motion, his left hand covered her mouth, stifling any possibility of a scream. His right hand reached for her breast, and . . .

What the unknown assailant hadn't counted on was that Lucille was no demure wallflower. In a flash, she had spun in her seat and turned to the intruder, somewhat loosening his grip. She raised both hands and moved her nails toward his face.

The struggle, though violent, was mercifully brief. The noise quickly drew people to her aid, and the brute was pulled off her and carted away. Lucille was swiftly rushed from the theater, safe from all. Safe, she bitterly realized, except for the whispers and innuendo that would no doubt follow her for years to come.

He didn't leave behind a note, so nobody knew why he took his own life. Or why he chose such a particularly painful, gruesome way to go.

It would have had to be planned very carefully. He had to get access to the place when no one would disturb him. And he would have had to have brought tools to fasten the handle of the knife to the back of the seat—firmly, because the sharpened point had to face upward just so, with no possibility that it would fall loose or tilt to one side.

And he couldn't just fall onto the blade haphazardly. He had to be sure of the angle. And to be certain the wound was fatal, he would have had to actually thrust himself against the knife's razor-sharp edge.

In short, he would have had to have practiced.

But that's how the stranger died, by throwing himself against a knife bolted to the back of one of the theater's seats—obviously distraught, possibly mad, definitely alone.

The Victoria Theatre has risen from the dead so often, no wonder it has so many ghosts. The first theater on the site was the Turner Opera House, built at Third and Main in downtown Dayton, Ohio, in 1866. The playhouse was in operation for only three years, however, before it was destroyed by fire.

Only the front facade remained. It was incorporated into a new theater, the Music Hall, which opened its doors on an adjacent lot at First and Main on November 28, 1871. The building wasn't an exact replica of the first. In fact, it had two fewer floors, and the auditorium was lowered to street level. The building has now survived for more than 130 years and played host to vaudeville's greatest stars.

The theater's name has been changed several times, starting in 1885 to the Grand Opera House. In 1899 it became the Victoria Opera House, and later the name altered slightly to the Victoria Theatre.

Then natural disaster struck. Like much of Dayton, the theater was damaged in the Flood of 1913 when the Great Miami River overflowed its banks. The river had flooded many times before—in fact, Dayton had flooded about once every twenty years since the city was founded—but this time turned out to be the worst in Ohio history. As the water crested, more than twenty feet covered central Dayton.

The theater bounced back, only to catch fire in 1918. It was refurbished and reopened the next year with a new name, the Victory Theatre, to celebrate America's win in World War I. By the 1930s the Victory had turned into a movie house, with only occasional live shows being performed there. Finally in 1972, like many midtown theaters past their prime, it was set to be knocked down.

In 1976 the Victory Theatre Association was founded to rescue the playhouse. Two years later they succeeded in buying the theater and immediately set about bringing back it's original Victorian glory.

A decade later a new group, the Arts Center Foundation, took over the playhouse and engineered a $17.5 million restoration, rechristening the building the Victoria Theatre in the process.

Today the 1,154-seat theater is home to the Dayton Ballet, a summer film festival, concerts, and Broadway touring shows. It also houses three ghosts.

The spectre of Vicky, the actress who's said to have vanished from her locked dressing room in the 1920s, has been seen throughout the theater, both during and after performances. Even before she appears, people usually can smell her rose perfume or hear her dress rustling as she makes her way across the floor.

Lucille survived her attack and lived into old age, but many patrons who have used the private box where she was assaulted say they felt a sense of panic or distress while sitting there—perhaps some sort of residual emotion. One person even claimed to have received a disembodied slap.

The face of the suicide victim supposedly used to appear in the folds of a set of backstage curtains that have since been removed. The good news is that, at least currently, this third phantom has disappeared.

For now, at least, he seems to rest in peace.

Chapter 20
Freddy the
Phantom

Since 2003 the State Theatre in Easton, Pennsylvania, has presented its annual Freddy Awards, named for its beloved longtime manager, J. Fred Osterstock. His apparition, however, took up residence in the historic building years ago.

Reports began to surface in the 1970s. Something odd was going on in the State Theatre in Easton, Pennsylvania.

The first few times the apparition was seen, maintenance men thought it was actually a living, breathing person. They'd catch sight of an unidentified man standing all alone in the back of the empty auditorium. Or they'd see the stranger walk into one of the theater's many closets, but when they swung open the door to catch him, the room was always empty.

Police were sometimes called in, but they never found an intruder. True, their dogs may have snarled as they peered down the dark, empty hallways, but dogs and cats do that all the time, don't they? Nothing and no one ever turned up.

After almost a dozen sightings, many by members of the theater's board of directors, it was just by chance that local historian Ken Klabunde happened to glimpse the spectre walking from the stage into the wings late one night. Later, as he was flipping through old photographs, a face jumped out at him. It was the mystery person Klabunde had seen back at the playhouse. His name was J. Fred Osterstock.

Osterstock was the type of dedicated, hardworking manager any theater organization would be proud to have on its staff. The distinguished gentleman, in all senses of that word, always had a friendly wave and a smile for anyone who passed by his office in the lobby. He held his post at the State Theatre from 1936 to 1965.

Although it's often said that someone "feels at home" at a particular place, the State Theatre actually *was* Fred's home for several weeks when a flood covered the first floor of his house in 1955. He later moved back into the theater on a permanent basis for the last few years of his life.

Easton is located on Pennsylvania's eastern border (hence, the city's name) at the confluence of the Lehigh River and the Delaware River, which forms the boundary between the Keystone State and New Jersey. It's about sixty miles north of Philadelphia and about seventy miles southwest of New York City. By the end of the nineteenth century, the city was a major commercial hub. Blessed by being on two rivers, three canals, and a major railroad line, Easton became a crossroads for the iron and coal industries even as, along with nearby Bethlehem, it became noted for steel production.

With all the money passing through the region in 1873, is it any wonder, then, that the State Theatre building began life as a bank? In 1910 the Northampton Bank was demolished to make way for a vaudeville house, which was called the Neumeyer Theatre. Only the bank's granite facade and foyer were saved and incorporated into the new structure.

Four years later, the name of the playhouse was changed to the Northampton Theatre; then within two years it had become the Colonial Theatre.

In 1925 Philadelphia architect William L. Lee was commissioned to completely redesign the space. As inspiration, he drew on Spanish influences as well as the fourteenth-century Davanzati Palace in Florence, Italy.

The refurbished theater finally got its current name in 1926. But by then, vaudeville was on its last legs, and around 1930 the playhouse was converted into a movie theater. By the 1960s the cinema was run-down, and it had sunk to showing second-run movies and adult-oriented films.

Sometime in the 1960s, the ornate Italian frescoes that local artists had painted on the theater's walls were covered over in dark blues and browns. Then in the 1970s the State Theatre went back to presenting live entertainment, albeit rock-and-roll concerts.

By the end of the decade, however, its owner decided the building had outlived its usefulness, and the theater closed in 1980. The following year it was turned over to the National Development Council.

Most people assumed the playhouse would be torn down, but wiser heads prevailed. A group of community organizers called the Friends of the State Theatre raised the capital to buy it.

In two phases, in 1986 and 1990, the theater was completely renovated, including the installation of new seats, carpeting, and curtains, plus up-to-date lighting and sound. And to top it off, the original playhouse artwork was uncovered and restored, returning it to its 1925 splendor.

The dapper denizen of the dark, J. "Freddy" Osterstock, was there through it all.

Although his apparition is still seen now and then, he doesn't always show up as a fully formed ghost. Sometimes he appears as a glowing orb of light, only about an inch in diameter. If anyone tries to catch the tiny shimmering sphere, however, it floats away, out of reach. Or it'll vanish completely, in the blink of an eye.

Of course, sometimes he doesn't materialize at all. Most often, people simply feel Freddy's presence. On rare occasions, actors or crew members feel the invisible spectre brush up against them.

In 2003 the State Theatre began to hold an annual awards ceremony to recognize outstanding accomplishment in local high school musical theater. Awards are given in eighteen categories including achievement in singing, lighting, and set design, among many others. Students are nominated by a panel that sees productions throughout the entire Lehigh Valley and Warren County, New Jersey.

In recognition of Osterstock's many years with the theater—and a tacit acknowledgment that his approving spirit is probably overseeing the proceedings—the honors were named the Freddy Awards.

Maybe it's too late for you to *compete* for a Freddy, but that doesn't mean you have to give up your chance to *see* Freddy. The State Theatre stages more than a hundred performances a year. If you're in the audience some night, let your eyes wander from the stage from time to time. You never know who—or what—might be sitting beside you.

Chapter 21
Phantoms
from the Fire

When a fire broke out in the opera house located on an upper floor of the Rhoads Building in downtown Boyertown, Pennsylvania, 171 people were killed. Some say that disembodied screams can still be heard at the site to this day.

"Hurry up, or we'll be late. We don't want to miss the show. Everyone we know is in it."

And they had to hurry if they wanted a good seat. It was Monday, January 13, 1908. Even though it was the depths of a Pennsylvania winter, whole families were bundling up and making their way down the sleepy evening streets of town to the Rhoads Opera House. It seemed that the entire community of around two thousand was trying to pack itself into the hall.

Like so many similarly named buildings across America at the time, it wasn't presenting opera, of course. Much of what toured as live entertainment was considered too bawdy and certainly too frivolous for many God-fearing, conservative people, so the theater had been called an opera house to convince mothers and fathers that the shows that would be presented there would be perfectly respectable.

And certainly that night's program would be. After all, it was being sponsored by St. John's Lutheran Church.

Boyertown, Pennsylvania, located in Berks County, is thirty-seven miles northeast of Philadelphia and just thirteen miles from Reading, close to the heart of the rustic Pennsylvania Dutch country. The main industry in the region at the turn of the twentieth century was farming, although the city itself was home to a respected cigar factory and the Boyertown Burial Casket Company, one of the top suppliers of coffins in the Northeast.

The home of the Boyertown Opera House was an auditorium on the second floor of a building owned by Dr. Thomas J. B. Rhoads. The brick structure, found at the corner of East Philadelphia Avenue and South Washington Street, was three stories tall and housed Farmers' National Bank and a hardware store on the first floor. A fraternal lodge took up the third floor, and four residential units were attached to the building at the rear of the bank.

By 8 p.m. just over three hundred audience members had crammed into the hall in eager anticipation. They were there to see their friends, mostly Sunday-school children, in the sixty-member cast of *The Scottish Reformation,* a play about Scotland's break from the Catholic Church in 1560. (Needless to say, this was a popular subject for the mainly Protestant local population.) Including the cast, theater crew, and others, there were probably about 425 people in the hall that fateful night.

Harriet E. Monroe, an internationally known dramatist based in Washington, D.C., wrote the play. Between acts, Harry C. Fisher, working for Monroe, would show slides of Scotland and Germany using an early projector called a stereopticon, or "magic lantern."

About 9:30, between the second and third acts—just before Queen Elizabeth was about to have Mary Queen of Scots beheaded—the calcium lights of the stereopticon snapped loudly and made a large sparkle. Startled audience members seated near the machine in the back of the house panicked and rushed toward the stage. Others at the front, alarmed by the chaotic movement, joined them. The children, who could see from their vantage point on the stage that nothing was wrong, tried desperately to motion the people back to their seats.

One survivor told newspapers that the subsequent fire was started when someone onstage peeked under the curtain to see what the commotion was about and the drape rolled over an eight-foot-long drum of coal oil at the front of the platform used to fuel the twelve footlights. (The building had no electricity.)

According to most accounts, however, a young boy in the cast accidentally kicked over one of the kerosene footlights in all the excitement. Men in the front row tried to move the drum of coal oil away from the platform before it, too, caught fire, but it broke open. Before long the entire stage was in flames.

The crowd turned and hurried toward the back of the room. But there were only two narrow exit doors, and both of them opened inward. Because of the crush from behind, people were never able to get the doors completely open. Even those few who eventually managed to get out had to work their way downstairs in darkness. The fire spread so quickly that many of them were consumed or were overcome by smoke within sight of the front entrance from the street.

Some people, seeing the doors from the hall were blocked, flew in terror to the windows. The fire escape, which Rhoads had added only under duress, wasn't visible and almost impossible to reach, however, because the high windows could be accessed only by climbing over three-foot-wide sills.

Soon the building was engulfed in flames. It was said that the screams of those caught inside could be heard a mile away. Firemen valiantly tried to fight the inferno. Even some people who had escaped rushed back in to try to save others. But as the fire grew, all became hopeless.

By the first rays of morning, the entire structure lay in ruins; 171 people lay dead, either from smoke inhalation or fire. At least half had been trapped and unable to escape the auditorium itself. Among the dead were 110 women, 23 children, and a firefighter who perished battling the blaze.

Three temporary morgues were set up to handle the deceased, who were laid out in white muslin for viewing by relatives and friends. Almost 10 percent of the town's population was lost in the fire. Full families were wiped out.

A hundred and five graves were quickly dug in the town's Fairview Cemetery. All of the bodies were identified, but twenty-five were so decomposed that they, along with body parts that had separated from corpses, were buried in a mass grave the following Saturday. (A large granite tombstone now marks the spot.) Others were buried in nearby Union Cemetery. For weeks afterward, the scent of burnt wood, scorched debris, and charred human flesh hung in the air.

The disaster made national headlines. Citizens were shocked and outraged. In the aftermath, reformers demanded new laws to ensure that such an event could never take place again. The Pennsylvania legislature immediately responded, and new fire-safety regulations were passed regarding access to exits, the placement of curtains, and the use of fire-resistant material. Among the new rules, all doors into public rooms had to be hung so they would open outward and stay unlocked while the room was occupied. All exits, including access to fire escapes outside the building, had to be marked, and fire extinguishers had to be mounted on the walls. The new legislation was signed into law by Governor Edwin Stuart on May 3, 1909, and would act as a model for governments around the country.

And who was found at fault? For a time it was thought that the oxygen tanks used to operate the projector had exploded. Monroe was briefly indicted for employing incompetent people, but the charge was never prosecuted. Rhoads was also arrested for criminal negligence.

Just months after the accident, people on the streets began to report hearing terrified screams and ghostly howls of pain coming from the burnt-out building. One old man moved into the devastated edifice and had to be taken out by force: He said the ghost of his wife, who had perished in the fire, had asked him to come there to be with her. Another woman was convinced that unsettled spirits from people who died in the calamity had invaded her house.

Today apartment buildings and stores occupy the block where the Rhoads building once stood. A plaque on one of the outer walls tells about the sad incident.

The catastrophe may have occurred a full century ago, yet some people swear that if you walk along the sidewalk in front of the current buildings on the site, spectral noises can still be heard in the air. Others say they occasionally hear moans and cries coming from the graves of the fire's victims at Fairview Cemetery.

Are any of the claims to be believed? The memory of the tragedy is certainly burned into the psyche of Boyertown. Perhaps some of the souls of those who died that frosty

January eve *do* still linger in the aether. If you pass through Boyertown, stop by the cemetery, pause by the commemorative plaque, and say a silent prayer: There but for the grace of God.

Chapter 22
Phantom at
the Fulton

Since 1873 the Fulton Opera House has played host to everything from vaudeville to touring companies of Broadway musicals. And since her death in 1933, an actress from the Great White Way who frequently performed there, Marie Cahill, has made it her domicile.

Though she's barely remembered today, in her time actress Marie Cahill was one of Broadway's most successful actresses. Born in 1874, she was only sixteen when producers spotted her in an amateur production of *Kathleen Mavoureen* in her native Brooklyn. Two years later she crossed the East River to make her Manhattan debut in a now-forgotten play called *C.O.D.* Before long, she abandoned the New York stage, opting for several years to act in London and Paris.

She returned to the Great White Way in 1896 to make her singing debut in Victor Herbert's *The Gold Bug,* in which she was lauded for her portrayal of a punningly named character, Lady Patty Larceny. Short, with a round, plain face, she was hardly the typical ingénue type, but her charm and cheekiness on the stage—no doubt helped by the years perfecting her craft in Europe—made her irresistible to audiences.

She found her first real acclaim when she introduced the song "Nancy Brown" while portraying a character by the same name in 1902's *The Wild Rose.* She was so well received that the composers, Frederic Brown and Henry K. Hadley, wrote another show based on the character, *Nancy Brown* (1903), expressly for her.

In between the two productions, two down-on-their-luck songwriters, Robert Cole and Rosamond Johnson, approached Cahill with a tune they had written based on an old spiritual. It was called "Under the Bamboo Tree." The actress fell in love with it and demanded that the song be interpolated into the score of her next show, *Sally in Our Alley*.

Shows containing songs composed by a number of composers were common at the time, but *Sally* already had a complete score by Ludwig Englander and George V. Hobart. Cahill was pugnacious, however, and she insisted that if "Bamboo Tree" wasn't placed in the musical, she would quit.

The producer, George Lederer, eventually relented, and it proved to be a wise decision. The song was the highlight of the show and, indeed, became the greatest hit of Cahill's career.

(Cahill was known for forcing producers to put "star turn" numbers from outside sources into already-completed scores for her shows. And because of her celebrity status, she could get away with it. In the case of "Under the Bamboo Tree," the song was so popular that it was also placed in *Nancy Brown* and was recycled into the classic 1944 Judy Garland movie *Meet Me in St. Louis*. If you don't remember the song from its title, it's the one whose chorus starts out "If you like-a me, like I like-a you and we like-a both the same . . .")

When Cahill's Broadway career went into a slump around 1915, she moved onto the vaudeville circuit and began a series of successful tours around the country.

It was one of those that brought her to the Fulton Opera House in Lancaster, Pennsylvania.

Fulton Hall, as the Victorian-style theater was first known, was designed by Samuel Sloan and built on the site of a Revolutionary War-era jail in 1852. It was named for Robert Fulton, who invented the first commercially success-ful steamboat and had been born in Lancaster County. Like most playhouses of the day, it was used for multiple pur-poses—lectures, plays, concerts, meetings, and civic events. It even had a shooting gallery above the theater.

After four years the Fulton was bought by Blasius Yecker and Hilaire Zaepfel, neither of whom had a theater back-ground. But they wanted to bring touring shows to their community, so they added seats, put in more ventilation, and increased the size of the stage.

It wasn't until 1873 that Edwin Forrest Durang, a noted theater designer, converted the Fulton into a professional-level opera house. In 1904 the theater underwent a major renovation and received its current form and a new neoclas-sical look. That same year it began to add silent movies to its bill of variety artists.

Because of its proximity to New York—Lancaster is only 130 miles away from the Big Apple—the new Ful-ton Opera House immediately began to attract the upper tier of touring artists and stage shows. Among the many notable names to grace its stage during these years were Sarah Bernhardt, Buffalo Bill Cody, George M. Cohan, Lil-lie Langtry, Anna Pavlova, John Philip Sousa, and Mark Twain.

And, of course, there was also Cahill.

By the 1930s the Fulton was beginning to show her age, and newer movie palaces in the area began to draw away the theater's audiences. But it soldiered on, switching to second-run and "B" movies. In the 1950s the cinema was spruced up a bit, and it became an "art house," showing independent and European films as well as holding an occasional concert. The following decade brought the theater's resurgence as a venue for live entertainment. A foundation was created to save the playhouse, and by 1969 it was home to a community theater group, the Actors Company of Pennsylvania. By the mid-1980s the Fulton Opera House had become a fully professional regional theater.

Beginning in 1989 a campaign was undertaken to restore the playhouse to its 1890s splendor while upgrading its stage and audience amenities for modern use. Between January and October 1995, the theater had a complete overhaul, followed by further refurbishment in 2004.

Reflecting back, Marie Cahill was among the plethora of stars who appeared at the Fulton during the Golden Age of vaudeville. She also was in the movies, making one silent film in 1915 and three more in 1917. Ten years later Cahill returned to the New York stage in *Merry-Go-Round*, and she made her last Broadway appearance in Cole Porter's *The New Yorkers* in 1930. In her final years she had her own half-hour radio show, "Cahillogues," based on a series of comic monologues she had recorded for the Victor label between 1917 and 1923. Cahill died in 1933 and is buried back in Brooklyn.

But her spirit has made a comeback at the Fulton. Why she's returned there is anyone's guess. Yes, she *had* performed there quite a few times during her vaudeville years, but otherwise she had no real, long-lasting connection with the theater. At least not while she was alive.

The phantom at the Fulton Opera that's thought to be Cahill always appears dressed in a white gown, which led at first to the spectre being called the Lady in White.

Somewhere along the line, the apparition became identified as the Broadway star.

Cahill's spectre is still a frequent guest of the Fulton, most often appearing in the wings, stage right. Her presence became so unsettling that, according to the theater's managing director, Aaron Young, the stage manager actually moved his desk to stage left.

Cahill is not the only opera ghost at the Fulton. *Several* spooks are said to swirl around the fly gallery, and a male phantom has appeared to a workman on a once-boarded-up staircase backstage.

Today the Fulton Theatre, as the opera house is also known, operates as a full-time Equity house. It's on the National Register of Historic Places and is said by some to be the oldest continuously operating theater in the United States.

And it's possible to take backstage tours. You, too, can stand on the very spot where Marie Cahill sang "Under the Bamboo Tree" for her adoring fans. You can visit the dressing room where she put on that long white dress. And you can stand in the wings where—if you're lucky—she'll take one more bow just for you.

Chapter 23
Ford's Phantom

Lincoln may not return to the scene of his assassination—would you?—but the ghost of John Wilkes Booth does stalk the stage at Ford's Theatre in Washington, D.C. His presence has been felt and heard throughout the playhouse, and his aura may have even turned up in an old Matthew Brady photograph.

So this was where it all started, Jennifer thought. As she stood in the Lincoln Museum in the basement of Ford's Theatre, tears involuntarily came to her eyes.

She hadn't expected that. She was, after all, a clinical psychologist, and she was used to dealing with tragedy on a daily basis. In her practice, she was always careful to keep a professional distance, allowing her to make a detached, if sympathetic, analysis of a crisis and help guide her clients toward awareness and recovery.

But researchers sometimes get more than they bargain for during the cut-and-dried examination of a case study. And that was, after all, what this visit to Ford's Theatre was all about.

Besides her personal practice, Jennifer had returned to the classroom—was it really five years ago now?—when she was asked to teach introductory sociology at the small college campus near her office. It was only two classes a week, the pay (though minimal for an adjunct instructor) was welcome, and it allowed her to keep herself in touch with changing trends among young adults, her specialty.

Her life had taken an unexpected turn just two years before when her dean called her in for a meeting.

"Jennifer, I know this is unusual. In fact, the university usually only expects it of tenured professors, or at least associate professors. But I've gotten a request, a recommendation really, from the department head that for you to continue here next year it would be to your advantage to publish."

She knew exactly what that meant. Publish or perish. In academic circles, depending upon the institution, many full professors spent much of their time in research and writing about their results. Their standing in the university was often judged by how many articles they had been able to get placed in scholarly periodicals or, if the subject was deemed worthy, bound by a university press. A faculty full of recognized experts didn't just give bragging rights to the school. It often translated into federal grants, alumni donations, and increased enrollment.

It was most uncommon for a mere lecturer—not yet even an assistant professor—to be asked to submit a major essay for peer review. But these were uncommon times. Campuses were downsizing; there was even talk of the course she taught being cut from the curriculum. The dean was on her side: He was passing along the advice because he was her friend and supporter. If he was suggesting that a paper was needed to secure her position, so be it.

It had started as simply as that. But then her thesis, "Killing Kennedys" (with its title taken from the famous quote by a worried Jacqueline Kennedy, "If they're killing Kennedys, then my children are next"), took on a life of its own.

Her angle was an examination of a national psyche that could lead to two Kennedys and a major civil rights leader being assassinated within the course of just under five years. As soon as he read the first draft, Jennifer's dean realized that the material was too good to have it disappear into a periodical. He recommended that she expand it into a full-blown book proposal. Amazingly, a contract with a small publisher quickly fell into place, and, well, the subject apparently struck a nerve with the public. Before she knew what had happened, her book was in stores nationwide. What was originally a series of offhand observations put to paper just to please the powers-that-be had made her, to her own astonishment, into a critically acclaimed author.

So now here she was in Washington, D.C., doing research for a follow-up work that would be worthy of the first. Her book agent had suggested that perhaps she had found her own unique genre: the nexus of psychology, government, and murder. *Why not go back to the beginning?* Jennifer thought. What were the forces that led John Wilkes Booth to become the first person to assassinate a U.S. president?

Jennifer moved from cabinet to cabinet in the museum. The core of the collection had come from one man, Colonel Osborn H. Oldroyd, who over a lifetime had assembled a mountain of Lincoln memorabilia and ephemera. At different points, Oldroyd had leased Lincoln's house in Springfield, Illinois, and in 1893 the Petersen House where Lincoln died across from Ford's Theatre. Oldroyd had exhibited his collection in both places. The federal government bought the Lincoln materials in 1926 and eight years later installed them in a makeshift museum in Ford's Theatre, which was then being used as an office building and storage facility.

Jennifer immediately recognized the Derringer that Booth had used to shoot Lincoln, the assassin's diary, the bloodstained pillow on which the president lay dying. Her thoughts strayed to the awful event that had occurred just overhead some 140 years earlier.

Ford's Theatre had originally been built in 1833 for the First Baptist Church. Twenty-eight years later it moved to a new sanctuary, and the old building was leased to John T. Ford. He remodeled it into a theater and named the playhouse Ford's Athenaeum. It was destroyed by fire just a year later, so he started from scratch, opening a new structure in 1863 as Ford's New Theatre, or more simply Ford's Theatre. The redbrick building stood at a towering three stories, with five arched doorways opening onto the street.

On the morning of April 14, 1865, the theater received a message that the president was going to attend that evening's performance of *Our American Cousin*. Interestingly, Lincoln had wanted to see the play that was appearing at the National Theatre instead that night, but his wife preferred to see the popular comedy. It was undoubtedly Booth's connections with Ford's Theatre that allowed him easy and complete backstage access, so history might have been changed had Lincoln gone with his original plans.

John Wilkes Booth, born in 1838, came from a renowned family of actors. His parents were British thespians who had moved to Maryland in 1821. The young Booth made his stage debut in Philadelphia at the age of seventeen and quickly became a matinee idol due to his good looks, tall frame, athletic physique, and agility on the stage. His two older brothers, Edwin and Junius Jr., were also actors; in fact, John was often in the shadow of Edwin, whom many considered to be the greatest American actor of the nineteenth century.

The Booths were great friends with Ford, and the staff of the theater knew the family well. So over the years John had unfettered access to the playhouse. In fact, during the war years, Booth often had his mail delivered there when he was on tour. Having performed at Ford's Theatre—the last time just a month before the assassination—Booth knew the playhouse intimately. (Lincoln, a great lover of theater, had actually seen Booth perform there in a play called *The Marble Heart* in November 1863.)

Booth was a strong proslavery supporter of the South. He made it a point to be at the hanging of John Brown, who had led an unsuccessful abolitionist raid of the federal armory at Harpers Ferry. (Brown's ghost, among others, now haunts the streets of that small town.) On his travels throughout the Civil War, Booth openly supported the Confederacy; he was just as vocal about his hatred for Lincoln.

By 1864 Booth had devised a plan to kidnap Lincoln so he could exchange the president for ten thousand Confederate prisoners of war. He thought he would finally have a chance to execute it on March 17, 1865, as Lincoln returned from a performance of the play *Still Waters Run Deep* at a hospital near the Soldiers' Home about three miles from the White House, but at the last minute Lincoln changed his plans and didn't attend the show.

Then on April 9 General Robert E. Lee surrendered at Appomattox. Two days later Booth was standing outside the White House when Lincoln announced that he was in favor of granting the vote to freed slaves. Enough was enough!

At 11 a.m. on April 14, Booth was picking up his mail at Ford's Theatre when he learned that Lincoln would be attending the show that night along with his wife and General and Mrs. Ulysses S. Grant. A plan to assassinate the president and the general immediately formed in his head.

He knew the play well. At around 10:15 p.m., during the second scene of the third act, one actor was alone on the stage. It was also a very funny scene, one that was sure to fill the hall with laughter. He would enter the Presidential Box, shoot the president, and then leap to the stage. A diagonal run would lead to the back door, from which he could make his escape.

Booth nonchalantly walked through his paces, checking the viability of his scheme. Meanwhile, the staff was making preparation for Lincoln's visit. Flags were added to the Presidential Box. A portrait of George Washington and two semicircular flags were hung from the front of the balustrade.

Leaving the theater, Booth rented a horse, telling the stables that he would return to pick it up later that evening. In the afternoon, he met coconspirators George Atzerodt and Lewis Paine and told them his plot. Atzerodt was to kill Vice President Andrew Johnson and, Paine, Secretary of State William Seward as close to 10:15 as possible. (Neither succeeded; in fact, Atzerodt didn't even try.) The intent was to throw the entire government into chaos, which would invigorate the South and inspire the Confederacy into restarting its fight against the North.

At 7 that evening, Booth dressed slowly. Black clothes and hat, tall boots, and new spurs. He looked at himself admiringly in the mirror at the National Hotel, where he was staying. *This face will be remembered forever as the savior of the nation*, he thought approvingly. He slipped a small lead ball into the single-shot .44-caliber Derringer, tucked it into his pants, and was off.

Having placed his horse at the ready by the stage door, Booth walked into the lobby of Ford's Theatre at just after 10 p.m. Roars of laughter cascaded from inside the auditorium. The actor made his way up the stairs to the back of the balcony. Slowly he approached the door to the Presidential Box. Slipping inside, Booth stepped from the darkness, aimed carefully at the back of the president's head just below the left ear, and fired.

Many people in the audience didn't hear the blast. They didn't see Booth's struggle with Major Henry Rathbone, who had been invited to join the Chief Executive when the Grants changed their plans. But they couldn't miss the maniacal figure leaping over the banister of the State Box down onto the stage. Some claimed they heard him scream, *"Sic semper tyranis"* ("Thus always to tyrants").

But Booth had been injured in the eleven-foot fall. He had not counted on his right spur catching on one of the flags hanging in front of the box, causing him to land badly and break his left leg.

Booth and David Herold, another of his fellow conspirators, separated from the others. They managed to elude capture for a week, but army forces finally tracked them to a farm in Port Royal, Virginia. Herold quickly gave up but Booth, holed up in a tobacco barn, refused to surrender. The soldiers set the building on fire to force him out. Whether Sergeant Boston Corbett was acting independently or on orders is still unclear, but he took aim and shot at Booth, striking him in the neck. The assassin was dragged from the blaze to the farmhouse porch, where he died three hours later.

Jennifer decided it was time to visit the scene of the crime. Making her way up to the theater itself, she was well aware that what she was seeing was actually a reproduction of the auditorium where Lincoln was shot. The building's original interior had been torn out years before.

After the assassination, the federal government took over the theater, eventually paying Ford $100,000. (In fact, he and his brothers were at first arrested for complicity in Lincoln's death and held for thirty-nine days before being released.) Closed as a theater, the building was refurbished for military use. From 1866 to 1887, War Department records were housed on the first floor, the library of the surgeon general was kept on the second floor, and the top floor became the Army Medical Museum. In 1887 the museum was relocated, and its rooms were made into offices for the War Department.

Six years later the front of the building collapsed without warning, killing twenty-two clerks and injuring sixty-eight others. After repairs, the former theater served as a warehouse for government records. Then in 1931 the lower level of the building was opened as the Lincoln Museum when the Oldroyd collection was moved across the street from Petersen House. The National Park Service took over its administration the following year.

After World War II there was a groundswell of interest in renovating the site, and after eight years of careful planning and restoration, Ford's Theatre was opened again to the public in 1968. Almost all of the furnishings found there today are copies, replicated in detail from period photographs, although the Presidential Box, decorated exactly as it was the night of the assassination, does have the original Washington portrait hanging out in front.

As Jennifer stared up at the box, contemplating the enormous ramifications Lincoln's death had for American society—both North and South—a dark, small haze seemed to form in the booth. Odd. People weren't allowed inside the box. Was it a shadow? Then, as quickly as she had noticed the darkened form, it was gone.

Then she remembered. According to a very old legend, the theater, including the Presidential Box, was said to be haunted. In fact, shortly after the assassination, pioneer photographer Matthew Brady took a series of archival shots inside the playhouse, and a small blur in the Presidential Box can plainly be seen in one of the photos. Some people think Brady captured the spectral figure of John Wilkes Booth—or perhaps even Abraham Lincoln. Perhaps he did: Over the years, many have claimed to see a spectral human life-form hovering in the booth.

Had Jennifer seen a ghost?

An endless stream of tourists visits Ford's Theatre every year. It operates as a legitimate playhouse as well, so hundreds of actors and staff members also get a chance to walk the hallowed halls. And many of them have had encounters with the phantom.

Very few people claim to have actually seen an apparition, but everyone seems to agree that it's John Wilkes Booth who has returned to stalk the theater. Disembodied footsteps are occasionally heard on the stairs, especially along the route Booth would have taken that April night. Even more mysteriously, the sound of laughter and, now and then, sobbing cuts through the air. There are distinct cold spots and sudden drops in temperature in the building. Lights go on and off by themselves, occasionally even in Box 7 (the Presidential Box). And the backstage crew has no explanation for what causes the front curtain to sometimes raise and lower on its own.

Actors attest to the fact that there is an evil, invisible residue or aura hanging over the diagonal path Booth followed as he dashed across the stage to make his escape. Even standing close to it, some actors have felt nervous, dizzy, or nauseous. They forget lines or, if they're in rehearsal, lose their places in the script. Even such respected performers as Hal Holbrook and Jack Aranson, who performed their respective one-man Mark Twain and *Moby Dick* shows in the theater, felt uneasy when they ventured near the intangible, malevolent line.

Jennifer never shared her encounter with anyone. After all, she was now a respected author. She couldn't afford to have her name mixed up with the supernatural. Still . . .

Maybe she could add a mystic or spiritual twist to her tale—how ghosts from the past, both real and imagined, continue to shape our social order. The Killer Instinct versus the Search for Survival. The Assassin versus the Afterlife. It might be just the hook she needed to wind up with another best-seller.

Chapter 24
School Spirit

Why is it that the spectre of "Jane," who haunts the Aycock Auditorium at the University of North Carolina at Greensboro, can be seen only by men? And unlike most theater ghosts, she seems to have had nothing to do with the venue itself while she was alive. Curious.

Greensboro, nestled in the forested Piedmont section of central North Carolina, lies midway between the Atlantic Ocean to the east and the Blue Ridge and Great Smoky Mountains to the west. Founded in 1808, the town was planned as the county seat with a courthouse on a center square. It was named for one of the great Continental Army commanders of the American Revolution, Major General Nathanael Greene. By the end of the nineteenth century, Greensboro had become a major crossroads for industry, especially textiles.

North Carolina's first state-supported school for the higher education of women was founded there in 1892 as the State Normal and Industrial School. Four years later the school's name was changed to the State Normal and Industrial College, and in 1919 it was renamed once again as the North Carolina College for Women.

Three separate state colleges were merged into a university system in 1931, so the Greensboro campus became the Women's College of the University of North Carolina. When state law led to the school's becoming co-ed in 1963, a final name change was made, which it retains today: the University of North Carolina at Greensboro.

The gender of the students at the university during its formative years is of particular relevance because the ghost that haunts the campus comes from its earliest days and is definitely female. And for some reason the spirit refuses to appear to other women.

Aycock Auditorium, located near the corner of Spring Garden and Tate Streets, has been the site of campus and community activities for more than eighty years. The 2,228-seat playhouse opened in 1927 and was named the following year for Charles Brantley Aycock, who served as governor of North Carolina from 1901 to 1905. The theater has played host to some of the world's greatest entertainers and lecturers, as well as plays, orchestras, ballets, and operas. The theater department also uses the playhouse to educate future generations of actors and stage technicians.

And it's haunted!

Jane, as the theater's ghost is known, has been a regular guest for so many years that practically all of the university's students and staff know about her. After all, she's been there practically since the day the playhouse opened its doors. And she's been the subject of several articles in the main local newspaper, the Greensboro *News & Record*. Certainly those who work, take classes, or perform in Aycock Auditorium are well aware of the phantom. Quite a few have actually seen her.

What makes her particularly unusual is that, according to legend, before her death Jane had nothing to do with the theater itself. She seems to be a residual spirit from a woman who lived in a building that was on the site before the auditorium was built. Supposedly, her name was Jane Aycock, and she was the daughter of the governor. Never mind that he had no daughters or that the house where she lived never belonged to the Aycock family.

What's important is that the elderly woman, lonely and despondent, hanged herself in the attic of the house that was removed to build the auditorium. It's not unheard of for people who've killed themselves to come back from the Beyond, but it *is* unusual when someone appears in a building that wasn't even there when the person was alive.

Jane may not have been outgoing in the past, but she's not very shy anymore. If she had a mind to, and she often does, she'll rush at people when they least expect it. Now and then she appears as a hazy form in a sort of white mist; other times it's a quite recognizable human form. Students who have had her pass by them often describe her as having light hair and a fair complexion. Others have felt her touch them on the shoulder from behind, but when they turned, no one was there.

A former manager of the playhouse has said that one night when he was alone in the otherwise empty auditorium, a single, loud note sounded on the theater's piano, which at the time had been temporarily moved into an aisle. Was Jane expressing her disapproval that it was out of place, or was she just trying to let him know she was there?

Like many ghosts, Jane enjoys toying with the lights. In fact, it happens so often that some techies have nicknamed one of the switches on the light board "Jane's dimmer."

And it's not just the lights she plays with. Electrical appliances such as radios occasionally come on by themselves and sewing machines in the costume rooms have started to run without assistance. She's scattered wardrobe after it's been sorted or stacked, and she'll rearrange people's personal possessions when they're not around just for the fun of it. Some folks have reported hearing—and sorry if this sounds like a cliché—clanking chains being dragged across the floor. And then there are the classic disembodied footsteps walking across the empty stage.

Jane's ghost has been seen all over the theater and by all sorts of people, but they have one thing in common: They're always male. Women may experience Jane's other mischief and manifestations, but she has materialized only to men and boys.

No one knows the reason, and there's nothing in the Jane Aycock story to suggest why. Is she just tired from so many years of seeing nothing but females on the college campus that she only wants to "show off" to men? Or does she simply prefer to interact with the opposite sex?

The auditorium was closed in 2006 for its first major renovation. Seats were replaced; dressing rooms, the orchestra pit, and acoustics were improved; more restrooms and an elevator for patrons were installed; and the electrical and ventilation systems were upgraded. The theater reopened in mid-2008, so it may be too soon to tell what Jane thinks of the improvements or whether she has even stuck around.

But it's worth trying to find out. If you're a guy and you want to see a ghost, hop in the car and take a trip to the Old North State. Aycock Auditorium is the place for you! Don't be surprised if, once inside, your school days suddenly turn into "school daze."

Chapter 25
The Schoolhouse
Hauntings

When the old schoolhouse was converted into a theater, it got a new lease on life—as well as a new resident spirit: its founder and champion, Broadway star Ruth Hunter. And what about those ghostly giggles? Are they coming from the phantoms of the school's former students?

Sanibel Island, located just off the coast of Fort Myers Beach in southwestern Florida, was well known by early Spanish explorers. Sure, it had pleasant beaches and a deep harbor. But that wasn't what the adventurers were looking for. They wanted gold, or at least a little silver. But unfortunately neither was to be found on the island, so it was of no real interest to the early Europeans.

Nevertheless, the small islet was duly noted on navigational charts. One 1765 map referred to it as Puerto de S. Nivel, which translates as South Plane Harbor. Later it appeared in a pilot's journal as Punto de Sanibel. By the end of the eighteenth century, it was simply being called Sanibel, and a company of investors founded the island's first town, which they also called Sanibel, in 1833.

In 1894 the one-room East Sanibel School was constructed at the corner of Bailey Road and Periwinkle Way for the education of the children of white residents. It was rebuilt two years later after being destroyed in a violent hurricane. Then in 1903 the building was lifted off its foundations and moved a few miles down Periwinkle.

The schoolhouse was typical for the period. It had a single large room with a raised platform at one end where the instructor stood. A small wood stove sat in the center of the room to provide heat as well as a place to warm liquids, and a bell in a tower on the roof called the students to class in the morning and back from afternoon recess. The teacher would instruct one age level while the others worked independently at their desks. In 1932 the structure was enlarged, adding on a second room and more windows.

Amazingly, the schoolhouse remained in operation until 1964, when the modern Sanibel Elementary School was built. Shortly thereafter, Broadway veteran Ruth Hunter and her husband, Philip, bought the old building to turn it into a theater, which they called the Pirate Playhouse.

Ruth Hunter had appeared in five shows on the Great White Way, including *The Wicked Age* (1927), *Adventure* (1928), *Veneer* (1929), and *The Up and Up* (1930). But it was her role as the daughter Ellie May in the enormous hit *Tobacco Road* that secured her place in Broadway history. The drama, about a lowlife family of sharecroppers, was one of the most successful plays ever to play New York, chalking up 3,182 performances between 1933 and 1941. It opened at the Theatre Masque (now the John Golden Theatre) before moving briefly to the 48th Street Theatre (now gone) and then on to the Forrest Theatre (now the Eugene O'Neill).

The Hunters threw themselves into the tiny theater. With approximately ninety seats crammed into the space, people in the audience were almost sitting on top of each other. But it didn't matter, because almost everyone knew one other. It was community theater in the truest sense of the word, because the Hunters encouraged local involvement in every department. The couple was hands-on as well: Philip worked the box office, and Ruth starred in many of the shows.

And then there were the ghosts.

Late at night, either during rehearsals or after the audience had left for the evening, actors and volunteers began to hear the disembodied sound of children laughing. Now and then they'd also notice the shuffle of small footsteps making their way up and down the aisles, even though no one was there. Some people even claimed to hear the old school bell clanging from time to time, though it had long been removed from the belfry.

The Hunters retired in 1984, and for a time it looked as if the Pirate Playhouse's days were numbered. But two actors, Robert Toperzer and Carrie Lund, took over the operations. They managed the theater successfully until 1991, when the theater company moved to a larger playhouse farther down the road on Periwinkle Way.

Lund and her husband, Robert Cacioppo, didn't give up on the old space, however. They brought in an artistic director, J. T. Smith, to breathe new life into the original venue, which they renamed the Old Schoolhouse Theater. Shows continued there until 2004.

During Smith's tenure, the ghostly occurrences continued. And it was during this period that Ruth and Philip are said to have returned to the theater as well—not in the flesh, but as spirits. Although neither of their spectres was ever seen, new unusual phenomena that started happening soon after their deaths were attributed to them.

Staff members would have the strange sensation of an invisible presence in the room or that they were being watched. Or sometimes the auditorium would inexplicably get exceptionally cold.

And the new phantoms certainly liked things tidy. If wardrobe was left lying on the floor overnight, the costumers would find it hung up neatly the next day. Props that had been left out somehow made their way back to where they belonged.

That being said, personal items would have a way of disappearing, only to turn up later in other parts of the theater. And on at least one occasion, an unseen hand ran a finger down the keyboard of the upright piano set to one side of the stage.

In 2004 the Old Schoolhouse Theater's acting company also moved into the Pirate Playhouse, which by then was being called the Periwinkle Playhouse. Today the building is known as the Schoolhouse Theater.

But what happened to the *old* schoolhouse theater?

In December 2004 it was moved to Dunlop Road and added to a collection of early twentieth-century houses called the Sanibel Museum & Historical Village. Opened in 1984, the open-air museum gives visitors an opportunity to see typical dwellings and other types of structures that were in use on the island, dating from 1898 to the 1920s. They include Miss Charlotta's Tea House, Old Bailey Store, the original post office, a packing house (a kind of warehouse), and three homes.

The Old Schoolhouse Theater has been lovingly restored to the way it looked before it was a playhouse. Since the renovations were made, there have been no reports of haunted activity. Maybe the spectres were unable to make the transition. Possibly the changes somehow helped the spirits of the actors and children move on to their Reward. Or, perhaps all of the hauntings were nothing more than people's imagination all along. We can never be sure. For now, unless another phantom pops up, school's out forever.

Part Three

CANADIAN CASPERS

If it's true that, as Shakespeare says, "All the world's a stage," then there must be ghosts haunting theaters worldwide. Let's take a quick trip north of the American border to check out some of the theater phantoms of the provinces.

We'll start in the Yukon, where Klondike Kate is still entertaining in her dance hall from the Gold Rush days. Heading east, there's a spectral caretaker backstage in Manitoba, Bloody Mary is still raising hairs in Lindsay, the ghost of a missing millionaire theater owner is in London, and a Lavender Lady haunts a double-decker theater in Toronto.

There's even a U.S. connection with the last of these theaters. When the Winter Garden was renovated, matching seats were brought in from the old Biograph Theater in Chicago. Did John Dillinger come along for the ride?

Chapter 26
The Queen of
the Klondike

Klondike Kate was known as the "Flower of the North." No won-der the dancer, muse, and financier of vaudeville theater owner Alexander Pantages still visits her old dressing room at the Palace Grand Theatre in the Yukon's Dawson City.

Gold!

Gold everywhere! Nuggets as big as your fist! All you have to do is bend down to pick them up.

At least, that's what everyone was saying.

The California Gold Rush that had begun in 1848 when James Marshall discovered the sparkling metal at Sutter's Mill in Coloma on the American River was long over. Within months of the discovery, tens of thousands of treasure hunt-ers had flooded the state seeking their fortunes. If you added in the families that accompanied many of them and the merchants and scoundrels who flocked to make money off them, more than three hundred thousand people migrated to the Golden State within seven years.

People came from all over the world. Regardless of where they were starting from, there was no easy way at the time to get to California. Either you sailed by ship, all the way around the tip of South America, came across the Pacific, passed over-land across the Isthmus of Panama, or attempted to cross the continental United States by a combination of train and trail. It took most people months to arrive—if they ever made it at all. Many took the better part of a year, which is why the bulk of the migrants became known as "forty-niners."

San Francisco was transformed overnight from a small shipping town into a metropolis as it became the gateway for immigrants heading for the gold-laden streams and, later, gold mines of central and northern California.

By 1850 most of the easy strikes were depleted.

So when word reached the City by the Bay in July 1897 that another gold strike—and this one perhaps ten times larger—had been discovered in the Yukon Territory the previous summer, the race was on.

In August 1896 a small party that included a native Tagish tribesman going by the name of Skookum Jim Mason, his sister Kate, her husband, George Carmack, and Jim's cousin Dawson Charlie met up with a Nova Scotian named Robert Henderson who had been looking for gold up the Indian River. According to the "code of the prospectors," you were supposed to share your food and any word of luck with others you came upon in the wilderness, and he confided to Carmack that he had found a few promising flakes.

Henderson soon left the scene, but the others decided to check out the possibilities in the region before winter set in. On August 21 they struck pay dirt in the beds of Bonanza Creek (at the time called Rabbit Creek) in the Yukon. It's unclear who actually made the discovery—to her dying day, Kate claimed that she'd actually found the first nuggets— but the three men agreed that Carmack, being a non-native, should stake all their claims in his name so they'd have the best chance of having them honored. (To his credit, Carmack never tried to cheat his friends and fully lived up to their unwritten agreement. Henderson, on the other hand, never profited from his initial discovery. He found out about the mother lode too late, and by the time he returned to the area, all of the best stakes had been taken.)

Word soon spread to the nearby mining camps along Fortynine Gulch and Stewart River about the Carmack claims. Before long, almost all of the available claims had been staked on the Bonanza, Hunker, and Eldorado Creeks. By the end of that year, a canvas and clapboard settlement had sprung up at the junction of the Klondike and Yukon Rivers to support the newcomers. Its name was Dawson City.

And that's where our ghost still "lives."

In July 1897 the first steamships of the season arrived in Seattle and San Francisco from Alaska. Onboard was what the *Seattle Post-Intelligencer* called "a solid ton of gold." Stunned onlookers claimed they saw men coming off the ships carrying suitcases and bags full of the precious ore.

It was that news which started the new stampede north. People came by the thousands, but just like with the earlier rush to California, it was hard to get to the Yukon. In fact, it was even worse. At least once you got to San Francisco, the journey to the California fields was pretty straightforward. Dawson City, on the other hand, was literally in the middle of nowhere. There were only three options to get there, none of them very good.

The "rich man's" way was to take a steamer up to St. Michael's, Alaska, at the mouth of the Yukon and then make the trip upstream. The most difficult way of all, which was soon abandoned because of the number of men who perished on it, was the "Canadian route" that cut across the Northwest Territory.

Most prospectors landed near Juneau on the Alaska panhandle and tried to make the perilous climb up White Pass out of Skagway or the Chilkoot Trail out of Dyea. If the prospectors made it to the top of the mountains, North West Mounted Police met them and demanded that they show a full year's provisions—about a ton of food—before they could proceed. Then the miners had another five hundred-plus grueling miles down the rapids of the Yukon River to get to Dawson City.

Despite all the odds, by the summer of 1898, the sleepy, muddy village of 1,500 had grown into a bustling, rough-and-tumble town of 40,000 souls.

Gold was plentiful, and the cheap shacks and tents were soon replaced with sturdy wooden houses. Saloons, restaurants, and dance halls sprang up, some boasting expensive, imported woods and chandeliers. Ladies of negotiable affection and gamblers mixed easily with the regular merchants and camp suppliers.

And at least one of the newcomers, Klondike Kate, wound up staying forever.

Kathleen Eloise Rockwell was born in Junction City, Kansas, on October 4, 1876, but she soon moved with her stepfather and mother to a large house in a prosperous neighborhood in Spokane, Washington. Even as a child, Kate was independent and strong-willed, and she often preferred to roughhouse with the neighborhood boys rather than play with girls her own age. As a teen, she was enrolled in boarding school, but she was sent home due to her refusal to follow the strict house rules.

In the 1890s her mother and stepfather divorced. She moved to New York with her mother, and it was there that she started her career as a chorus girl. She then joined a troupe of dancers and traveled to Seattle in 1899.

After she arrived on the West Coast, she quickly became disenchanted with her new job. She discovered that much more was expected of her than just dancing in the line. She not only had to sing, for which she wasn't trained, but she also had to go out into the audience between sets to flirt with the men and push drinks.

Along with everyone else, she heard the rumors about the money to be made in the Yukon, and, always an impulsive spirit, she decided to try her luck.

At first three other dancers accompanied her, but they almost immediately turned back. The headstrong Kate persisted, determined to make it to Dawson City. And get there she did, by literally tap dancing her way via Skagway, and then Whitehorse. According to legend, she was stopped by a Mountie at one point because she was a woman: He was sure she was planning to be a "camp follower" rather than a prospector, and he disapproved. Undaunted, Kate snuck away, disguised herself as a boy, and jumped aboard a boat headed downriver.

She arrived in Dawson in 1900.

By the time she reached the town, gold fever had passed its peak. Most of the easy gold was gone, and there were no more new stakes to be had, with the best claims having already been taken the previous autumn. The "rush" was over as quickly as it had begun, and within a year only about eight thousand people remained behind in Dawson City. Nevertheless, a city that size still needed entertainment, and Kate was willing to oblige. Her weeks at the raunchy club in Seattle had taught her how to keep her pride while fleecing.

As opposed to the "working girls" who made their way to the "Paris of the North" for more nefarious purposes, Kate actually had talent. She was quickly hired to perform at the Palace Grand Theatre.

The dance hall had been built in 1899 by a Wild West showman named Arizona Charlie Meadows. Rockwell, or "Klondike Kate," as she came to be known, was soon the star of his Savoy Theatrical Company.

What made Kate famous was her flame dance. When the colorful, curvaceous entertainer hit the stage, any hint of the girlhood tomboy still left in her was gone. She first appeared covered by a full-length cape. She dropped it to the floor to reveal a tight, red-sequined dress. In her hands she held a cane, to which was attached two hundred yards of red chiffon. As she twisted and twirled to the strains of spirited music, the cloth unfurled and swirled around her, making it look as though she were engulfed in fire. As the music swelled, the tempo increased, and her movements became increasingly, well, heated, she drove the stampeders wild. No wonder she became known as the "Flame of the Yukon."

Miners threw gold nuggets at her feet. Between shows she would charge men a dollar a dance and encourage them to drink champagne that she personally supplied at $7.50 a bottle. Despite having had her misgivings about doing the exact same thing back in Seattle, Kate had learned her lesson well.

Before long, she had enough money to buy a vaudeville-burlesque playhouse in town called the Orpheum Theatre.

It's said that within the first four months she was in Dawson City, the flamboyant "Flower of the North," as Klondike Kate was also being called, had received over a hundred proposals of marriage.

She had eyes for only one man, however. But as affairs of the heart sometimes have it, he was not the best choice. She fell for Alexander Pantages.

Born Pericles Pantages on the island of Andros in 1867, the handsome Greek ran away at the age of nine and went to sea. He eventually signed up on merchant ships and for a time worked with the French digging the Suez Canal. Eventually he settled in San Francisco as a waiter and, briefly and unsuccessfully, a boxer.

Like so many others, he was drawn to the Yukon in the first wave of prospectors, and he soon found himself in Dawson City. When Rockwell met him, he was a bartender and server at one of the saloons, but she was already headlining in Dawson throughout the Pacific Northwest, wearing what she claimed were $1,500 Paris gowns and priceless gold jewelry.

Her star status didn't stop her from beginning a torrid love affair with the sultry young man, however. Their relationship was intense, with bouts of deep passion interspersed with bursts of extreme jealousy. But when they were together, they made a great team, not only personally, but professionally as well. They became business partners, with Pantages becoming manager of the Orpheum.

By 1902 the population of Dawson City had dwindled to around five thousand. Klondike Kate headed south for greener pastures and opened a storefront movie theater in British Columbia. Pantages left Dawson shortly thereafter but headed to Seattle, where he started the Crystal Theater; there he exhibited a combination of variety acts and films.

Kate had always been tolerant, though unhappy, about Pantages's wandering eye. But she had always assumed that one day they would marry. That possibility came to an end when she discovered in late 1902 that Pantages had married a violinist named Lois Mendenhall.

Kate was devastated. In 1905 she sued for breach of promise as well as the theft of $25,000 of her assets. The suit was settled out of court. She managed to retrieve a bit of her money, but nothing like what was actually owed her. She never saw Pantages again, except once, and then just for a few minutes in Los Angeles, during his trial for rape in 1929.

Klondike Kate moved to eastern Oregon. Although she was no longer famous, she remained proud of her past. By the 1920s she was passing out postcards of herself as the "Belle of the Klondike" and sharing her tales of the Gold Rush days with anyone who would listen. But her glory days were behind her, and she began to fade into obscurity.

Pantages's fortunes were quite different. In 1904 he built his first eponymous Pantages Theatre in Seattle. Within two decades he had built more than thirty theaters and controlled the booking of another sixty, allowing him to put together the largest vaudeville chain west of the Mississippi, the Pantages circuit. Its route extended up into Canada; in fact, his artists' tours traditionally started in Winnipeg.

Around 1920 Pantages became involved with Paramount Studios and Famous Players distributors, and suddenly his old vaudeville houses were a major motion picture chain. This brought the attention of RKO and it's major shareholder (Joseph P. Kennedy) which had already acquired the Keith-Albee-Orpheum vaudeville circuit and, in the process, wrestled away control of New York's Palace Theatre from Martin Beck.

They made Pantages an offer to buy his theaters in 1929, but he tried to hold out. Perhaps it's just a coincidence, but that same year Pantages was accused of rape by a seventeen-year-old dancer in Los Angeles named Eunice Pringle. After two trials, he was found not guilty, but the proceedings had cost Pantages his life savings and his reputation. In the end, he was forced to sell his theater chain to RKO for less than he had originally been offered. He died a broken man in 1936.

Meanwhile, in the 1930s, a series of reunions were held by the "Sourdoughs" who had braved the Yukon at the turn of the century, and for a time the name of Klondike Kate was back on everyone's lips. In 1931 she received an invitation to attend one of their get-togethers in Portland, Oregon, from a former miner, John Matson, who confided that he had always loved her from afar. They continued to correspond, and two years later they married. Some people say Matson eventually returned to the Yukon while Kate stayed in Oregon. Regardless, Matson died in 1946, and Kate remarried some years later.

In the 1940s Kate briefly parlayed her former success as an entertainer into a career training wannabe Hollywood starlets. She died quietly in February 1957.

But she didn't stay in Oregon.

She's said to have returned to haunt the dressing rooms of the Palace Grand, the theater where she had her first triumphs in her youth. But, although it's on the exact same site, the theater she's come back to isn't the original. The 1899 theater had been built on permafrost, and it was giving way by the 1950s, so Parks Canada replaced it with an almost exact replica in 1962.

Rockwell had a sharp eye and a canny business sense when she was alive, so she's probably aware that it's not the same old haunt. But it's no doubt close enough for her to call it home.

Although Dawson City now has a resident population of only about two thousand, the figure swells during the summer tourist season when more than sixty thousand visitors come. If you find yourself among them and you decide to tour the old Palace Grand Theatre, look closely: If you see someone with blazing red hair backstage surrounded by red chiffon, you just might have stumbled across the ghost of the "Darling of Dawson" herself, Klondike Kate.

Chapter 27

By George!

It's not often that, when a theater changes location, its ghost moves right along with it. But leave it to George, the son of a caretaker at the old Dominion Theatre in Winnipeg, to do just that. When the theater company transferred to the new Manitoba Theatre Centre, he came along for the ride.

"By George, I think he's got it!"

"I wish you'd quit quoting—actually, *mis*quoting— *My Fair Lady*. We're not even doing a musical. Besides, the thought that the kid's ghost might actually *be* here and moving things around the theater creeps me out."

"Oh, come on," taunted his friend. "How could you not like little George? He must really like MTC if he bothered to follow us here."

True enough, the actor conceded. But it still didn't make him feel any more comfortable.

Not that he had personally seen or experienced anything. But lots of others had. *You're new to the company*, his friend had told him. *Just wait*. He'd run into him, or have something strange, odd, or curious happen sooner or later; George loved to pull pranks. After all, boys will be boys. Even if they're no longer alive.

George's case was unusual, because his is one of the few known instances in which a ghost has actually moved with the occupants when they changed from to one location to another. Usually they just stay put.

Or many times, if the original building is demolished, a spectre will stay at that property and then reappear in a new structure built on the exact same site. It's almost unheard of for a phantom to pack its bags and relocate.

But that's just what happened in Winnipeg a mere forty years ago.

Found in central Canada, Winnipeg is the capital and largest city of Manitoba, which lies just north of Minnesota and North Dakota. On the eastern edge of the Canadian prairies, the city is surrounded by hundreds of lakes and several unspoiled rivers.

Though far from the large populations back in the East and around Vancouver to the west, the relatively isolated metropolis nevertheless became a thriving center for arts and culture. The first known amateur theater groups in Winnipeg date to 1866, and over the years several playhouses were built or converted from existing venues to provide live, homegrown entertainment. Among the earliest were Red River Hall, the Theatre Royal, Manitoba Hall (later the Opera House), Dufferin Hall, the Princess Opera House, Victoria Hall (later the Bijou), the Grand Theatre, the Winnipeg Theatre . . . well, you get the drift. The place has had an active theater community since its earliest days, even before the city was officially incorporated.

Conveniently located on the Canadian Pacific Railway, Winnipeg also soon became a major stop for touring theatrical companies. As the city grew, it became home to festivals for writers, jazz, folk music, and theater. In fact, the Winnipeg Fringe Theatre Festival is the second-largest fringe festival in North America.

In 1957 John Hirsch and Tom Hendry founded a small acting company, Theatre 77, so named because its theater was just seventy-seven steps from the corner of Portage Avenue East and Main Street. The following year they merged with the Winnipeg Little Theatre (which had flourished from 1921 to 1937, then again in 1948) to form the Manitoba Theatre Centre. Their mission was to create a fully professional theater in Winnipeg, and in the process it became the first regional theater in the country. MTC, as it became known, also quickly established a school, play-reading societies, and outreach programs in the community. By the end of 1958 they had moved into the Dominion Theatre, located at the intersection of Portage and Main in downtown.

The theater, built of brick, had first opened its doors on December 12, 1904, as a vaudeville house, advertising shows that were suitable for viewing by the entire family. The auditorium sat 1,100 people on a main floor, balcony, and high gallery. The Dominion had already housed several resident theater companies by the time MTC moved in, including the Permanent Players from 1910 to 1912 and, in the 1930s, the John Holden Players. Then, for a time, like so many other former vaudeville and legitimate houses in the mid-twentieth century, it was turned into a movie theater.

In 1960 the Manitoba Theatre Centre had to move temporarily to the nearby Beacon Theatre while the Dominion's roof was being repaired. Otherwise, it happily remained in the Dominion Theatre until the structure was razed so the Richard Building and the Lombard Hotel could be constructed on the site.

Among the many resident staff members of the Dominion during MTC's stay there was a longtime caretaker. He and his young teenage son, whose name was—you guessed it—George, lived in an apartment over the theater. The boy's not-so-secret ambition in life, it's said, was to become an actor.

Unfortunately, his dream was never to come true. When a fire broke out in the building, George, who used a wheelchair, was unable to escape. He died, tragically cutting short any chance he might have had for a life in the theater.

Or at least an *actual* life.

Manitoba Theatre Centre moved for a time to Centennial Concert Hall when the Dominion was demolished, but a new theater, its current home on Market Avenue, was already in the planning stages. The Mainstage theater of the new $2.8 million complex, designed by the Number Ten Architectural Group, opened on November 2, 1970. In addition to the 789-seat house, the center would eventually also contain scenery and wardrobe shops, rehearsal spaces, and offices. Since 1969 the theater company has also operated a separate 286-seat theater, known as the MTC Warehouse on Rupert Avenue.

But here comes the weird part of the story.

Two or three years after MTC was in its new home, people started noticing strange goings-on. Ghostlike things. Then, after a couple of sightings, they realized George had somehow found them and their new playhouse, and he had come back to be with his friends. As such, he's not so much haunting the theater as he is just hanging out.

Today George's ghost is seldom visible, and audiences almost never see it. But people backstage can sense when he's in the room. And he likes to get into mischief, perhaps just to let people know he hasn't abandoned them. He'll play havoc with electrical devices, flip theater seats up and down, and secretly move small props and personal items around the playhouse.

But no one has ever really minded. Everyone loved the boy back at the Dominion; he was one of them. And now he's become the unlikely friend of the entire staff at the new theater as well.

Maybe someday he'll get his chance to perform onstage after all. Anyone out there looking to write a play for a blithe spirit?

Chapter 28

The Mischief of Bloody Mary

The spot of light in the balcony appeared to the entire cast onstage at the Academy Theatre in Ontario. Only after rehearsal did they learn the story of the house's resident spirit, "Bloody Mary."

Sally looked past the other actors into the auditorium. Empty. Dark. As much as she loved being in front of a live audience, this was actually the part she enjoyed most: the rehearsal. It was here, when she and her fellow actors were exploring the script, experimenting, trying to find their characters, *this* was when the real magic happened. Out of nothing, a character is conjured out of simple words on a page and fleshed out into three dimensions.

Sally was portraying the role of the teacher in the Academy Theatre's production of Richard Harris's play *Stepping Out*. In the story, a weekly tap-dancing class in a tiny neighborhood church hall in North London serves as the backdrop for eight students sharing their lives and emotions.

In the scene the actors were working on, the teacher is showing them a new step. Sally stood center stage facing out into the auditorium, as the others turned toward her, standing in a straight line.

All of a sudden, a small, fuzzy, solitary light in the balcony caught her eye. Puzzled, Sally called out to the other actors as it slowly started to float from one side of the balcony to the other.

"Look, over your shoulders. What's that?"

Everyone turned. The pulsating glow paused, then, as they watched, quickly faded out. Whatever it had been, it was gone. The eerie illumination had been there for mere seconds.

The incident was forgotten by most of the actors as their rehearsal resumed. They had a lot of work to do before opening night, and they jumped back into the run-through.

Afterward, however, Sally dropped in on one of the tech staff and casually asked about the curious luminescence she and the others had seen. She assumed it was just a lamp the crew had been setting, but it was unlike any she had seen before.

It was only then that she learned that what she'd seen was no spotlight. It had been the theater's ghost.

And her name was Bloody Mary.

The Academy Theatre is located in Lindsay, a small town of about seventeen thousand on the Scugog River in the Kawartha Lakes area of southern Ontario, Canada. The first settlement was in 1827, when an American family named Purdy built a dam and later a sawmill there. Streets and lots for Purdy's Mill, as the village became known, were laid out in 1834, and during the process one of the surveyor's assistants, a Mr. Lindsay, was accidentally shot in the leg. The limb became infected, and before long the poor man had died and was buried alongside the river. The village's name was soon changed to Lindsay in his memory.

So even from the beginning, the town's history included, if not a ghost, then at least an accidental death that affected the whole community. But it wasn't *his* ghost that chose to return.

The Great Fire of 1861 destroyed most of Lindsay, including its first pub, a log cabin that had been built on the southeast corner of Lindsay Street and Kent Street East around 1834. When two residents, R. J. Matchett and Fred Knowlton, decided the town needed a permanent theater in 1892, the lot on which the tavern had stood was still available, so it was chosen as the site for their Academy of Music. Within a year the opera house was up and running.

Designed by architect W. Blackwell from nearby Peterborough, the playhouse is a three-story redbrick structure with a peaked roof. But its plain exterior belies what lies within.

At the time of its opening, the Academy was reputed to be the most technically advanced theater in all of Canada, and the reports may very well have been true. A fly gallery towered twenty-two feet above the thirty-eight-by-forty-foot stage. There were five drops (curtains) at the director's disposal, as well as the ability to move twelve sets of scenery in and out through four slots in the wooden floor. Four dressing rooms were located under the stage, and the entire building was lit with incandescent bulbs.

From the audience's point of view, it was certainly a jewel box of a theater. The interior frescos and other decorations by R. Elliot & Son of Toronto were in the French Empire style. Nine hundred seats were spread over two levels: 166 were in the stalls (orchestra), and 218 more were arranged in a wide curve on the slightly raised parquet at the back of the house. An upper level of five hundred seats ringed the theater's walls in a horseshoe shape, and there were also two private boxes, one on each side of the proscenium.

It was the heating system, however, that inadvertently led to the hauntings Sally, the rest of her cast, and so many other staffers have experienced over the years. There were three coal furnaces in the theater, and a married couple was hired to tend to them. Because of the constant need to stoke and refuel the flames, the husband and wife were housed in a third-floor apartment in the building. It was while rushing down the stairs to the basement that the female caretaker tripped and fell down, fatally injuring herself. She died on her way to the hospital.

(Like all good legends, there's another version to the story. Some say that, instead, she died from falling off a tall ladder while changing a lightbulb in the auditorium.)

But Mary, or Bloody Mary as some call her, has never deserted the theater, and she continues to help out at the playhouse. Well, "help out" might not be the right words, because—although she's a friendly spirit—she's quite pesky and prankish. Mary tends to move small objects around the theater or hide them from their owners, though anything she takes always reappears eventually. And, of course, it's believed she's responsible for other phenomena that are typical of many theater hauntings: doors that slam on their own, lights that switch on and off by themselves, and seats that raise and lower without the aid of human hands. If Mary gets too frisky, though, all someone has to do is ask her to stop the antics, and she always obeys.

Her apparition is seldom seen, and when it is, the ghost merely appears as an indistinct blur of light, almost always in the balcony. But if you want to feel her presence, just take seat number 13 in any row when the house is empty. It's said that if you quietly sit there long enough she'll let herself be known.

She's certainly faithful to the Academy. There have been many renovations and travails over the years. In 1931 a new ceiling, an orchestra pit, and a smaller stage were installed. The auditorium was also completely overhauled. The design of the gallery was changed and the number of seats reduced, so the playhouse's capacity was cut to around six hundred. Mary's stuck around through it all.

Competition from a nearby movie theater along with the public's changing tastes in entertainment forced the theater to close its doors in 1955. Seven years later it went up for sale. Civic-minded individuals, fearful that the building would soon fall to the wrecking ball, formed a foundation to save it. Fortunately, they were successful. They purchased the playhouse, and after careful refurbishment, the newly christened Academy Theatre for Performing Arts reopened its doors. It has flourished as a mostly volunteer, nonprofit organization ever since, with about fifty thousand souls attending shows there every year—50,001, if you count Bloody Mary.

Chapter 29

The Return of
Ambrose Small

In December 1919 Ambrose Small sold his theater chain for $1.7 million. The next day he simply disappeared. At least in the flesh. He's come back to inhabit the playhouse he loved best.

Fifty-six-year-old Ambrose Joseph Small had everything to live for. He and his wife, Theresa, were in the upper echelon of turn-of-the-twentieth-century Toronto society. They lived in the Rosedale section of town, and he belonged to such posh associations as the Yacht Club, the Empire Club, and the Canadian Club.

Ostensibly, Small was a respectable impresario—a theater and real estate magnate. He owned theaters in seven cities throughout Ontario, including the Grand Opera House in Toronto and the Grand Opera House (now known as the Grand Theatre) in London, and he held the title to more than sixty other properties.

In late November 1919, Small sold off all of his theaters to Trans-Canada Theatres Limited for $1.7 million. He received a check for the amount on December 1, and the next morning Small's wife deposited it in the bank while he went shopping. That afternoon Small met with his lawyer, F. W. M. Flock, in his own office in the Toronto Grand Opera House. Flock departed around 5:30 p.m.

And Ambrose Small was never seen again.

Needless to say, there was an almost immediate inquiry into his disappearance. Almost, because his wife didn't report it right away as she was afraid of scandal. In fact, the investigation was not made public for two weeks. It had been an open secret that Small's business dealings were not always completely on the up-and-up, as everyone was supposed to believe. His first money was earned as a book-maker on horse races while working as an usher and barman at the Grand Opera House (which he would come to own in 1903). It's said that his friendship with Thomas Flynn, Ontario's commissioner of horse racing, led to his obtaining a financial interest in several gambling halls just outside of Toronto's authority.

Nevertheless, Small had made his real fortune by owning theaters and putting together a circuit of thirty-five play-houses for which he controlled the booking. And he knew how to give the audience what it (really) wanted. Despite the Victorian times, many of the plays he presented at his opera house in Toronto had scandalous subject matter and titillating titles, such as *Nellie the Beautiful Cloak Model* and *Bertha the Sewing-Machine Girl*.

His private life was also not as upright as it seemed. True, he was married to an impeccably proper, charitable, and deeply religious woman from the highest social register. But he apparently also carried on a series of affairs with chorus and working-class girls. He even kept a secret room in the Opera House for his clandestine assignations.

Regardless, police were baffled by the way he vanished. There was no ransom note, so it didn't seem to be a kidnapping. There was no sign of a struggle or violence in his office or any of the other rooms in that part of the theater. No one saw him leave the building. (A vendor at a newspaper stand on the street who claimed to have seen him later that night was soon discredited.)

Perhaps most curious of all: No money was missing from Small's bank account. His private secretary, John Doughty, did pilfer $100,000 in bonds from the office after Small went missing, but it seemed to be unrelated to the case.

So if Small had decided to vanish voluntarily, why hadn't he taken any of his money with him? Had he somehow set up accounts on the sly or kept wads of cash? No evidence that he had done either was ever discovered.

Although vicious rumors swirled about that his wife was somehow involved in the disappearance, possibly with a boyfriend—one story had them burning Small's body in the furnace under London's Grand Opera House, although how they managed to get the body there from Toronto was never explained—she was thoroughly investigated and seemed to be beyond reproach.

It was Flynn who convinced police, not knowing whether Small was living or dead, to take an unconventional approach and call in mediums, to try to discover whether the missing businessman was on this side of the Veil or the next. One said Small had taken off on his own and was living in another country incognito. (Indeed, in 1920 magician Harry Blackstone Sr. swore in an affidavit that he had run into the theater owner, whom he knew well from his Canadian appearances, in a Juarez, Mexico, casino.) Another clairvoyant also claimed Small was alive but that he wasn't getting in touch with anyone because he had amnesia.

Most of them thought he was dead. One had him being shot in the back on one of the theater's stairwells; another had him going up in flames in a house fire in Montreal. A few, perhaps colored by what they had read in the tabloids about his alleged early shady connections, "saw" that he had been slain by gamblers or other underworld figures. None of these "visions" resulted in real leads.

Toronto newspapers, always eager for a headline, approached Sir Arthur Conan Doyle, who was an avid Spiritualist and, more importantly, the creator of the detective Sherlock Holmes, about working on the case. The author, in New York City at the time, was intrigued but passed.

The case has never been solved.

According to legend, the Grand Opera House in London was Small's favorite. It was built by Small and C. J. Whitney of Detroit to replace the old 1881 opera house on the site that had been all but destroyed by fire on February 23, 1900. The new 839-seat theater opened its doors on September 9, 1901, and in its heyday was one of the premier playhouses on the circuit for both vaudeville and legitimate touring companies.

It was sold to the Famous Players film syndicate in 1924 and converted into a movie house six years later. In 1945 the playhouse became the property of the London Little Theatre Group, now known as Theatre London, and their seasons consisted of original works augmented by traveling shows. In 1974 the playhouse became a fully professional regional theater. It closed three years later for renovations, reopening as the Grand Theatre on January 28, 1979, with both a main auditorium and a separate McManus Studio Theatre located on a lower floor. The only remaining piece from the original house is the proscenium arch in front of the main stage.

It also has Small's ghost.

At the Grand, Small's lively spirit is more lighthearted than annoying. He'll mess around with the sound or lights, a common spook activity in theaters. There have been unexplainable hissing noises in the theater and the sound of someone walking in the balcony, even when there's no one there. These phenomena, too, have been attributed to Small.

Now and then, his unseen hands will gently tug at a person's hair or clothing. One time Deb Fox, now an upstairs receptionist, was working late at night in the box office. She had to deliver seating charts to the call center, which was in the old part of the building. As she walked alone, halfway down a corridor beneath the stage level she sensed a warm (rather than the usual cold) presence and then felt herself being visually scanned from top to bottom. (It's little wonder she underwent such close scrutiny if the unseen spirit was Small. He *was* quite the womanizer.) Needless to say, Fox has never gone down that hallway alone since.

Occasionally, Small has stepped out of the shadows and become visible. He's been known to fully materialize in dressing rooms, hover over the stage, or take a stroll on the catwalks.

And he's not alone in the theater. From time to time, actors and crew also see the ghost of a woman on the stairs backstage. She's believed to be a former cleaning lady, but beyond that there's nothing known about her. It's even been claimed that at one point during the run of a play about the Black Connellys, a family of Irish immigrants who settled in nearby Luncan in the 1840s, the ghosts of the entire clan turned up onstage with the actors.

Small got around. The Grand Theatre is only one of *two* places he chose to haunt. Apparently, for several years, he also used to hang out at the Tivoli Theatre in Hamilton, Ontario. The building dated back to 1907, when it held a carriage factory and a nickelodeon. It was converted into a vaudeville house in 1924 or 1925 and later incorporated movies into its programs. (In fact, it's the theater where "talkies" were first shown in Hamilton.) It became a cinema full-time in 1950 and remained open until 1990. It then closed for five years before reopening as a seven hundred-seat playhouse. In August 2004 part of the wall of the main entrance collapsed, and efforts were made to try to save the theater. Unfortunately, the attempts were unsuccessful, and the Tivoli was eventually torn down.

Now here's the Ambrose Small connection. Actors and backstage staff reported ghostly goings-on there for years, including disembodied footsteps and strange whispers. An apparition was also seen all over the theater: a male figure in Victorian clothing with a long, thick moustache slightly curled at both ends. Everyone who saw the spectre and was then shown a photograph of Small agreed that, yes, he was the man!

And, once again, even in that theater he had a friend. The phantom of a beautiful young woman in a long period dress was also caught floating around the theater from time to time.

Small's body has never been found. But someday the mystery surrounding his sudden disappearance may be solved. In the meantime, there's always a chance to meet his ghost if you're in London, Ontario, and up for a night at the theater.

Chapter 30

Wraiths at the Winter Garden

Among the many spectres in the Elgin and the Winter Garden Theatre Center in Toronto is that of a lavender-scented woman who was murdered in one of its ladies' rooms. And some of the seats in the playhouse came from the movie theater John Dillinger attended just before he died. The chairs open and fold up on their own. Are they haunted too?

"So how are those seats working out?"

The theater architect knew exactly what the man was talking about. Earlier that year his Toronto company had bought some used chairs and shipped them all the way from Chicago for use in a landmark theater they were renovating. They were exactly the style theater chairs they had needed.

"And how about the special one?"

"Special one?"

"Yes, you know: the one that was upholstered differently than all the others. Since you put the chairs in your theater, have you noticed anything, well, unusual?"

"What do you mean?"

"Well, I don't know how to say this," asked the man from the Biograph, "but have you seen any ghosts?"

The Toronto architect was stunned. How did this stranger all the way down in Chicago know?

The Elgin and Winter Garden Theatres on Yonge Street in the North York district of Toronto are the world's last remaining Edwardian-style double-decker, or stacked, theaters. They are, and were from their inception, two separate, complete theaters, one right above the other, located in the same building.

Marcus Loew invited architect Thomas W. Lamb north to build a theater similar in design to the renovation he had done on the American Theatre on Forty-Second Street in New York City. That playhouse had opened in 1893 with a 2,070-seat auditorium and an open-air rooftop theater, but when William Morris (of later actors' agency fame) bought it in 1908, he hired Lamb to convert the upper theater into an enclosed space seating 1,400. The main stage downstairs was tastefully traditional, but in the rooftop theater Lamb was allowed to let his imagination run wild. Forest tableaux were painted on the walls, and small lights meant to resemble stars were set into a blue ceiling. The effect was supposed to make the audience feel that they were watching the performance under an open sky.

In 1912 the theaters were sold to Marcus Loew, who operated them for twenty-seven years. Following a 1930 fire, the building was torn down, and today there's a parking lot on the site.

Loew wanted another double-theater complex to act as the flagship for his chain, but this time, instead of having to refurbish existing spaces, Lamb was able to conceive the auditoriums as complementary theaters from the very beginning.

The 1,561-seat street-level playhouse today known as the Elgin opened as Loew's Yonge Street Theatre on December 15, 1913. It was richly decorated in red with gold leaf ornamentation, and painted cherubs, tiered side boxes, and a spectacular domed ceiling.

The Winter Garden Theatre, an enclosed rooftop play-house located seven floors above the Yonge Street Theatre, opened just two months later, on February 16, 1914. It was about half the size with just 992 seats, but its interior couldn't have looked more different. The walls were decorated with botanical images of vines and other flora, and the ceiling—including the section under the mezzanine overhang—was festooned with hanging orange and green leaves. Originally, five thousand fireproofed beech boughs with actual leaves attached were used in the decor. Small lights scattered among the leaves resembled ornamental lanterns. The concept was that the audience should think it was sitting in a lush garden retreat as it watched the show.

When Loew bought the American Theatre from Morris back in New York, he had changed the bill of fare to vaudeville and stage revues, and that's what he brought to both the Yonge Street and the Winter Garden Theatres from their inception. They played host to the top entertainers in the field, including George Burns, Milton Berle, Sophie Tucker, Edgar Bergen, and Bill "Bojangles" Robinson.

But just as the American Theatre was forced to close with the changing times, so too the public's fascination with talking movies took their toll on its Canadian counterpart.

In 1928 the Winter Garden was simply boarded up. Although it was occasionally used as a movie location and served as a canteen for soldiers during World War II, the theater was basically left just as it was, with everything in place. Eventually, even the staircase leading up to the play-house was walled over.

Loew's Yonge Street Theatre, like so many legitimate playhouses of the era, was transformed into a cinema, beginning a movie-only format in 1930. It fell into disrepair and disrepute, and in 1969 Loew sold the theater to the Famous Players movie theater chain. By the 1970s it had become a derelict house showing second-run and adult (though not pornographic) films. In 1978 the theater's name was changed to the Elgin.

But as in life, many theaters also have a second act. In 1981 the Ontario Heritage Association, an agency of the Ministry of Culture, bought the building and by the following year had succeeded in having it named a National Historic Site. The $29 million restoration of both theaters took two and a half years, finally opening to the public in 1989.

To quickly bring at least one of the theaters back to life, conservators temporarily retrofitted the Elgin Theatre to allow the Canadian premiere of Andrew Lloyd Webber's *Cats* to take place. After that musical's two-year run, work started in earnest on both theaters under the careful eye of the architectural firm Janis A. Barlow & Associates.

Work began with the Elgin Theatre. Twenty-eight layers of paint were stripped off to get back to the lobby's original coloration, and more than 300,000 sheets of aluminum leaf were pounded into shape while re-gilding.

But when they entered the long-closed doors to the rooftop Winter Garden Theatre, it was like breaking into King Tut's tomb: It was filled, as Egyptian archaeologist Howard Carter had exclaimed when first peeking into his fabulous discovery, with "wonderful things."

Fifty-nine years had gone by, and the Winter Garden was a veritable time capsule of the vaudeville era. There were stacks of vintage playbills and ticket stubs still strewn on countertops. Sequined gowns, feather boas, and the baggy pants of long-forgotten comedians filled the costume racks. Props and scenery were scattered around backstage. The mirrors in the empty dressing room were still rimmed by dozens of bare lightbulbs, and the still-operational projection booth stood as a mute testament to the theater's days as a silent-movie house.

To summon back the look of the original decor, the overhead foliage was painstakingly replaced, one leaf at a time. The Belgian company that supplied the floor covering was able to match all-new carpeting to the original. The walls bearing hand-painted watercolor frescoes of roses and vines were delicately cleaned using rolled bread dough to reveal the paintings' soft pastel hues.

The seats posed more of a problem. It was definitely necessary to replace the worn and rickety seats, but preservationists wanted chairs that matched the originals as closely as possible. The search was on.

Their hunt led them, of all places, to the Biograph Theater in Chicago. The movie theater had recently been refurbished itself, including all-new seats, and it had placed its vintage chairs in storage. And that included the one that at one point they had deliberately upholstered in a different color: the seat John Dillinger had occupied while watching *Manhattan Melodrama*, right before he walked outside to his death.

Although the gangster's saga was well known, along with the legend that his ghost haunts the nearby alley in which he was killed, when the Winter Garden received the seats its restorers didn't connect the single distinct chair with the Dillinger story. They simply assumed it had worn out and was recovered with a different pattern because no matching fabric was available at the time. They didn't know the Biograph had expressly fitted the chair so audiences would be able to pick it out.

Unfortunately, once all of the chairs were stripped to their frames and refinished in Toronto, the celebrated chair was hopelessly mixed in with the others, so its identity has been lost to history.

Or has it?

No one has ever claimed that Dillinger's spectre visited the inside of the Biograph, much less sat in his old chair. But once comfortably ensconced in the Winter Garden, some of the old Biograph chairs seemed to have a mind of their own. Ushers say several seats sometimes drop down without assistance as if unseen persons were settling into them. Then, just a few seconds later, the seats would just as suddenly fold back up, once again without being touched.

When it happens, are Dillinger and his two lady escorts from that July 1934 night in the house? Or is it the notorious "special chair" wanting to make itself known?

If the lively chairs aren't enough to give you the willies, maybe the Lavender Lady will. According to an apocryphal tale, a young woman was stabbed to death in one of the restrooms back in the Winter Garden Theatre's halcyon days. Mortally wounded, she stumbled to the elevator in the upper lobby and managed to press the call button before sinking to the floor. By the time the elevator operator arrived at the rooftop and opened the gated door, the girl was dead.

The mystery woman has returned, as phantoms of murder victims often do, to the site of the tragedy. People know she's in the room when they catch a whiff of her lavender-scented perfume.

The Lavender Lady has also been known to materialize; bur when she does, it's usually downstairs at the main box office. She's been described as being in her mid-twenties, blonde, with her hair up in a bun and her clothes all disheveled, as if she had tried to fight off her attacker.

Perhaps she's the one haunting the elevator as well. The old-style elevators were designed to require attendants to operate them. But sometimes the lifts simply start to move without help, stopping at different floors. Spookier still, on lonely nights, when the Winter Garden is dark and no staff or crew are on the rooftop level, occasionally the upstairs call button will signal for the elevator. Any operator brave enough to climb in the cage and ride to the top will find that no one's there waiting. Nevertheless, it's become a Winter Garden tradition for the attendant to briefly open the door as a nod to the unseen Lavender Lady.

It's not just the Winter Garden Theatre that's haunted. There are at least seven other ghosts making their home downstairs in the Elgin and in the main lobby.

Ladies before gentlemen.

The shadowy figure of a young woman has been seen floating out of the coat checkroom on the Elgin's mezzanine level. The space was once used for actors who had to make quick costume changes, so it's thought that the spectre is an actress who used to perform in the theater.

Another spectral lady, this one dressed in clothing from the Edwardian era, sometimes appears in the downstairs lobby. Patrons as well as staff have sighted her before she evaporated. Because of her appearance, she's thought to be a different spirit than the Lavender Lady who haunts the lobby upstairs.

And speaking of flowers, the unexplainable scent of lilacs is occasionally carried on the breeze through the refurbished dressing rooms. Lavender; lilacs: Perhaps ghosts have eclectic tastes in flora.

A nameless male phantom hovers around and sometimes appears inside the ladies' washroom on the second floor. But he's no Peeping Tom. It's believed that he was a theater technician, so he might be there making sure everything is running smoothly.

The ghost of a man dressed in a plain brown suit has been spotted sitting in the auditorium on several occasions. Because he usually appears during rehearsals, some think he may have had a professional association with the Elgin, but no one's ever gotten close enough to identify him. If you get too near, he simply vanishes.

Sam, or Samuel, was a trombone player at the Elgin who died when he lost his balance and toppled into the open orchestra pit in the 1920s. Staff members at the theater claim they still see him occasionally or hear the wailing of his horn.

Perhaps the most recent addition to the Elgin's assemblage of apparitions is "Stan," who was part of the crew restoring the theater. He fell to his death from the mezzanine, and he must not be too happy about it because he makes life miserable for the staff by taunting them. He'll sneak up behind one of them on the stairs, fall into step, and then pick up speed. Soon the person has to start running to stay one step ahead of the phantom.

And we mustn't forget the little child. The phantom of a youngster has been noticed in and around one of the side boxes in the mezzanine, or running on the staircase between the balcony and the mezzanine. (Onlookers have never been sure whether it's a boy or a girl). The story goes that the child has returned to that area because he or she fell from one of those upper boxes down to the orchestra-level floor far below.

The next time you're in Toronto, why not take a tour of the Elgin and Winter Garden Theatres? Or better yet, catch a show there. You might get a chance to sit in Dillinger's chair and not even know it. And for an encore, maybe you'll get a chance to see one of the theaters' many actors from the Afterlife.

Part Four

THERE'LL ALWAYS
BE AN ENGLAND

What Broadway is to New York City, the West End is to London. The great theaters of London have an extra century or two of history attached to them, however they've picked up a few more ghosts than their Manhattan counterparts.

Actor-manager Sir Herbert Beerbohm never left Her Majesty's Theatre, and his counterpart John Baldwin Buckstone is still taking bows at the Haymarket. Actor William Terriss swore he would come back after being stabbed outside the Adelphi—and he did! Over at the Duke of York's, there was a haunted jacket that crushed anyone who tried it on. And at least four actors haunt Drury Lane, along with its most famous spectral visitor, the mysterious Man in Gray.

Ready for your final nights at the theater?

Chapter 31

"I Shall Come Back"

The late nineteenth-century British actor William Terriss, noted for his romantic leads and legions of female admirers, was fatally stabbed outside the stage door of the Adelphi Theatre in 1897. As he died in the arms of his leading lady, Terriss swore that he would return. And apparently he has.

As the deranged assassin Richard Prince emerged from the shadows, he knew what he had to do. Terriss must die. After all, wasn't he the one who was standing in his way to glory and fame? Wasn't Terriss's tacit approval the reason the other actors—and sometimes even people in the street—scorned him? Wasn't the only way to end the pain and humiliation to kill the much-loved actor?

William Terriss was indeed the man of the hour. Born William Charles James Lewin in London in 1847, Terriss didn't immediately set out to become an actor. Blessed with a bold spirit and wanderlust to match, he set sail as a crew member on a merchant ship. By the time he was twenty, he had raised sheep in the Falklands, planted tea in Bengal, and mined silver in America. In 1867 he returned to England, where he realized that with his masculine good looks, rich voice, and charismatic swagger, he was well suited for a life in the theater.

Taking the stage name William Terriss, he saw his reputation grow as he was cast in a succession of melodramas and swashbuckling roles. His London debut came at the Prince of Wales Theatre in 1871 in the long-forgotten Tom Robertson play *Society*. Major roles in *Robin Hood* and *Rebecca* (based on Sir Walter Scott's *Ivanhoe*) followed.

Along the way, he had acquired a family. In 1868 he had married Isabel Lewis, and before long they had two children, both of whom followed him onto the stage. His daughter, Ellaline, became a well-known actress in the musical theater, and his son, Tom, would also become a writer and film director, besides being an actor.

The 1880s were incredibly successful for Terriss, making him a star. He joined the company of the renowned actor-manager Henry Irving at the Lyceum Theatre, where he made his mark in such Shakespeare roles as Cassio and Mercutio. Terriss soon became a favorite of Irving, and their professional and personal association remained strong for the rest of the younger man's life.

That life, however, was about to intersect with the man who would prove his doom: Richard Prince.

Born Richard Millar Archer near Dundee, Scotland, the young man moved to London to make his fortune as an actor. Though calling himself William Archer Flint for a time, he eventually settled on the stage name Richard Prince. He was a mediocre, though willing, actor, and by the early 1880s he had begun to appear regularly in walk-ons, bit parts, and supernumerary roles. At some point he became acquainted with Terriss, who was already starring in West End productions. Although not friends by any means, the famous actor nevertheless recommended the struggling Prince whenever possible for shows with which he was involved.

One of these was the production of *The Harbour Lights*, which opened in December 1885. Instead of being grateful, however, with his mental problems beginning to surface and cast in only a minor role, Prince allowed the seeds of jealousy to take root in his mind.

He believed himself to be a great actor—he wasn't—and he felt that he was every bit as good as, or better than, Terriss himself. Prince is said to have asked the company manager if he could understudy Terriss, but the man, aware that the actor was barely good enough to perform the small role in which he was already cast, turned him down.

Prince's rejection only resulted in his berating Terriss more—to anyone who would listen, including members of the cast. Without any thought as to the possible consequences, the bemused actors encouraged the disillusioned Prince for their own entertainment. At first, Terriss was completely unaware of the seething malice brewing in Prince's heart. But one night, after he let out a barrage of insults to Terriss's face, Prince found himself being ignominiously dropped from the show.

The confrontation would come back to haunt Terriss.

But the leading man had neither the time nor the inclination to dwell on the falling-out, because his costar was the beautiful, twenty-four-year-old Jessie Milward. They had immediate chemistry, both onstage and off, and before long they were lovers. The public couldn't get enough of them together, and they appeared as romantic leads opposite each other in a succession of plays. In addition to performing in London, they first toured the provinces, then followed with engagements in America.

If ever there was such a thing as a "matinee idol," it was Terriss. He was a very good actor, utterly charming, and it didn't hurt that he was also incredibly handsome. And he wasn't just "playing" the hero. Kind and generous to a fault, he was also adored by his fellow cast members, stage crew, and theater staff. He soon earned a nickname, "Breezy Bill," for his natural, cheerful manner.

With his accumulated wealth and fame, he leased the Adelphi and started his own company in 1890 (although some sources suggest he was merely engaged by the theater's owners). Regardless, both the public and the critics loved his work, and he enjoyed seven successful, productive years, performing primarily at the Adelphi.

This was the man the disgruntled Richard Archer Prince, hiding in Maiden Lane beside the Adelphi Theatre, felt he had to destroy.

Prince's hatred for Terriss was no doubt further enflamed by the embarrassment and shame he must have felt over having had to accept charity from the Actors' Benevolent Fund (ABF), a compassionate association set up to discreetly assist impoverished actors. Despite having fired him from his own show, Terriss had continued to suggest Prince for other roles and personally recommended him for assistance by the ABF. It was no doubt in large part due to the suggestion of such an esteemed member of the theater community that Prince was given enough money to cover his daily expenses on several occasions.

It's little wonder that Prince was in dire financial straits. Much is forgiven if you're talented, but Prince was not. His coarse and loutish behavior usually led to his being dismissed. The theater community is very small; actors and managers talk; and before long, Prince found himself unemployable.

And whom did he blame? Certainly not himself. On any given night, in taverns all across the West End, the inebriated Prince could be heard berating the man who had by that time become affectionately known around town as "No. 1, Adelphi Terriss."

By the end of 1897, Prince had fallen into madness. On December 13, foul-mouthed and no doubt intoxicated, he caused a commotion in the lobby of the Vaudeville Theatre and was thrown out. The next night he wheedled his way into Terriss's dressing room at the Adelphi, where he loudly argued with his former employer and sometime benefactor.

On December 16, the day of the murder, Prince, destitute, showed up at the ABF council offices pleading for money. The secretary turned him away, saying that he would have to wait until after the following day's meeting. Whether Prince thought Terriss was responsible for cutting him off is unknown. But the rejection may have been the straw that broke the proverbial camel's back.

Clearly, by this time, the man was completely insane. "Mad Archer," as Prince would become known, bought a knife and, just after nightfall, lay in wait for his victim.

William Terriss was a hit at the Adelphi in a new melodrama titled *Secret Service*. That night, in the hours before his performance, he dined at Rules restaurant in Covent Garden with his son-in-law, Seymour Hicks, who had married Ellaline in 1893. Hicks, already a successful actor, would later be partnered with his wife for many years in a series of romantic comedies.

At the time of Terriss's murder, Hicks was appearing at the Gaiety Theatre opposite the Adelphi. After supper they parted company in the street, bound for their respective theaters. Terriss walked alone down the darkened Maiden Lane toward the Adelphi, where he had a private entrance, separate from the stage door in Bull Inn Court. As Terriss inserted his key into the lock, Prince jumped out and stabbed him three times, once each in the back, side, and chest.

It was the last of these that proved to be fatal. The scuffle had not gone unheard, and the wounded actor was quickly carried inside. So loud was the commotion that Hicks became aware of it across the street. He ran to the Adelphi to discover Terriss lying in the arms of his beloved Jessie Milward in a pool of blood. A doctor who had rushed from the nearby Charing Cross Hospital was at Terriss's side, desperately trying to mend the wounds.

One of those standing by the dying actor was Terriss's understudy, an actor named Lane. The night before the attack, he had dreamt of Terriss bleeding to death in the theater, surrounded by friends. When he had told others about it, they scoffed.

Now, as he struggled for breath, Terriss drew his leading lady close to him. He whispered his final words in her ear, but they echoed to everyone in the circle around him.

"I shall come back."

Then the great actor was dead.

Silence pervaded the theater. Then an astral voice rang in Hicks's ears. It was Terriss, speaking the words of a man who had suddenly had the Other World revealed to him. Was it a question, a declaration, or both?

"Can any man be so foolish as to believe that there is no Afterlife?!"

Amazingly, Prince had not fled. Instead, he stood by the open stage door, surveying the panicked scene inside. Spectators grabbed him, and when police arrived from the nearby Bow Street station, they had no trouble arresting the crazed murderer.

"I did it for revenge," Prince shouted as they dragged him away. "He has kept me out of employment for fourteen years, and I had either to die in the street or kill him.

"He has had due warning," he's reported to have said, "and if he is dead, he knew what to expect from me. He prevented me getting money from the Fund today, and I have stopped him."

Prince was soon tried. At his initial hearing, he pleaded "guilty with provocation," but his lawyers convinced him to change his plea to not guilty. During the trial, his counsel—and even Prince's own mother—entered testimony that the man was out of his mind.

The jury found him "guilty, but according to the medical evidence, not responsible for his actions." The killer was imprisoned in Broadmoor Criminal Lunatic Asylum. Ironically, Prince was a model prisoner during his lifelong incarceration and even became active in the prisoners' theatrical society, both performing in shows and conducting the inmates' orchestra. One of the many plays in which he starred there turned out to be—*Secret Service*. The man who had deprived London of one of its most famous actors lived until the age of eighty-one, dying in 1937.

Behind the doors of an insane asylum, Richard Archer Prince became the star he never was in the outside world.

Terriss was buried in Brompton Cemetery in London. Today his portrait hangs in Denville Hall, the home for retired actors and actresses. And there's a plaque on the wall outside the stage door of the Adelphi Theatre, commemorating the events of that ill-fated night in 1897.

But true to his word, Terriss has returned to the theater. Or at least the theater that is now in that location.

The current Adelphi is the fourth building on that site. The first theater was opened in November 1806 as the Sans Pareil (meaning "without compare"), built by a merchant, John Scott, for his daughter Jane, who sang, danced, wrote, and performed in many of its early musical shows. Scott sold the theater thirteen years later to two men, Jones and Rodwell, and they changed its name to mirror the adjacent Adelphi buildings. The playhouse became renowned for its melodramas, including many of the first theatrical adaptations of several Charles Dickens novels.

In 1844 the French dancer Céline Céleste and actor-manager Ben Webster took over the theater. They named John Baldwin Buckstone, who had had success with his Dickens plays there, as the resident playwright. (Buckstone would later become more associated with the Theatre Royal, Haymarket, and after his death became its resident ghost.)

Just over a decade later, with Céleste having departed, Webster decided the theater had fallen into such "incurable disrepair" that it had to be replaced. It was torn down, and the New Adelphi rose in its place in November 1858. The interior was a vast improvement over the small, shabby old auditorium. It featured seating for 1,500 as well as a brilliant gas-jet chandelier that hung over the heads of the audience.

That theater, the one in which Terriss performed and died, was demolished at the end of the 1890s, and the aptly named Century Theatre took its place in September 1901. Three years later it once again reverted to the Adelphi name, and for almost three decades it housed a series of light musical comedies. It, too, was replaced, in December 1930, by an Art Deco palace designed by theater architect

Ernest Schaufelberg. Opened as the Royal Adelphi Theatre, ten years later it changed its name back to simply the Adelphi Theatre.

Despite his death, William Terriss has been there throughout all of the changes. The apparition is tall, wears a top hat and frock coat, and carries a walking cane. Although he's occasionally spotted outside the stage door (or sometimes just heard pacing in the alleyway), the ghost is most often seen inside the theater. And he turns up everywhere: in the backstage corridors, standing in the wings, and walking in the house along the front of the stage after the audience has gone for the night. Now and then he passes through the empty lobby into the street.

He has a particular attachment to his old dressing room. People sitting inside the room sometimes hear disembodied footsteps outside in the corridor. And the couch sometimes seems to have a life of its own: In one frightening incident in 1928, a roomful of onlookers watched in amazement as it bounced while a young woman was sitting on it. On other occasions, the furniture was discovered to have shifted its position overnight while the room was unoccupied.

Then there is the tapping. Terriss used to rap twice on his leading lady's door as he passed to let her know he was there, and he often did the same on the way out. Actors who have since used the star's dressing room have heard similar unexplainable knocking. They rush to the door and open it, only to find an empty passageway.

That being said, Terriss is occasionally seen in the hallway. In fact, he's been caught walking into his old dressing room by taking a shortcut through the wall.

Other paranormal activity in the theater includes lights that come on and go off by themselves, wide swings in temperature in a very short amount of time, an elevator that moves when it's unoccupied or hasn't been called, and green orbs of light that hover over tables in the dressing rooms.

Starting around 1955, Terriss's ghost also appeared from time to time on the platform of the Charing Cross underground station—the train Terriss would have taken to his residence after an evening's performance at the Adelphi. The spectre was always described as a man wearing a gray suit, a shirt with an old-fashioned collar, and white gloves. For some reason the manifestations seemed to stop around 1972.

Is the apparition really William Terriss making good on his promise to return? Well, no one can say for sure. The spirit never stops and never talks, and it's seldom recognized as Terriss until later when the witness sees a photograph of the actor.

But this much is certain: *Something*—or some*one*—haunts the Adelphi. Terriss loved that theater. He lived and died for it. Perhaps, true to his promise, he did make the ultimate "comeback."

Chapter 32

Buckstone's Back

The ghost of actor-manager John Baldwin Buckstone first appeared at the Theatre Royal, Haymarket, in London, within a year of his death, way back in 1879. Apparently, he's not going anywhere soon.

It was just too foggy for Dame Margaret Rutherford to make it home. Fog was a way of life in London, but this was just too much.

Normally after the evening performance was over, the celebrated character actress would be able to walk out the stage door and be home in Gerrards Cross just west of London within an hour. But tonight was different. Outside, the air was as thick as the proverbial pea soup.

Reluctantly, she and her husband, the actor Stringer Davis, decided to spend the night in her dressing room backstage rather than risk having an accident on the road.

Rutherford was no stranger to dressing rooms. Born in Balham, a suburb south of London, in 1892, she made her stage debut with the Old Vic at the age of thirty-three. She was hardly the leading-lady type. In fact, she was rather dowdy with a frumpy frame, but her flair for physical comedy made her much in demand. By 1936 she was also appearing regularly in films.

In 1941 she made an indelible impression in the role of the eccentric medium Madame Arcati in the original stage production of Noël Coward's *Blithe Spirit* at the Savoy Theatre. (She later repeated the role in the 1945 movie version.) The story concerns a writer, Charles Condomine, who organizes a séance to gather material for a book. A rather peculiar medium, flamboyantly portrayed by Rutherford, accidentally conjures up the ghost of his deceased first wife, Elvira, who proceeds to create havoc. Repeated attempts by the medium to send her back to the Other Side are unsuccessful. At first the phantom merely seems mischievous, but by the play's end, Elvira has turned lethal. She cuts the brake lines in Charles's car, hoping he'll have a fatal accident and join her in the Next World. Instead, his new wife, Ruth, crashes the vehicle and dies. When her ghost shows up as well, a tug of war between the two spectres ensues. In a final coup de grâce, the medium manages to send both phantoms back to the Beyond.

Over the next twenty years, more than a dozen films and triumph after triumph on the stage followed for Rutherford. Then in 1961 she first portrayed the movie role for which she is probably best remembered: the spinster amateur detective character created by Agatha Christie, Miss Marple. That year the actress was made an Officer of the Order of the British Empire (OBE). (She would be made a Dame Commander, DBE, six years after that.)

Nineteen sixty-three was a big year for Rutherford. In addition to appearing in her second Miss Marple film, *Murder at the Gallop*—there would eventually be four in all—she won an Academy Award for Best Supporting Actress for her role as an absentminded duchess in *The V.I.P.s*. It's also the year she saw Buckstone's ghost.

Near the end of her life, Rutherford suffered from Alzheimer's disease. The symptoms were already beginning to surface when she made her last stage appearance in a revival of Sheridan's *The Rivals* opposite Ralph Richardson at the Haymarket. After just a few difficult weeks, she was forced to withdraw from the production. She died in 1972 and is buried next to her husband in the cemetery at St. John's Church in Gerrards Cross.

But fortunately for fans of ghost lore, she had not only told theater friends at the time that she saw Buckstone's phantom, but she later talked about it in an interview with the paranormal magazine *Psychic News*.

It was during a run at the Theatre Royal, Haymarket. Forced to spend that foggy night at the theater, she made up the divans in her dressing room into makeshift beds for herself and her husband. Before long they were both blissfully asleep.

Waking in the middle of the night, she was instantly aware that something was not quite right. They were not alone in the room. As she looked over to the wardrobe cabinet, she saw the hairy leg and calf-length breeches of a wispy male figure appear in the open door. As the spectre moved, she noticed that it was dressed in the clothes of a gentleman from the late nineteenth century. Her eyes followed the form up to his face and immediately recognized him from faded photographs she had seen in the past. It was the ghost of the former manager of that very theater, John Baldwin Buckstone.

Buckstone had been born in the Hoxton district of London in 1802, and, as a youth, he was apprenticed to a solicitor. The law didn't suit him, however, and at the age of nineteen he made his first professional appearance as an actor. Two years later he made his London debut at the Surrey Theatre.

In 1827 Buckstone was invited to join the company at the Adelphi Theatre, the playhouse the ghost of William

Terriss would begin to haunt some ninety years later. Buckstone spent five years there, most often cast as the comic lead. During that period, several of his original plays were also produced at the Adelphi. In fact, he became a quite prolific playwright. By the end of his career, Buckstone would write more than 150 shows.

His association with the Theatre Royal, Haymarket, began when he first performed there in 1833. Over the next twenty years, Buckstone would appear in several West End theaters and even toured America, but he would always return to the Haymarket.

The Theatre Royal, Haymarket (also known as simply the Haymarket Theatre), is the third-oldest theater still operating in London today. The playhouse was originally called the Little Theatre in the Haymarket when John Potter built it just off Piccadilly Circus in 1720. The theater received its royal patent in 1766, and it was under the management of David Morris that the current playhouse, designed by court architect John Nash, was built a few doors south on Haymarket in 1821.

(Beginning in 1660, during the English Restoration of Charles II, only theaters that had received a "patent" were allowed to perform "spoken drama" and refer to itself as a "Theatre Royal." All others were allowed to perform only light entertainment, such as comedy, musicals, dance, pantomime, or melodrama.)

The new theater's facade boasted a portico with six tall Corinthian pillars, and inside, the stage was completely surrounded by a proscenium arch—the first time ever in any theater. It's that theater which Buckstone, by then wealthy and famous, leased in 1853. As was common at the time, he not only ran the theater, he was also an "actor-manager," heading a company of actors and casting himself in the lead of many of their productions, especially those plays he wrote himself.

Perhaps Buckstone's biggest moneymaker was the 1862 premiere of *Our American Cousin*, the play Abraham Lincoln was watching when he was assassinated three years later at Ford's Theatre. The production was a huge success, running for four hundred performances. (For those of you into theater trivia, one of the play's characters was a boring nobleman named Lord Dundreary, from which we got the word "dreary.")

Buckstone was a friendly, gregarious man, and his actors and staff loved him. He was to remain attached to the theater until a year before his death in 1879—and, according to Margaret Rutherford and many others, even beyond.

Within a year of his death, Buckstone returned. His spectre first manifested itself in 1880 in the royal box. And why not? The Haymarket was Queen Victoria's favorite theater, and Buckstone was often asked to sit in the royal box when Her Majesty was in attendance.

Besides Rutherford, several other people have gone on record admitting they've seen Buckstone's ghost. One was Olga Barnett, an assistant manager who saw an unfamiliar man dressed in a mid-Victorian-era frock coat standing behind actor Michael Flanders (who was seated in a wheelchair about to go onstage) during the run of *A Drop of Another Hat*. She knew no one was supposed to be there, and she was just about to tell the errant actor to move, when the shadow vanished. When she mentioned the phenomenon to the rest of the company, several people, including Flanders, revealed that they had also seen the "tall gentleman in the old frock coat."

Dame Flora Robson and Sir Donald Sinden later claimed to have seen the spectre as well. The latter wrote in his 1982 autobiography, *A Touch of the Memoirs* (Hodder & Stoughton), that he and actress Gillian Howell saw Buckstone's ghost in 1949 while performing in *The Heiress*. Their dressing rooms were at the top of a set of stairs. One evening as they were going down to make their entrance, they passed the dressing room of Sir Ralph Richardson, who was starring in the production.

He stood with his back to them, dressed in his 1860s wardrobe. Sinden and Howell passed within two feet and greeted him as they went by. There was no reply, but they weren't surprised. Actors are often lost in silent contemplation as they prepare to go on. The pair continued down another flight and a half of stairs, making their way into the wings. It was then that they noticed Richardson was already onstage.

Then who had they seen? Sinden quickly ran up the stairs, but whoever had been there was gone. Given the costume the apparition was wearing and the fact that it was outside the star dressing room, Sinden realized that it must have been John Baldwin Buckstone.

One actor, whose name has now been lost, once opened his dressing room and was startled to see a mysterious figure dressed in that ever-present frock coat sitting in a chair. He immediately slammed the door shut, locked it from the outside, and rushed to get witnesses. He called the backstage fireman on duty, and the two ran to the dressing room. When they opened the door, the phantom was gone.

Not that Buckstone is shy around firemen. Two of them were once standing outside the theater when they saw the face of a stranger inside, peering through one of the windows. Shown a photograph of Buckstone, they were able to identify him as the spectral intruder.

Buckstone's ghost always manifests to people in the cast, the backstage crew, or staff, not the audience. It seldom appears, but when it does, there's no mistaking it.

Usually, the former actor-manager is content to produce other paranormal activity, just to let others know he's still around. Lights flicker on and off by themselves, doors swing open and shut, and doorknobs jiggle, as if being moved by spirit hands. Objects will disappear from one area of the theater, only to be found in another, and hushed whispers and phantom footsteps are heard in the hallways. Actors in the theater sometimes have the feeling that a benevolent but invisible presence is peeking in on them in their dressing rooms.

And Buckstone's old dressing room—probably the one occupied by Margaret Rutherford that frightful night—is especially haunted. People still feel his strong presence there. Items left there will sometimes move around inside closed cupboards, and pages of books flip over as if being turned by ghostly fingers.

None of which is of much concern to anyone, because Buckstone's appearance is considered to be a good omen. He most often turns up during the run of successful shows. So if you're visiting the Theatre Royal, Haymarket during the long run of a hit play, keep your eyes peeled for an ethereal figure dressed in a period frock coat. Buckstone's back!

Chapter 33
The Phantom at the Opera

For more than two decades, The Phantom of the Opera *has been going strong at Her Majesty's Theatre in London. But it's not that opera ghost that's haunting its darkened halls. Rather, it's the spectre of the actor-manager who built the playhouse in 1897. Has he returned to enjoy "The Music of the Night"?*

Deep in the bowels of Her Majesty's Theatre, far below the massive stage, the creaking machinery designed back in the Victorian era to produce special effects for spectacle-hungry audiences is still working. Who knew that a century after it was installed it could be used to make a mist-shrouded boat seemingly drift on what appears to be the fathomless depths of an underground lake?

Dangling high above the heads of the audience, a crystal chandelier blazes in sheer opulence, making the audience believe if only for a few hours that they are really sitting inside the grand opera house of Paris.

Any moment the mysterious stranger wearing a white mask to hide his deformed face will jump out, revealing himself on a perch high above the proscenium. The chain holding up the massive chandelier will snap, and it will begin to crash onto the heads of the terrified audience below.

Christine smiled. Not the character in the musical onstage, mind you. No, this Christine was a young woman in the audience who just happened to share her name with the heroine in the Gothic tale. And perhaps that was part of her attraction to the show. In any case, she sat mesmerized as the first act raced toward its climax.

Andrew Lloyd Webber's *The Phantom of the Opera*, based on the 1910 French novel by Gaston Leroux, had been playing continuously in the London playhouse, Her Majesty's Theatre, since its premiere on October 9, 1986. And Christine had seen it *many* times.

She had been there—what?—maybe twenty, twenty-five times? And in between, she was always saving up for her next visit. But trips were becoming more rare as London ticket prices were beginning to soar. Every time she came now, she was giving herself a special treat. That night, she didn't know how special the evening was going to be.

Christine had seen the musical from just about every spot in the theater, but her favorite was always where she was sitting now, about halfway back in the stalls (what in America would be called the orchestra) just in front of the overhang of the dress circle (or, as Americans say, the mezzanine). That way, the giant chandelier was always in her sight, and she had the best view in the house as it plummeted.

Over the years, people have made hundreds of jokes about that chandelier, but there was so much *more* to the show. Christine knew every line of the libretto, every nuance of the score, and every movement the actors would make on the stage.

The story for those who didn't know—and could there be anyone who didn't?—is a tragic love triangle: the title character, a man with a misshapen face who hides in a lair beneath the Paris opera house; his protégée, the beautiful waif Christine; and her childhood sweetheart Raoul, who has suddenly come back into her life as the patron of the opera house. The jealous Phantom, Christine's "angel of music," uses a combination of magic and malice to ensure her rise to stardom even as he demands her devotion.

The music was swelling to a climax. The Phantom was just about to reveal himself.

Out in the audience, Christine noticed something odd just out of the corner of her eye. Behind her, off to her far left, a dark shadow seemed to appear just behind the last row of seats. It was a male figure, tall. Even though he was only in silhouette, she could tell that his wardrobe, from the long jacket to the traveling cape, seemed to be from a long ago era. A hat was pulled down over his brow, slightly hiding a white mask. It was the Phantom! But what was he doing out in the house?

She knew it couldn't be him. She quickly looked up to the rafters, where she knew the actor was supposed to appear any second. Yes, there he was: She could just make out the actor's fedora peeking out from his hiding place at the top of the proscenium. Then who was that person walking behind her? Although she hated to tear her eyes away from the stage, she forced herself to turn back to the wall. The strange shape was gone. Had she simply imagined it? Or had she seen an actual phantom?

A crack of lightning. Screams. The chandelier started its deadly plunge. And darkness.

The title character in the musical does seem at times to have supernatural powers, and he's often referred to as an "opera ghost." But he's only a character in a play. The theater, however, is actually haunted.

Her Majesty's Theatre has quite a history—more than three hundred years of it—plenty of time to pick up a ghost or two. But the spectre haunting the playhouse has nothing

to do with its current record-holding tenant. Rather, its resident spirit is the man who built the theater and served as
its first actor-manager.

The playhouse, one of the most ornate in all of London, is actually the fourth to stand on that site in the
Haymarket. Its roots date back to the beginning of the eighteenth century, when playwright and architect John Van-
brugh established the Queen's Theatre there in 1705. From
the beginning, it was referred to as Her Majesty's Theatre,
even though it didn't have a royal patent. In 1714, when
George I took the throne, the theater changed its name to
His Majesty's Theatre, and ever since, the theater has been
rechristened whenever necessary to reflect the gender of the
current monarch.

The original structure, as well as the two that replaced
it, were all consumed by fire, the first two times due to
arson. The third Her Majesty's Theatre was razed in 1892 to
make way for the current magnificent building.

Which is where our ghost makes his entrance—or at
least the man who would become its ghost.

Born Herbert Draper Beerbohm in London in 1852, Tree
(which he took as a stage surname) made his theater debut
with an amateur company in the English provinces at the
age of twenty-four. In 1884 he had his first performance
in the West End, and his star rose quickly. Within three
years he was managing the Theatre Royal, Haymarket. (He
would be followed by John Baldwin Buckstone, whose ghost
haunts the Haymarket to this day.) Tree's greatest success
at the Haymarket was the 1895 melodrama *Trilby*, in which
he played the role of Svengali.

With the money earned from that production, he
was able to build his own playhouse across the street in

1897—what would be the fourth (and, so far, final) Her Majesty's Theatre. It was designed by Charles J. Phipps, with four stories and an attic, topped by a square dome, all in the French Renaissance style. The exterior was decorated with a row of four Corinthian columns in front of the dress circle foyer.

The interior was spacious and luxurious, with high paneled ceilings and mirrored walls. The stage was wide and, perhaps for the first time in a London theater, flat rather than raked, which in later years made it perfect for large-scale musicals. The auditorium, with (at the time) approximately 1,300 seats on four levels, was said to have been designed to emulate the opera house at Versailles.

As a traditional actor-manager, Herbert Beerbohm Tree ran the theater, headed a company, and often acted in the lead roles. Tree was not a natural leading-man "type." Tall and thin with a reedy voice, he was most successful when he performed "character roles." He was well versed in the art of make-up, so he was able to play a wide variety of parts over his career, and he was prone to grand, histrionic gestures. Under his management the theater became known for its elaborate sets and special effects as well as its productions of the Shakespeare canon.

Like all the great actor-managers of the British stage, Tree made a lingering impression on his theater, and it blossomed under his leadership. In 1904 he founded the Royal Academy of Dramatic Arts there, and five years later he was knighted. He died in 1917, but it was far from his final curtain at Her Majesty's.

He has returned.

In the 1970s the entire cast of Sir Terence Rattigan's last play, *Cause Célèbre*, including its star, Glynis Johns, saw

Tree's ghost slowly make its way along the back wall of the stalls.

Tree's spirit will turn up from time to time in the wardrobe department, which is housed in the upper rooms that were once Tree's private apartment. He often travels the stairs that connect the dress circle to the stalls or will cross behind the last row of seats.

The ghost is also noticed many times backstage on Fridays, which was the day Tree would usually make his rounds to pay salaries.

But usually, Tree doesn't like to show his face. His presence, however, is very often—and very strongly—felt throughout what he called "my beautiful, beautiful theater." At least one recent actor playing the Phantom has said he was often aware of an unsettling essence standing behind him in the star dressing room.

Tree's preferred haunt, seems to be what was his favorite seat in the upper left-hand box. Patrons sitting there these days often complain that the door to the compartment will fly open by itself and the air will turn frigid. (In fact, whenever Tree is encountered anywhere in the theater, in any form, there's a sudden and distinct drop in temperature.)

The Phantom of the Opera has been playing at Her Majesty's Theatre in London for more than twenty years with no end in sight. So why not take in the show for yourself on your next visit to the West End? Perhaps you'll get to see two phantoms for the price of one.

Chapter 34
The Strangler Jacket

The wardrobe department at the Duke of York's Theatre in London was home to one of the strangest pieces of theatrical paranormal paraphernalia ever to exist: a lady's bolero jacket that constricted and tried to squeeze to death anyone who dared to try it on. And then there's the house ghost: its former manager Violet Melnotte.

"Take it off. Take it off! I can't breathe!"

The wardrobe mistress tore the small coat off the actress's bodice. Whatever could be wrong?

"I swear, that jacket was getting tighter and tighter. And the collar was closing in around my neck. It was trying to strangle me!"

And with that, the actress flew out of the fitting room.

The costumer backstage at the Duke of York's Theatre put the coat back on its rack, this time making sure to separate it from the rest. This was far from the first time someone had had that reaction while trying on the jacket. Perhaps it really *was* haunted.

No one was sure exactly where the small black bolero jacket originally came from. Some say it had been found in a market stall by the wardrobe department of the Embassy Theatre (now part of the Central School of Speech and Drama) and became the property of the Duke of York's costumers when one of its shows transferred there in the 1920s.

More likely, it had been designed by a costume house for a West End production of *Charley's Aunt* sometime before World War I. The Duke of York's supposedly came by it when its wardrobe department rented the jacket for use in a new play, *The Queen Came By*. Every woman in the cast of that show who tried on the jacket complained of discomfort. During her fittings, the play's star, Thora Hind, had no problems with the jacket, but once the show was under way, the coat seemed to fit tighter every time she put it on.

Three other actresses who wore the jacket were also overcome with feelings of fear and trepidation. It seemed to them as if they were being suffocated, as if the jacket was somehow closing in on them. Each one claimed the sensation disappeared the instant she took the jacket off.

The levelheaded wife of the play's producer scoffed at the idea and put on the jacket herself to prove that there was nothing wrong with it.

"There! You see? I didn't feel a thing. I told you that those girls are all hysterics," she triumphantly swaggered. It was only as she handed the jacket back to the dresser that she noticed the terrified look on the other woman's face. "What?"

She spun to the full-length mirror propped up against the wall beside her. Even though she had felt nothing, large red welts covered her neck, as if invisible hands had attempted to strangle her. Instinctively, she clutched her hand to her throat.

At last, she too believed. To find out who—or what—was haunting the jacket, it was decided that a séance should be held inside the theater. According to the tale still making theatrical rounds, the sitters contacted the spirit of the young actress who first wore the coat. She told them that her jealous boyfriend had strangled her inside the theater while she had the coat on. He removed the identifying garment before he stole her body from the theater, placed it in a barrel, and dumped it into a river. Somehow the malice that the man exuded during the attack—as well as the method by which the girl was killed—were absorbed into the fabric of the bolero coat and has affected everyone who has worn it since.

Where is the costume today? According to British author and parapsychologist Peter Underwood, an American identified only by the name Lloyd bought the dreaded jacket. He, his wife, and their daughter all supposedly reported the same feelings of strangulation and panic when they tried it on.

With the jacket gone, actors and staff at the Duke of York's Theatre thought they were safe. But unfortunately, the hauntings were just getting started.

But this time they knew exactly who was causing them.

In 1892 Frank Wyatt and his wife, Violet Melnotte, built the playhouse, calling it the Trafalgar Square Theatre, on St. Martin's Lane, a narrow, winding road outside of what was, at the time, the main theater district. Within two years of its opening, Melnotte had become the theater's driving force. Its name was shortened to simply the Trafalgar, then in 1895 the theater was renamed the Duke of York's, in honor of the man who would later become King George V. (The change was made with royal permission, but without the patent that would have made it a Theatre Royal.)

From the start, the graceful four-level, nine hundred–seat theater, designed by architect Walter Emden, was considered a Victorian jewel. The brick facade of the exterior boasted a loggia and four Ionic columns fronting the first floor (what in America would be called the second story). Inside, the auditorium was painted a cool cream with gold embellishments.

In 1900 the theater housed the London production of David Belasco's *Madame Butterfly*. It was there that Puccini first saw the play that he turned into perhaps his most famous opera. Three years later, J. M. Barrie's most famous work, *Peter Pan, or The Boy Who Wouldn't Grow Up*, had its premiere there. In the 1930s the theater hosted opera, ballet, and Grand Guignol.

Hovering at the edges throughout it all was the eccentric Melnotte.

Violet Melnotte, whose real name was Emma Solomon, was born in Birmingham in 1855. She made her professional debut as a pantomime actress at the Theatre Royal, Hull, in the early 1870s. She made her London debut in 1876.

Over the next ten years, she appeared as an actress in pantomime and light opera in the West End, on tour in the provinces, and in America. But by 1885 she was already involved in theater management, and by the time she opened the Trafalgar Square Theatre with her husband, she was a seasoned theater administrator with several different theaters behind her. During her tenure at the Duke of York's, she became known as a powerful, brash owner. Even though she usually leased out the theater to other managers and producers, she somehow still seemed to have a hand in all facets of the productions. "Madame," as she was politely referred to, more or less controlled the theater (except for the years 1928–1933) until her death in 1935.

Because the spooky activity started in the theater shortly after she died, most of it has been attributed to her over the years. She was certainly strong-willed and determined when she was alive. If she wanted to come back, it was thought, what could have stopped her? Besides, she had lived in an apartment above the theater. Maybe she was just staying close to home.

She doesn't often become visible, but when she does, it's usually in the dress circle bar, and her shadowlike figure is dressed in black.

More often, she announces herself with loud knocking sounds, much more pronounced than what could be explained by the usual creaks and groans of an old theater. No one is sure whether Violet's attempting to communicate or just letting the current staff and actors know she's still around.

Melnotte liked to watch the shows from a particular private box. Today, sometimes its door will occasionally close on its own accord, even when it's occupied. Maybe she doesn't like others to intrude.

There is one other unusual phenomenon. Sometimes the spectral sound of an iron fire door slamming shut can be heard at around ten o'clock at night. The oddest thing about the noise, however, is that the door in question is no longer there. It was removed years ago. It's said that on one occasion an antique skeleton key materialized out of thin air right where the door used to be and fell at the feet of the theater manager.

The Duke of York's was damaged during World War II, requiring extensive repairs. At some other point, the seating was reduced to about 650 on three levels, making it one of the more intimate major theaters in the West End.

Throughout it all, the hauntings continued.

Then in the late 1970s Capital Radio purchased the theater. They restored the auditorium to its original colors and improved sight lines in the stalls by removing pillars that had once been architecturally necessary to hold up the dress circle.

According to head carpenter Max Alfonso, a terrible accident was prevented during the renovation by paranormal intervention. He was working late, standing on a thirty-foot scaffold. As he painted the huge back wall of the stage, he realized that the wheels on the temporary platform had not been locked into place, and it had started to roll away from the wall.

As it did, the framework started to tilt, leaning against the wall. Alfonso knew it would only be a moment before the entire structure fell over, and he would fall, most likely to his death.

Then, for some reason, as if time were suspended, the scaffolding simply stopped, still slanted at a perilous angle. Nothing had blocked the wheels. Nothing could be seen holding it back. But Alfonso didn't question the saving grace.

In those few seconds, he looked above him and noticed a water pipe at his fingertips, and he lunged for it. He stretched farther than he thought possible, and as his fingers curled around the providential pipe and he swung to safety, the scaffold toppled and fell in a heap.

She may have been a cranky old bird when she was alive, but was it Violet looking out for one of her own? All Alfonso knew was he had been saved by supernatural means.

The refurbished Duke of York's reopened in 1980. Two years later it was bought by the Ambassador Theatre Group chain, which still uses it as its headquarters and flagship theater.

Tapping and other spectral noises are still reported from time to time, but they're not as frequent as they once were.

And what about that haunted jacket? Is it still out there somewhere?

No one seems to know. But if someday you pick up a turn-of-the-twentieth-century bolero coat from some secondhand store and it fits just a little too snugly, watch out. It may be the last jacket you ever wear.

Chapter 35

The Most Haunted
Theater in the World

The Theatre Royal, Drury Lane, in London is the most haunted theater in England—some say, in the world. There's the bad-tempered spirit of actor Charles Macklin, who killed a fellow cast member, and the comforting, guiding hands of the great clown Joseph Grimaldi. Then, too, there are the spectres of the famed actors Dan Leno and Charles Kean. But its most frequent unearthly visitor is the ethereal presence of an anonymous Man in Gray.

"My God, get a torch! There's a body in here!"

The 1848 (or, according to some sources, 1850) renovations in the Upper Circle of the Theatre Royal, Drury Lane, had been uneventful up to that point. A little gold gilding here; a splash of paint there. Nothing major. After all, the new theater had opened only about thirty years earlier. It wasn't until the workmen happened to tap on one of the walls to check whether it was sound that they became curious. Their rapping produced a dull echo, almost as if there were a secret chamber hidden behind the wall.

But how could that be? Nothing showed up on architect Benjamin Wyatt's original blueprints, and nobody had any memory of an annex having been closed over.

Nevertheless, the noise was unmistakable.

Being careful not to make too much damage in case their hunch was wrong, the crew gently pried back a single board.

Then two. And there it was plain as day: a gaping, hollow space about the size of a large armoire.

The foreman asked the others to step aside, and he peered into the hole. As his eyes adjusted to the darkness, he slowly made out a form crumpled on the floor. White. Bones!

Within moments everyone was pressing against the crack, each taking a turn peeking inside. Then, satisfied that there was indeed a corpse behind the wall—or at least what was left of one—they began ripping at the boards. Soon a large opening exposed the remains.

The man's skeleton, covered by a few patches of rotted cloth dating back to the previous century, lay slumped in a small pile. Playing cards and a few coins were strewn at his feet.

"Well, who is he? Or rather, *was* he?"

"Why are you looking at me, mate? How the bloody 'ell would I know?"

It was then that a glint of steel sparkled in the reflection of the torch. *What was that coming from?* they wondered. Suddenly, in horror, the men realized a small dagger was lodged in the skeleton's rib cage. The man had been murdered!

Or so it seemed. In due course, the coroner would record an open verdict regarding the cause of death. But one thing was certain: The guy sure didn't seal himself up behind the wall.

The remains were discreetly removed from the theater and given a Christian burial nearby. The whole incident was hushed up and, after a few years, largely forgotten—that is, until the ghost started to appear.

It didn't show up until the 1930s, almost eighty years after the skeleton was uncovered, so no one knows for sure that it's the same person. After all, any number of people could have died and returned to haunt the theater in that much time.

But there's one key phenomenon that makes people believe the ghost is the man whose skeleton was recovered. When he's seen, the phantom always appears in the Upper Circle, crossing a row from one side to the other. He sometimes makes a detour through the circle bar, but he starts his stroll by the spot in the wall where the hidden chamber was located.

The spectre is called the Man in Gray because he's dressed in a long gray cloak, usually with the hint of a sword protruding from underneath. He also wears knee-length breeches, ruffled sleeves, buckled shoes or riding boots, a powdered wig, and a tricorner hat (which he sometimes carries), all dating from the late eighteenth century.

Who was it? Well, no one knows. The most popular theory is that he was a young dandy, a social gadfly, or possibly even a nobleman who was killed in a fight over one of the actresses appearing at the Theatre Royal, Drury Lane. He was then supposedly walled up in what was then a seldom-used passageway exiting from the right side of the Upper Circle. And there he remained until he was uncovered.

Oddly for a ghost, he appears only in the daytime, between 9 a.m. and 6 p.m. Few members of the general public have run into the Man in Gray because he normally arrives on the scene only during the rehearsals for a new play or musical. Believe it or not, actors and management are thrilled to see him, because he seems to turn up only if the show is going to be a huge hit! Among the rehearsals at which he materialized were those for the original long-running West End productions of *Oklahoma!*, *Carousel*, *South Pacific*, *The King and I*, and *My Fair Lady*.

On occasion, however, the spirit does come back to see the finished product. In 1950, when the run of *Carousel* was regularly selling out, Morgan Davies (who was one of the stars) was surprised to see an empty seat in one of the boxes at a performance. The next time he had a chance to look up in that direction, he saw a figure in a long gray cloak and an open-front shirt with long sleeves and ruffled cuffs sitting there. The shadow stood up and raised his arm. It was transparent!

Noted Irish tenor and comic actor Sir Harry Secombe, along with his dresser, admitted seeing the Man in Gray in the 1960s.

Interestingly, no one is able to get closer than about forty (and certainly no more than ten) feet to him. If you try, he instantly disappears. He's also apparently publicity shy, because he won't turn up if there's press, royalty, or even cameras in the house. One rare exception was in 1939, when the cast of *The Dancing Years* was assembled onstage for photographs. More than half the actors saw the phantom cross the Upper Circle. However, no one managed to snap a picture of him.

Although the Man in Gray is the most frequently seen ghost, several others also haunt the theater. In fact, there are so many spirits roaming around the Theatre Royal, Drury Lane, that it's thought to be the most haunted theater in England.

Of course, the theater has had more than three hundred years to produce those spirits.

Indeed, the Theatre Royal, Drury Lane, is the oldest theater in use in London today. There has been a playhouse on the Drury Lane site in the Covent Garden district since the one built by Thomas Killigrew in 1663. It opened as one of only two theaters in the city to have a royal patent allowing them to present serious, nonmusical drama.

It quickly became the favorite theater of King Charles II, if for no other reason than his mistress, Nell Gwynne, was an actress there. (Actually, she had been selling oranges in the pit until the king "discovered" her and launched her career in 1665. Her ghost has never haunted Drury Lane, but for a time in the 1980s it was claimed that she had reappeared at a strip club named Gargoyle in London's Soho. It's unclear why people thought the manifestation was Gwynne, because her apparition was never seen. They merely smelled a lavender perfume that Gwynne was said to have favored.)

The original Drury Lane theater burned to the ground in 1672. A new theater designed by the famous architect Sir Christopher Wren was built on the Drury Lane lot two years later.

One of the other ghosts in the current Theatre Royal, Drury Lane, comes from this second theater. Charles Macklin was an Irish actor of mercurial temper. He got into an argument and killed fellow cast member Thomas Hallam in a backstage hallway in 1735. (Some remember the fight as having taken place in the green room, where actors can lounge backstage and meet visitors after the show.) During the row, Macklin struck Hallam with his cane, piercing the man through his left eye and up into the brain. And they were only fighting over a wig!

At his trial, the normally quarrelsome and hot-blooded Macklin coolly defended himself and managed to get off with manslaughter. His sentence was a fine and cold branding— an unusual punishment of the period in which an unheated piece of iron was used to stamp a letter on the offender's skin, marking him or her for life.

Macklin lived to be 107 years old, and he was still working up to the age of ninety. But die he eventually did. No sooner was he in the ground than his spectre was back in the theater.

His ghost, described as ugly, tall, and thin, still walks the backstage corridors near where he killed his colleague. So far he hasn't hurt anyone, but it's probably best to steer clear if you see the felon phantom coming toward you. And time your visit carefully: He usually appears in the early evening, which was when the fight took place.

Macklin's victim may have returned to the theater as well. Some people think the Man in Gray has nothing to do with the skeleton that was discovered in the Upper Circle. They think the phantom is actually the wandering spirit of the murdered actor, Thomas Hallam.

Then there are the other ghosts that date from this period. Although he doesn't appear very often, Charles II himself shows up in the audience from time to time, along with his retinue. The most frequently mentioned manifestation of the royal party occurred in 1948 during the run of *Oklahoma!*

Another phantom from the eighteenth century is Sarah Siddons, who was one of Britain's great tragediennes. She's manifested at least once in the dressing room of Elizabeth Larner during the run of *Camelot* in 1960. Larner discovered the ghost sitting in her dressing room chair, dressed in period costume. The spirit rose, walked up to a wall, and vanished as it passed through. Larner had immediately recongnized the apparition as being Siddons from an oil portrait hanging elsewhere in the theater.

In 1791 the second Theatre Royal, Drury Lane, was razed to build a larger theater. This third playhouse, designed by

Henry Holland, was short-lived, however. It was destroyed by fire in 1809. The current structure, designed by Benjamin Wyatt, opened three years later with a production of *Hamlet*—one of Shakespeare's many plays that features a ghost in its dramatis personae.

There are plenty of other famous apparitions at Drury Lane as well. And one of them is quite frisky.

Oklahoma! was the first of several Broadway musicals to make it across the pond after the end of World War II. Opening on April 30, 1947, the musical starred Howard (then Harold) Keel as the leading man, Curly. Betty Jo Jones, an American actress in the production, told the show's publicity agent, Walter Macqueen-Pope, that for three nights in a row during a comedy scene, invisible hands gently but forcibly guided her farther downstage, closer to the audience, so she would get a better reaction. (One has to wonder what the other actors, stage crew, and the director thought of this, since all movements onstage are very carefully blocked.) To reward her for taking his advice, the spirit gave Jones a firm pat on the back.

Also according to Macqueen-Pope (in his 1955 book, *Pillars of Drury Lane*), a similar thing happened to actress Doreen Duke when she was onstage auditioning for *The King and I*. It wasn't going well, when unseen hands began to guide her into a new location on the stage that showed her to a better advantage. She got the role. The ghostly hands returned several times during rehearsals and then again on opening night to move her and give her encouraging pats and strokes.

Apparently the spirit became quite attached to her.

This same spectral presence has been felt both on the stage and in dressing rooms but has never been seen. It's always been presumed to be that of a male actor. Many have felt the ghost come up behind them and place a coat or cloak over their shoulders, tie up the back of a costume, or help with a button or zipper. But when the actor turned to thank the Good Samaritan, there would be no one there.

The phantom is usually a reassuring figure, giving nervous actors a friendly slap on the back or a quick kiss to a lady's cheek. But he's also been known to boot people in the behind if he disapproves of something or wants them to notice him.

Once in the 1890s, the British actor-manager Herbert Beerbohm Tree was the unwelcome recipient of a swift kick while giving a soliloquy from Shakespeare's *Falstaff* during a matinee royal gala performance. When Sir Henry Irving heard what had happened to his stage rival, he laughingly pronounced, "The ghost isn't an actor; he's a critic!"

Sometimes the spectre will tug at a performer's costume. Tony Britton had the tails of his coat pulled by invisible hands during the curtain call in a 1973 production of *No, No, Nanette*. The nearest actor at the time was five to six feet away.

During the opening night of *My Fair Lady*, two stage managers reported hearing unexplainable creaking noises coming from a particular piece of the set: the front staircase of the house where Henry Higgins, the lead character, supposedly lived. It sounded to them as if some unseen person were walking down the steps. As they stood there, puzzled by the unwelcome sounds, one of the men felt an invisible hand reach into his pocket. The other was smacked on the shoulder. Actress Betty Woolf, who portrayed the housekeeper Mrs. Pierce and was standing nearby, was pinched on the bottom. (This wasn't all that unusual, though, because the spectre seems to like "goosing" chorus girls.)

He also likes to pull pranks. While appearing in *Oklahoma!* Gloria Stuart received her pay, as usual, one Friday afternoon. She locked the money in a desk drawer in her dressing room, then locked the room itself while she was onstage. When she went to retrieve the money later that night, it was gone. She and the company manager thoroughly searched the room, only to find the missing cash in Stuart's pocketbook.

Because he remains invisible, the identity of this mischievous ghost has always been a mystery. But over the years, tradition has decided that it's most likely the spirit of Joseph Grimaldi, who was a celebrated pantomime clown and actor who often appeared at the Theatre Royal, Drury Lane, from the late 1700s up to his death in 1837. He was well known for helping out and encouraging young, inexperienced actors and actresses.

You could almost say Grimaldi was born at Drury Lane. His father was ballet-master at the theater, his mother was a dancer in the corps, and he first appeared in a scene on the Drury Lane stage in 1780, when he was only two years old. His fortunes were later tied to the competing Sadler Well's Theatre and as a young man he married the daughter of its principal owner.

But given Grimaldi's love for the Drury Lane, his early connections to it, and its financial support when he was in ill health in his last years, there's every reason to believe that *if* Grimaldi were able to return from the Beyond, Theatre Royal, Drury Lane, would be a more likely place for him to settle.

Okay, so far we have the Man in Gray, Charles Macklin, Charles II, Sarah Siddons, and the ghost of Grimaldi. What other spirits hang out at Drury Lane?

One phantom that's definitely attached to it is Dan Leno, a comedian who was perhaps the most famous British music hall star ever. He reigned at the end of the nineteenth century and was beloved for his cockney humor and performing in obvious, comic drag during the pantomime season. He died, probably of a brain tumor after a complete nervous breakdown, in 1904 at only forty-three years of age.

Leno began his career at the age of four, dancing in an act with his brother and uncle. By the age of eighteen, he was a champion clog dancer, and it's the distinctive sound of his wooden shoes that's sometimes heard in his old dressing room. Actors have also occasionally noticed the strong odor of lavender cologne onstage, which he used to cover up the smell from a bladder condition. (Although the aroma of their fragrances were similar, tradition holds that the scent comes from Leno's ghost, not Neil Gwynne's.)

Leno does materialize now and then. Actor Stanley Lupino, in his 1934 autobiography, *Stocks to the Stars*, relates how he saw the spectre. While performing in a pantomime one winter, Lupino's car skidded on the way home and he had an accident. Unhurt but unable to have the car repaired until morning, he made his way back to the theater and decided to sleep in his dressing room. He made a small fire, locked the door, and lay down on the divan.

Suddenly he heard the sound of his costumes on the clothes rack being slid to one side. Then he noticed the legs of a man—only the legs—standing in front of the fire. Almost immediately the limbs disappeared into the darkness in the corner of the room. But then, after a moment or two, the door opened and closed on its own. Lupino leapt to the door, only to find that it was still bolted from the inside.

At the time, Lupino had no idea who his visitor had been. But the ghost visited again, the second time during the day just before a matinee. As Lupino looked in the mirror in the dressing room, he saw another face hovering above his. It was in full makeup and wore a little smile. Lupino instantly recognized the face from the many photographs and paintings he had seen: It was Dan Leno! Lupino turned; no one was behind him. Then he realized that the dressing room he was in had been one of Leno's favorites and the last one he had used before his death.

Two nights later Lupino's wife and a friend of hers were in the dressing room with him, and as he left to go to the stage he heard the companion gasp. She had seen a man walk from behind the clothes rack and follow Lupino out of the room.

Yes, the room is definitely haunted. Once, after Britton's dresser replaced a hanger on the rack, it began to vibrate, picking up speed for over a minute. Similarly, one of the hangers came to life when Secombe was using the dressing room in 1967 during the run of *The Four Musketeers*. At the same time as the hanger was hopping about, there was a distinct tapping emanating from the wall.

At least one other actor, a female dancer, claimed to have seen Leno's spectre, which still stops in once in a while. His spirit, like Grimaldi's, has also been known to offer physical taps of encouragement to actors he likes.

Edmund Kean was regarded by many as the finest British actor in his generation. It was his 1814 Shylock at Theatre Royal, Drury Lane (and the subsequent three years performing at the theater) that secured his reputation. His ghost has been recognized in the theater on at least one occasion.

The ghost of his son, actor Charles Kean, was first spotted sitting in the stalls around 1900. He was dressed in mid-nineteenth-century clothing, sporting white hair. Kean was born in Ireland in 1811 and made his London theater debut at Drury Lane at the age of sixteen. Eleven years later it was the site of Kean's celebrated portrayal of Hamlet (another Shakespeare play with a ghost as one of its characters).

Charles Kean was more associated with the Haymarket Theatre than Theatre Royal, Drury Lane, and for a time he co-leased the Princess Theatre. But after his death in 1868, he apparently chose to return to the theater where he'd had his most notable success as a tragedian.

One woman who saw his ghost sitting at the end of her row at first thought it was an actor in eighteenth-century costume. When the man was nowhere to be seen at the end of the act, she mentioned him to the manager. After she gave a very detailed description of the actor, he showed her a photograph of Charles Kean.

"Yes," she confirmed. "That's him!"

The manager's office itself seems to be haunted by Arthur Collins, who was manager of Drury Lane from 1897 to 1923. Loose objects such as pens and coins will sometimes come to life on the desk if someone is in the room late at night. These disturbances are explained by the fact that Collins always kept strict hours and was upset if people stayed late. He felt that if you did your job expeditiously, everything could get done during normal working hours.

Collins was actually seen by two actresses in the cast of the original West End *My Fair Lady*. While waiting in the office, they saw a man unknown to them enter. He didn't acknowledge them; he simply looked in a cupboard and then left. Only when they described him did others realize that the strange visitor had been Collins.

Another spectre is worth mentioning because of the weird circumstances of its one and only appearance. Back in 1937, Clifford Heatherley was portraying the ghost of Henry VIII in the Ivor Novello musical *Crest of the Wave*. Early in the show's run, the actor died during a matinee performance. It was decided that until the role could be recast, the short scene in which he had appeared would be cut. But that evening Henry VIII appeared as scheduled nevertheless. That is to say, the ghost of Heatherley—recognizable to all of his fellow actors—walked onstage at the appropriate time.

These phantoms are just the beginning. Over the years there have also been unconfirmed rumors of other spirits appearing throughout the theater, including those of:

- Freddy Fredericks, a short, stocky ghost that sometimes appears around the witching hour
- George Grossmith, another former manager of the theater
- a Miss or Mrs. Jordan, who was head of the cleaning staff
- "a royal waiter," one of the ushers dressed in eighteenth-century livery to attend to the king and other royals

Finally, the whole theater, but especially the Upper Circle, is prone to sudden unexplained cold spots. A sound technician coming down from the gallery once saw a pair of spectral feet walking toward him. And in 1964, during preparations for *Camelot,* two stage electricians were working after hours with one of the fly men. At 5 a.m. the air became icy cold and a roaring noise, like a hurricane, rushed toward them from the back of the dress circle. When they looked into the house to see what had caused the sound, a gigantic gray mist was floating across the seats.

So there you have it. Almost a dozen identifiable spectres and who knows how many more unknown spirits. If you take in a show at the Theatre Royal, Drury Lane, or go on one of its daytime tours, don't be surprised if you come face to face with a ghost or feel its icy hands guiding your path. After all, you're in what may be the most haunted theater in the world!

Appendix A

"Boo"ks!

Among the literally hundreds of books about ghosts, poltergeists, and related paranormal phenomena, only a few deal specifically with performing arts venues that are haunted. Fortunately, those are detailed and thorough.

Some concentrate on the spirits; others focus on the playhouses themselves. All contribute to the folklore that has grown up about haunted theaters.

A few volumes, such as those by Guiley and Hauck, are perennial favorites and are available in most major bookstores. Many of the others are now out of print, but all can be located without too much difficulty in libraries or from online booksellers.

BOOKS

Alexander, Diane. *Playhouse*. Los Angeles: Dorleac-MacLeish, 1984. A thorough history of the Pasadena Playhouse and the life of Gilmor Brown.

Belasco, David. *Six Plays*. Includes *The Return of Peter Grimm*. Boston: Little, 1928. The original play about Peter Grimm can also be found in numerous anthologies. It was also novelized as *Return of Peter Grimm* (New York: Grosset & Dunlap, 1912). Now long out of print and copyright, both the play and novel can be found free of charge on various Web sites.

Bergen, Ronald. *The Great Theatres of London*. London: Admiral (Multimedia Books Ltd.), 1987. An illustrated

tome detailing the stories and architecture of the great
theaters of the West End.

Botto, Louis. *At This Theatre*. New York: Applause Theatre
& Cinema Books, 2002. The longtime editor of *Playbill*
magazine, Botto gathered his historical columns that
have appeared for many years in the programs given out
at Broadway performances and expanded them to create
this illustrated coffee-table–style book.

Guiley, Rosemary Ellen. *The Encyclopedia of Ghosts and
Spirits*. New York: Facts on File, 1992. This one-volume
encyclopedia is a classic. It collects ghost stories,
primarily from America and the United Kingdom, along
with essays of important figures in ghost folklore as well
as paranormal research and Spiritualism.

Hauck, Dennis William. *Haunted Places: The National
Directory*. New York: Penguin, 1996.

———. *The International Directory of Haunted Places*.
New York: Penguin, 2000. Hauck's national directory
along with its smaller international companion volume
together list almost three thousand haunted locations,
plus sites where UFOs and mysterious creatures have
been sighted around the world. The books are considered
essential to any ghost hunter's complete library.

Huggett, Richard. *Supernatural on Stage: Ghosts and
Superstitions of the Theatre*. New York: Taplinger
Publishing Company, 1975. Few ghosts are mentioned,
but just about every possible theater superstition is
included—from never wishing an actor "good luck" to
not whistling or saying the name of the play *Macbeth*
in a theater. Many of the beliefs are accompanied by
explanations of how they may have come about.

Johnstone, Shiela M.F. *Let's Go to the Grand!: 100 Years of Entertainment at London's Grand Theatre.* Toronto: Natural Heritage Books, 2001.

Lamont-Brown, Raymond. *Phantoms of the Theater.* Nashville: Thomas Nelson Inc., 1977. Hopping back and forth from the United States to England and Europe, the dozens of tales of ghosts, Spiritualism, and the supernatural found in this short volume range in size from a few paragraphs to several pages.

Lewis, Roy Harley. *Theatre Ghosts.* Newton Abbot, Devon, England: David & Charles, 1988. An exhaustive researcher, Lewis checked and doubled-checked his sources, obtaining first-person accounts whenever possible to corroborate many of the legends of British theater ghosts. These stories come from all across the United Kingdom, stretching from the West End to smaller, out-of-the-way theaters in the far provinces.

Maple, Eric. *Superstition and the Superstitious.* South Brunswick, NJ: A. S. Barnes and Co., 1972. Although not specific to the theater, this well-regarded book contains superstitions from all walks of life and investigates some of their possible origins.

Ogden, Tom. *The Complete Idiot's Guide to Ghosts and Hauntings.* Indianapolis: Alpha Books, 2004. This expanded edition contains first-person accounts of ghost sightings, some published for the first time, in addition to better-known tales from around the globe. Chapters separate the stories by the types of venues the spirits haunt.

O'Sullivan, Judy. *The Pasadena Playhouse.* Pasadena: The Pasadena Playhouse, 1992. Written as a commemorative edition celebrating the playhouse's seventy-fifth anniversary, this heavily illustrated edition covers the entire history of the official State Theatre of California, from its humble beginnings, through its Golden Age and derelict years, up to its renovation and resurgence.

Smith, Barbara. *Haunted Theaters*. Edmonton, Alberta, Canada: Ghost House Books, 2002. A spirited collection of the most famous ghost tales from theaters throughout the United States, Canada, and the United Kingdom.

Spencer, John and Anne. *Encyclopedia of Ghosts and Spirits*. Vol. 2. London: Headline Book Publishing, 2001. More than three hundred short ghost stories and tales of poltergeist activity fill this large volume.

Zepke, Terrance. *Best Ghost Tales of North Carolina*. Sarasota, FL: Pineapple Press, 2006. As its name suggests, this book surveys phantoms of the Tar Heel State, including Jane, the spectre residing at Aycock Auditorium.

Although they vary greatly in actual physical size, the following reference books could all be considered "pocket guides" to the theaters they cover, containing such information as the names of playhouses, addresses, seating charts, and contact information. In some cases, brief histories and descriptions of the theaters' interiors are included.

Elms, Susie. *The London Theatre Scene*. Chislehurst, Kent, England: Frank Cook Publications (Frank Cook Travel Guides), 1979.

The Complete Guide to West End Theatres. Ginette Goulston-Lincoln, Jane Moss, and Susan Whiddington, eds. London: Society of London Theatres, 1994.

Stubs: New York City Seating Guide. Long Island City, New York: American Map Corporation (imprint of Langenscheidt Publishers Inc.), 2002.

Where to Sit. Compiled and edited by Carl Princi and Roz Burstein. Los Angeles: KFAC, 1980. A seat-plan guide to Southern California entertainment venues.

TELEVISION

"Phantoms of the Opera" episode of *Weird Travels.* Travel Channel, 2004. This program, one of several on the Travel Channel visiting haunted sites, concentrates on six theaters: the Orpheum Theatre (Memphis, Tennessee), the Old Schoolhouse Theater (Sanibel Island, Florida), the Brady Theater (Tulsa, Oklahoma), the Avon Theater and the Lincoln Square Theatre (Decatur, Illinois), and the Pasadena Playhouse (Pasadena, California).

WEB SITES

I also consulted several Web sites while compiling this book. The official sites of individual theaters are noted in Appendix B, "Spooky Sites." The following are of more general interest and contain directories of haunted locations.

www.haunted-places.com

Besides showing state-by-state as well as international listings, haunted-places.com gives information on related books as well as TV and radio programs devoted to the paranormal and the supernatural. It also offers a subscription to a newsletter, the *Haunted-Places Report.*

www.theshadowlands.net

Founded by Dave Juliano in 1994
Dave Juliano and Tina Carlson, codirectors

The Shadowlands is perhaps the largest Internet listing of haunted places—more than thirteen thousand—from all over the world. The individual stories are broken down by the country, state, and city in which the hauntings occur. The site also offers links to information on UFOs and unexplained creatures such as Bigfoot and the Loch Ness monster.

Appendix B
Spooky Sites

Fellow ghost hunters, you're in luck! Almost all of the haunted theaters mentioned in the stories in this book are still operating and open for business. You just might be able to catch a few of these phantoms for yourself.

There are a few exceptions, such as the original Guthrie Theater and the Metropolitan Opera House, both of which no longer exist. Please forgive me if I found a few instances where the spooky tales were either too compelling or even legendary to leave out, even though the playhouses themselves are long gone.

Bear in mind that to enter most theaters, it's necessary to attend a performance of a show. But a few theaters do offer backstage tours. I've listed those that I've been able to confirm, but it's always advisable to check directly with the theater's box office or Web site.

In the following listings, I've tried to be as complete as possible. All telephone numbers and Web sites were correct at the time of publication, but please be aware that these are often subject to change. In cases where the theater doesn't have an official Web site, I've tried to provide an alternate site that contains all of the background information you'll need to help plan a visit.

Theater telephone numbers are for the box office unless otherwise indicated. Please be aware that the numbers are listed as they would be dialed from within the United States; the long distance and international prefixes (1) and (011) have been omitted. When dialing a West End number within

London, the country code (44) is not necessary, but currently a prefix (0) must be added before the two- or three-digit city code.

Also, seating capacities in the theaters vary. The numbers generally don't include boxes, special accommodations made for wheelchair access, and seats that are blocked or have a restricted view for individual productions.

Some of the cities mentioned in this book offer ghost tours that point out haunted sites, although the interiors of buildings are not generally visited. Two tours are worth mentioning before we begin looking at haunted theaters chapter by chapter:

Street Smarts
(212) 969-8262
www.streetsmartsny.com

Street Smarts offers "Ghosts on Broadway," a walking tour of the haunted theaters of midtown Manhattan.

London Walks
P.O. Box 1708
London, NW6 4LW
United Kingdom
(20) 7624-3978
(20) 7624-9255 or (20) 7624-WALKS (recorded information)
www.walks.com

London Walks offers an "Apparitions, Alleyways and Ale" tour, which covers the heart of the theater district in London, England. Along the route, the tour discusses the ghosts of the Adelphi Theatre; the Theatre Royal, Drury Lane; the Theatre Royal, Haymarket; Her Majesty's Theatre; and the Duke of York's. It currently departs Monday and Thursday from the Embankment station of the Underground.

So it's time to dress up for a night of theater. If you're in luck, you'll find yourself front row and center for a haunting.

CHAPTER 1: THE BISHOP OF BROADWAY

Belasco Theatre
111 West Forty-Fourth Street
New York, NY 10036
www.shubertorganization.com/theatres/belasco.asp

Capacity: 1,016
Nearest subway: Forty-Second Street/Times Square on the 1/2/3/7/9/N/R/S lines
The theater is on the north side of West Forty-Fourth Street, east of Broadway between Sixth and Seventh Avenues.

For a brief description of the theater and a list of all the shows that have played the Belasco, visit the Internet Broadway Database at www.ibdb.com/venue.php?id=1360.

Chapter 2: The Ziegfeld Girl

New Amsterdam Theatre
214 West Forty-Second Street
New York, NY 10036
(212) 282-2900
www.disney.go.com/theatre/newamsterdam

Capacity: 1,747 on three levels
Nearest subway: Forty-Second Street/Times Square on the
1/2/3/7/9/N/R/S lines
The theater is on the south side of West Forty-Second
Street, between Seventh and Eighth Avenues.

For a brief description of the theater and a list of all the
shows that have played the New Amsterdam Theatre, visit at
www.ibdb.com/venue.php?id=1294.

Although tours of the New Amsterdam have been available in the past, none are currently being offered.

Chapter 3: Playing the Palace

Palace Theatre
1564 Broadway (at Forty-Seventh Street)
New York, NY 10036
(212) 730-8200
www.palacetheatreonbroadway.com

Capacity: 1,740 on three levels
Nearest subway: Forty-Ninth Street on the N/R lines
The theater is on the east side of Broadway in Duffy
Square between Forty-Sixth and Forty-Seventh Streets.

For a brief description of the theater and a list of all the shows that have played the Palace Theatre, visit the Internet Broadway Database at www.ibdb.com/venue.php?id=1317.

Royal Alexandra Theatre
260 King Street West
Toronto, Ontario
Canada
(416) 872-1212
www.mirvish.com

The Royal Alex, as the theater's also known, is said to be haunted by the ghost of Al Jolson, who performed there during his vaudeville days.

CHAPTER 4: A NIGHT AT THE OPERA

Metropolitan Opera House (Original)
1411 Broadway
New York, NY 10018

Nearest subway: Forty-Second Street/Times Square on the 1/2/3/7/9/N/R/S lines

The old Metropolitan Opera House, which has been demolished, was between West Thirty-Ninth Street and West Fortieth Street, on the west side of Broadway. Today the site is an open plaza in front of modern office skyscrapers.

Information on the history of both the old and current Metropolitan Opera Houses can be found on the theater's official Web site, www.metopera.org.

Chapter 5: No Exit

Harvard Exit Theatre
807 East Roy Street
Seattle, WA 98102
(206) 323-0587
www.landmarktheaters.com/market/Seattle/HarvardExit
Theatre.htm

Several companies offer ghost tours of haunted Seattle. At least one definitely includes the Harvard Exit Theatre in its itinerary:

Haunted History of Capitol Hill
Operated by the Seattle Museum of the Mysteries
623 Broadway East
Seattle, WA 98102
(206) 328-6499
www.seattlechatclub.org

At least two other tours of haunted Seattle might be of interest:

Market Ghost Tour
Departs from Gum Wall outside Pike Place Market
1501 Pike Place
Seattle, WA 98101
Tour information and reservations: (206) 322-1218
www.seattleghost.com

Chapter 6: Vex Not His Ghost

Elizabethan Stage/Allen Pavilion
Oregon Shakespeare Festival
15 South Pioneer Street
Ashland, OR 97520
Box office: (541) 482-4331 or (800) 219-8161
Administrative office: (541) 482-2111
www.osfashland.org

Chapter 7: "Not Now, Gilmor"

Pasadena Playhouse
39 South El Molino Avenue
Pasadena, CA 91101
(626) 356-7529
www.pasadenaplayhouse.org

Capacity: 654

The Pasadena Playhouse is just south of Colorado Boulevard, which is the major street through the city's central business district. In the 1960s the theater converted to continental-style seating (long rows with no central aisles), and this design has been maintained in the refurbished auditorium.

Chapter 8: Only a Ghost in a Gilded Cage

Bird Cage Theatre
Bird Cage Theater Museum
517 East Allen Street
Tombstone, AZ 85638
(520) 457-3421

To reach Tombstone from Tucson, travel east on I-10, then south on Highway 80 for about twenty miles. The theater is on Allen at Sixth Street. Tours are available daily, generally from around 8 a.m. to 6 p.m., though times may vary. The theater also offers evening ghost tours on Thursday, Friday, and Saturday nights at 8 p.m. Additional tours at 9:30 p.m. and 11 p.m. are added as needed.

Two other popular historic sites in Tombstone are said to be haunted:

O.K. Corral
326 East Allen Street
Tombstone, AZ 85638
(520) 457-3456
ok-corral.com

The actual corral is now fenced from view, and admission is charged for entry. Shows re-create the famous 1881 gunfight at 2 p.m. and 4 p.m. daily. The gun battle actually began in a vacant lot behind the corral and spilled out onto Fremont Street, so even if you don't attend a performance you can still stand where part of the clash took place.

Boot Hill Graveyard
P.O. Box 250
Tombstone, AZ 85638
(520) 457-3300

The cemetery is on Highway 80 just north of downtown Tombstone. The graveyard is open to the public, free of charge, but visitors should be as respectful of the grounds as they would be of any other cemetery.

For more information on Tombstone, contact:

Tombstone Visitors Center
Corner of Fourth and Allen Streets
Tombstone, AZ 85638
(520) 457-3929 or (800) 457-3423
www.cityoftombstone.com

Chamber of Commerce
P.O. Box 995
Tombstone, AZ 85638
(888) 457-3929
www.cityoftombstone.com

More information is available at www.tombstoneaz.net.

CHAPTER 9: LITTLE BOY LOST

KiMo Theatre
423 Central Avenue Northwest
Albuquerque, NM 87102
Event information: (505) 768-3544
Administrative office: (505) 768-3522
www.cabq.gov/kimo

Two walking ghost tours of Old Town are available, both run by:

Tours of Old Town
(505) 246-8687 (246-TOUR)
www.toursofoldtown.com

Chapter 10: Take Me Back to Tulsa

Brady Theater
105 West Brady Street
Tulsa, OK 74103
(918) 582-7239
www.bradytheater.com

Chapter 11: Exit, Dying

Grand Opera House
100 High Avenue
Oshkosh, WI 54901
(920) 424-2350
www.grandoperahouse.org

Chapter 12: The Stained-Glass Spirit

Grandstreet Theatre
325 North Park Avenue (at West Sixth Avenue)
Helena, MT 59601
Box office: (406) 447-1574
Administrative office: (406) 442-4270
www.grandstreet.net

Last Chance Tour Train
(888) 423-1023
Last Chance Tour Train, a ghost tour of Helena led by local historian and ghost author Ellen Baumler, visits Catholic Hill and passes by Carroll College, the Benton Avenue Cemetery, and, of course, the Grandstreet Theatre.

CHAPTER 13: THE HOUSE OF USHER

Guthrie Theater (original)
725 Vineland Place
Minneapolis, MN 55403

The old Guthrie has been razed, with plans to create a park on the site. The theater was just off I-94, south of the intersection with I-394 and across the street from Loring Park. The new Guthrie, which isn't haunted, is along the West River Parkway overlooking the Mississippi River.

For more information on the old and current Guthrie Theaters, contact:

Guthrie Theater
(612) 377-2224
www.guthrietheater.org

CHAPTER 14: THE GHOST OF DD113

Woodstock Opera House
121 Van Buren Street
Woodstock, IL 60098
(815) 338-5300
www.woodstockoperahouse.com

Woodstock is approximately fifty miles northwest of Chicago.

Chapter 15: The Apparition of the Alley

Biograph Theater
2433 North Lincoln Avenue
Chicago, IL 60614
Box office: (773) 871-3000
Administrative office: (773) 549-5788

Today the former cinema is a venue for live theater called Victory Gardens at the Biograph. The haunted alleyway runs between the buildings at 2423 (which was Mee Wong Chop restaurant at the time of Dillinger's death) and 2427 on North Lincoln Avenue.

Information on the theater company that now owns and operates the Biograph is at www.victorygardens.org.

Chapter 16: Mary, Mary, Quite Contrary

Orpheum Theatre
203 South Main Street
Memphis, TN 38103
(901) 525-7800
www.orpheum-memphis.com

Chapter 17: Nightmares in Nashville

Ryman Auditorium
116 Fifth Avenue North
Nashville, TN 37219
Box office: (615) 889-3060
www.ryman.com

The Ryman Auditorium, located in the heart of Nashville, is open as a museum from 9 a.m. to 4 p.m. daily except for New Year's Day, Thanksgiving, and Christmas. It's also an active venue for concerts in the evenings.

Tours are available from 9:30 a.m. to 3:30 p.m. and depart from the lobby of the auditorium. Reservations are not taken in advance. For more information, call (615) 458-8700.

CHAPTER 18: THE SPECTRAL SWEEPER

Akron Civic Theatre
182 South Main Street
Akron, OH 44308
(330) 535-3179 or (330) 253-2488
www.akroncivic.com

CHAPTER 19: WITHOUT A TRACE

Victoria Theatre
1 North Ludlow Street
Dayton, OH 45402
Box office: (937) 228-3630 or (888) 228-3630
Administrative office: (937) 228-7591
www.victoriatheatre.com

CHAPTER 20: FREDDY THE PHANTOM

State Theatre (Center for the Arts)
453 Northampton Street
Easton, PA 18042
Box office: (610) 252-3132
Administrative office: (610) 258-7766
www.statetheatre.org

Chapter 21: Phantoms from the Fire

Site of the Rhoads Opera House
Corner of East Philadelphia Avenue and South Washington
Street
Boyertown, PA 19512

Although there is no longer a theater at the address, a commemorative plaque is on the side of the building at the site of the old opera house.

Fairview Cemetery
317 West Philadelphia Avenue
Boyertown, PA 19512

Boyertown Area Historical Society
43 South Chestnut Street
Boyertown, PA 19512
(610) 367-5255
www.boyertownhistory.org

In its collection, the society, whose headquarters are usually open Sunday afternoons, has photographs of the blaze and its aftermath, newspaper articles about the fire, and clothing worn by the some of the mourners at the victims' funerals.

CHAPTER 22: PHANTOM AT THE FULTON

Fulton Opera House
12 North Prince Street
Lancaster, PA 17603
Box office and tour information: (717) 397-7425
www.thefulton.org
www.fultontheatre.org

Backstage tours are conducted Monday through Friday at 11 a.m. The schedule may vary, though, depending upon rehearsals or special programs in the theater, so it's best to call for reservations.

CHAPTER 23: FORD'S PHANTOM

Ford's Theatre
511 Tenth Street Northwest
Washington, DC 20004
(202) 347-4833
Theater's Web site: www.fordstheatre.com or www.fords.org
National Park Service visitors information: www.nps.gov/foth

Ford's Theatre is owned by the U.S. Department of the Interior and is operated under a partnership between the U.S. National Park Service and the not-for-profit Ford's Theater Society. The interior of theater is a modern replica of the original playhouse in which President Lincoln was shot, totally reconstructed from period photographs. Although the National Park Service maintains the facility as a museum, the auditorium is also a working playhouse, so the theater is closed during performances.

Admission to the theater and the Petersen House across the street (where Lincoln died) is free. Same-day timed tickets are available at the box office beginning at 8:30 a.m. Advance tickets for a specific date and time incur a service fee and can be reserved at the box office, at the theater's Web site, or through Ticketmaster at (202) 397-7328.

CHAPTER 24: SCHOOL SPIRIT

Aycock Auditorium
University of North Carolina-Greensboro
Near the corner of Tate and Spring Garden Streets
Greensboro, NC 27402
(336) 334-4849
http://www.uncg.edu/euc/boxoffice/venues/index
.php?go=aycock

As with most college and university campuses, parking is restricted. During weekends and after 5 p.m., it's possible for Aycock Auditorium visitors to park behind the Weatherspoon Art Museum, at the intersection of Spring Garden and Tate. Aycock is close to the museum on Tate. During school hours, your safest bet is the parking structure at the corner of McIver and West Market Streets. Limited parking is also available on area streets.

Chapter 25: The Schoolhouse Hauntings

Old Schoolhouse Theater
Sanibel Museum & Historical Village
850 Dunlop Road
(Near the intersection of Periwinkle Way)
Sanibel, FL 33957
(239) 472-4648
www.sanibelmuseum.org

The interior of the former theater has been restored to the way it looked when it operated as a school, and the building no longer seems to be haunted. Open from early November to mid-August, Wednesday through Saturday. Hours vary seasonally.

The new Schoolhouse Theater is not haunted, but historical information about both playhouses can be located at www.theschoolhousetheater.com.

Sanibel Island is on Florida's southwest coast, across San Carlos Bay from Fort Myers Beach. To get there, exit off I-75 onto Daniels Parkway, then take Summerlin Road across the bridge onto the island.

Chapter 26: The Queen of the Klondike

Palace Grand Theatre
255 King Street
Dawson City, Yukon Territory Y0B 1G0
Canada

The original theater was built on permafrost, and after years of the ground thawing and refreezing, the building's foundations gave way. The current theater, located on the same spot, is an exact replica of the original (except for modern conveniences, of course) built by Parks Canada in 1962.

Although no regular theater productions are performed there, the playhouse is used for occasional evening shows and concerts. It is also open daily for tours.

For more information, contact:

Parks Canada
SS Keno National Historic Site of Canada
Box 390
Dawson City, YT Y0B 1G0
Canada
(867) 993-7200
www.pc.gc.ca

Klondike Visitors Association
P.O. Box 389C
Dawson City, YT Y0B 1G0
Canada
(867) 993-5575
www.dawsoncity.ca

CHAPTER 27: BY GEORGE!

Manitoba Theatre Centre
174 Market Avenue
Winnipeg, Manitoba R3B 0P8
Canada
Box office: (204) 942-6537 or (877) 446-4500
Administrative office: (204) 956-1340
www.mtc.mb.ca

The primary auditorium, called the Mainstage, is now known officially as the John Hirsch Theatre.

The Dominion Theatre, where George first became attached to the company, was at Portage Avenue East and Main Street, but it was demolished in 1968 to make way for the construction of the Richardson Building/Lombard Hotel complex.

Chapter 28: The Mischief of Bloody Mary

Academy Theatre (of Performing Arts)
2 Lindsay Street South
Lindsay, Ontario K9V 4S1
Canada
(705) 324-9111 or (877) 888-0038
www.academytheatre.ca

Chapter 29: The Return of Ambrose Small

Grand Theatre
371 Richmond Street
London, Ontario N6A 3E4
Canada
(519) 672-8800 or (800) 265-1593
www.grandtheatre.com

The Grand Theatre was originally known as the Grand Opera House when it was founded by Ambrose Small and Colonel C. J. Whitney in 1901. Although Small disappeared from the Grand Opera House in Toronto, which was demolished in 1927, he's said to haunt the Grand Theatre in London. The Tivoli Theatre, which Small's ghost was also said to haunt, has recently been demolished. It was at 108 James Street North in Hamilton, Ontario.

Chapter 30: Wraiths at the Winter Garden

Elgin and Winter Garden Theatre Centre
189 Yonge Street
North York
Toronto, Ontario M5B 1M4
Canada
Administrative office: (416) 314-2901
www.heritagefdn.on.ca/userfiles/html/nts_1_2374_1.html

Nearest Underground: Queen
    Ninety-minute tours are generally conducted Saturdays at 10:45 a.m. and may be joined without reservations in the theater lobby. Visitors get to see the original and current lobbies, the interior of the auditoriums, a dressing room, the old silent-movie projector, theatrical ephemera, and some of the original vaudeville scenery from the center's valuable collection.
    For more information on the theaters' history and current operation, contact:

Ontario Heritage Trust
10 Adelaide Street East
Toronto, Ontario M5C 1J3
Canada
(416) 325-5000
www.heritagefdn.on.ca

Chapter 31: "I Shall Come Back"

Adelphi Theatre
Strand
London, England WC2R 0NS
United Kingdom
(44)(871) 297-0749
www.rutheatres.com/venueinfo/ade.htm

Capacity: 1,500 on three levels
Nearest Underground: Charing Cross, with Embankment nearby

The Adelphi Theatre was purchased by Andrew Lloyd Webber's Really Useful Theatres group in 1993 and was completely renovated before reopening with his musical *Sunset Boulevard*. Today the theater is owned and managed by the Adelphi Theatre Company Limited, a partnership between the Really Useful group and Nederlander International. The theater's exterior is usually covered by a giant billboard, advertising whatever show is playing within. To get an idea of what the original columned facade looked like, check out the front of the buildings next door.

Chapter 32: Buckstone's Back

Theatre Royal, Haymarket
Haymarket
London, England SW1Y 4HT
United Kingdom
(44)(845) 481-1870
www.trh.co.uk/
Capacity: 888 on four levels
Nearest Underground: Piccadilly Circus and Leicester Square, although Charing Cross is also nearby

Tours are available.

Chapter 33: The Phantom at the Opera

Her Majesty's Theatre
Haymarket
London, England SW1Y 4QR
United Kingdom
(44)(844) 412-4653
www.rutheatres.com/venueinfo/hmt.htm

Capacity: 1,148 on four levels
Nearest Underground: Piccadilly Circus

Tours of the theater are sold only in conjunction with tickets to a performance of *Phantom of the Opera* and are arranged through:

Red Letter Days
(44)(845) 640-8000 or (44)(845) 266-7000 (Monday through Friday, 9 a.m. to 5:30 p.m. GMT)
www.redletterdays.co.uk

Chapter 34: The Strangler Jacket

Duke of York's
St Martin's Lane
London, England WC2N 4BG
United Kingdom
(44)(870) 060-6623
www.theambassadors.com/dukeofyorks/info/index.html

Capacity: 647 on three levels
Nearest Underground: Leicester Square

Special tours by prior arrangement.

Chapter 35: The Most Haunted Theater in the World

Theatre Royal, Drury Lane
Catherine Street
London, England WC2B 5JF
United Kingdom
(44)(870) 890-1109
www.rutheatres.com/venueinfo/dru.htm
Capacity: 2,196 on four levels
Nearest Underground: Covent Garden

There are tours daily (Sunday by special arrangement) that visit the interior of the theater, including backstage areas. The one-hour tour is interactive, with actors portraying several historical characters who explain the theater's history. Tour tickets are also available through many London ticket agencies and at the theater.

Theatre Royal, Drury Lane, is owned and operated by the Really Useful Group Theatres, which can be contacted at:
22 Tower Street
London WC2H 9TW
United Kingdom
Phone: (44)(20) 7240-0880
www.rutheatres.com

About the Author

Tom Ogden is one of America's most celebrated magicians. He has performed professionally for thirty-five years, from the tinsel and sawdust of the circus ring to the glitter and sequins of Las Vegas, Atlantic City, and Lake Tahoe. He has opened for such acts as Robin Williams, Billy Crystal, and the Osmonds.

Ogden's television work has included appearances on NBC's The World's Greatest Magic and FOX's The Great Magic of Las Vegas, as well as numerous commercials. He has twice been voted Parlour Magician of the Year at the famed Magic Castle in Hollywood and has received more than a dozen nominations in other categories. He has also appeared as a humorist and motivational speaker for corporations such as Disney, Xerox, Pepsi, KFC, and Sears.

Ogden's books include *200 Years of the American Circus* (which was named a Best Reference Work by both the American Library Association and the New York Public Library), *Wizards and Sorcerers*, *The Complete Idiot's Guide to Magic Tricks*, *The Complete Idiot's Guide to Ghosts and Hauntings*, and *The Complete Idiot's Guide to Street Magic*. He has also been profiled in *Writer's Market*.

Tom Ogden resides in Los Angeles.